"Touch me," Tanya urged.

Stede brought her to him, holding her tight. She slipped a hand between them and caressed the front of him, panting when she felt him rigid and straining. His strangled cry sounded twice as loud in the silence of her loft, and it satisfied her even more than his touch when he pushed her hand away.

He wanted her, and she felt her heart singing with the knowledge of it. "Thought you wanted to show me your treasures," she whispered.

"Perhaps it's your pleasure chest I'm thinking of now, Tanya," he taunted, the burning spear of his tongue warm against her ear as he slipped her blouse from her shoulders....

Blaze™

Dear Reader,

Just as I finished this book, my great-aunt, to whom it's dedicated, passed on. Some forty-odd books ago, I dedicated my first novel to Carrie Winifred Dunlap as well, since she taught me so much about love.

Winnie loved romances, especially the one that led her to the altar in 1941 with the man (and dentist) she married, my uncle "Doc." Oh, there were other suitors. Guy, Duke and Rex, in particular. I know because she saved their letters in a polished wooden box. But Winnie enjoyed tales of others' romances, too, and would have appreciated the love story you're about to read, which concerns a time-traveling privateer.

In her drawer I found a tiny, folded paper that had, in turn, been found by Winnie in her own mother's drawer years before. In my great-grandmother's hand it said, "To live in the hearts you leave behind is not to die." Someone else had penned, "A beautiful thought!"

These could be words spoken by the sexy privateer you're about to meet. I hope you'll agree with him (and me) that true love transcends time and lives on forever in your heart. This one's for all the kindnesses remembered—

My very best,

Jule McBride

THE PLEASURE CHEST
Jule McBride

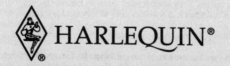

TORONTO • NEW YORK • LONDON
AMSTERDAM • PARIS • SYDNEY • HAMBURG
STOCKHOLM • ATHENS • TOKYO • MILAN • MADRID
PRAGUE • WARSAW • BUDAPEST • AUCKLAND

ISBN-13: 978-0-373-79285-6
ISBN-10:   0-373-79285-9

THE PLEASURE CHEST

www.eHarlequin.com

Printed in U.S.A.

In loving memory of my favorite person in the world, my great-aunt, Carrie Winifred Dunlap, 1917–to eternity in the hearts of others.

And to the man who helped her so much, and thought of those beautiful yellow roses, her best friend, George "Bono" Hall.

Prologue

New York, 1791

"PUT AWAY YER MUSKET, Basil Drake, and say you won't be shootin' me today," called Stede O'Flannery. He hazarded a glance from behind the trunk of an oak, squinting green eyes that Basil's fiancée, Lucinda, had vowed were the color of sunlit shamrocks. He shook his head, unable to believe Basil had brought a smoothbore musket to the woods, a sixty-nine caliber French Charleyville by the looks of it, equipped with a bayonet. So much for using comparable weapons. Stede only had a flintlock pistol.

"Show yourself, O'Flannery," yelled Basil. "You're a damn rascal, and I insist on this interview."

Oh, Sweet Betsy Ross, Stede thought grumpily. Raising his voice, he shouted, "I didn't dishonor Lucinda!"

"You were caught red-handed in her bedchamber, man!"

Literally, since he'd been lying on top of her, unlacing her bodice with wind-chapped fingers.

"She was shivering, O'Flannery!"

With cold, though, not sexual need. She'd been drenched from the plunge she'd taken into the freezing Hudson River, after saying she'd sooner kill herself than marry Basil. Not that anyone had bothered to credit Stede with saving her life. "No good deed goes unpunished," he mused. When Basil's voice sounded again, Stede pushed aside a vision of blond tresses trailing over creamy bare bosoms.

"You're a no-account scoundrel!"

True. But could Stede help it if war had made him wealthy? Or if his reputation excited women more than when they entertained bores like Basil? Or if, in addition to being a privateer, he could paint landscapes that came alive and made ladies swoon? Besides, Lucinda was his patroness, nothing more. One of many. Because Stede's own mama, rest her soul, had been Lucinda's nurse, he'd known Lucinda for years. It was she who'd encouraged him to paint, claiming that fruits in his still lifes made her mouth water as if from a lover's kiss. But who was her lover? After reading her private letters, Basil had assumed Stede was the man.

"Maybe I should kill you now and be done with it, Basil."

"It's you they'll carry from here in a pine box!"

"Doubtful." Dueling was illegal in New York, so they'd crossed the river to Jersey, and now Stede glanced where early morning fog was rolling from the Hudson's choppy waters, looking as thick as pipe smoke. Because he was tall, slender, blond and clothed in white, Basil looked ethereal, like an unlit taper in the shadowy dawn. Neither he nor Stede had brought seconds. This way, Stede had figured Basil could back down without losing face. Basil had claimed the same, but judging by how he'd handled himself on fox hunts with Lucinda's father, General Barrington, Stede knew Basil couldn't shoot his way out of a burlap sack, not even with a good musket.

"C'mon, Basil. I really don't want to kill you on this fine mornin'." Not that it would be any great loss. The officious fool was twice Lucinda's age, but her father had been impressed by his supposed good name and rumored inheritance. Meantime, Stede heard the family had fled to the colonies years ago to escape Basil Senior's gaming debts. Well, Stede thought, as Poor Richard always said, "Light purse, heavy heart." Maybe debting accounted for Basil's lack of decent humor.

"Show yourself, O'Flannery!"

Stede's trigger finger itched on his pistol. Truth was, every fellow who drank in McMulligan's would thank Stede for killing Basil. "He who drinks fast, pays slow," said Stede, voicing another Poor Richard-ism. It was why Mark McMulligan hated Basil even more than Lucinda did. Stede sighed. The revolution might be over, but hatred lasted forever. Even now, a fleet was in New York harbor, and captains were ready with letters of marque that would allow them to intercept merchant vessels for plunder. While Stede could board any one of them tonight and escape Basil's wrath, not to mention General Barrington's, he'd buried war booty nearby on Manhattan Island; some of it was hard-won by his father, rest his soul, and Stede had hoped to use the treasure to build a home and settle down.

"Is that too much for a man to ask?" he exploded, sensing that his dreams were going up in smoke. Damn if this situation wasn't about as welcome as the Stamp Act. What had that fellow, Rousseau, said? Yes... "Man's born free, but everywhere in chains."

"When they're not conscripting you into somebody else's army," he muttered, "a bunch of jealous suitors and worried papas start gunning for you."

Long moments passed. As usual. Duels took forever. A man could sail to China and back before they were over, which was why Stede preferred pub brawls any day.

Leaves rustled. Birds took flight. In the silence, his heart ticked like a clock, saying it was too early to be in the woods on a cold morning when he could be tucked in his cot above McMulligan's with some sweet serving wench. Tired of waiting, he stepped from behind the oak, deciding he'd better throw away his fire. Yes, he'd offer a delope, which is what Basil would call it, since he insisted on using all the latest fancy French dueling terminology.

Slowly, so Basil could see, Stede stepped fully into view and raised his arm, pointing the pistol skyward. The autumn air was misty, but sharp, carrying scents of winter. Colors burst inside his mind, and for a second, he imagined painting a picture of the russet and gold canopy of leaves. He'd make the trees look like uniformed soldiers surrounding the foggy clearing, preparing to march to a massacre across a soft blur of grass. Yes, the red leaves were redcoats....

He squeezed the trigger.

The retort was swift, the blast threatening to knock him back a pace, but he stood firm.

"Ah. So you concede!" yelled Basil. Grandly Basil pushed aside his waistcoat, then prepared to shoulder his musket while striding forward to shake hands. Good. Stede would rather swallow a spoonful of his pride than prolong this idiocy. At twenty paces, Basil stopped, a glint in his eyes that Stede could see even at this distance. Suddenly Basil released a war whoop and charged, coming at a dead run. If the ball didn't kill Stede, the bayonet mounted to the musket barrel surely would.

"Bloody bastard!" Stede gasped, pivoting and darting toward the woods. He'd conceded by shooting skyward, but Basil was going to kill him, anyway! And there was no time for Stede to reload. He'd brought no witnesses. "Lout!" Stede shouted as Basil closed the distance.

He whirled in time to see Basil aim at his heart, then hit the dirt as Basil fired. *Boom!* Air whooshed overhead as a bullet passed, then another blast sounded, but from where? Basil hadn't had time to reload, either. Now he shrieked and dropped his pistol. He was hit! Someone had fired at Basil from the trees. Who?

Stede scanned the woods, then looked at Basil. He was staggering backward, clutching his chest, blood spilling through his splayed fingers. "Sweet Betsy Ross," Stede cursed. Basil was a horse's behind, but he didn't deserve to die. His knees were buckling, though, and he fell backward. As he rolled onto his belly, Stede holstered his pistol and approached at a crouching run. Kneeling, he took Basil's pulse.

"Dead." There was still no sound from the woods. He shouted, "Who's there?"

A heartbeat passed, then Lucinda Barrington ran into the clearing. With the color drained from her face and clad in a white cloak, she looked like a ghost, the vision marred only by the mud splattered around the dress's hem, and the fact that her slender shaking hands held a flintlock pistol much like Stede's; it probably belonged to her father.

Before he could say anything, another male voice sounded from the woods. "Lucinda!"

Ignoring the cry, she raced toward Stede, her hair flying behind her. "Hurry," she urged as he registered her pursuer's footsteps in the underbrush, then the thunder of horses' hooves.

LUCINDA STARED at Basil, stricken. "I meant to scare him," she whispered shakily. "But I didn't mean to…" Tears sprang into her blue eyes. "I hit him, didn't I? I really hit him! He was going to kill you, though. And since he didn't, now my father will. Oh, Stede! Everyone thinks you and I…"

Are lovers, he finished mentally.

"You've got to get out of here!" She tossed a wild glance toward the trees. Men were approaching, probably with her father. He wouldn't be the first to think his daughter's virgin heart had been captured by a swarthy privateer, either.

"Basil hired that witch, Missus Llassa, too," Lucinda raced on, her startled eyes still fixed on Basil. "He paid her to put a hex on you, Stede, just in case you killed Basil, instead of the other way around."

His heart missed a beat. "Missus Llassa put a hex on me?"

"You know you don't believe in hexes," said Lucinda.

Stede knew no such thing. Besides, many claimed Missus Llassa's evil magic could kill a man from a hundred miles away. There was no time to argue the point, though, because Jonathan Wilson, a local furniture maker, emerged from the fog wearing a top-hat and black cape, looking as if he, too, were materializing from an old-fashioned ghost tale. His face turned chalk-white when he saw Basil, then he ran forward, just as Stede had, kneeled and took the man's pulse once more.

"Holy sons of liberty," he whispered simply, his eyes

widening as he took in the blood pooling beneath Basil's chest. He stared at Lucinda. "You killed him, darling."

Darling? So, Lucinda's secret lover was Jonathan Wilson! Well, good for her, Stede thought. It had been months since Basil and General Barrington had announced Lucinda's engagement to Basil without even consulting her. But all along, the smart girl had other plans—to marry Jonathan, at least judging by the glance they were exchanging. Too bad Basil was what General Barrington had wanted for his daughter's future, Stede suddenly fumed. While Jonathan Wilson was a Presbyterian, Basil Drake had remained an Episcopalian, and like every other scoundrel from the Church of England, he'd always been a closet loyalist, too. Not that Stede, himself, had a religion of preference. The way he figured it, if he went inside any kind of church, the roof would cave in.

"Basil's really dead," Lucinda said in a stunned whisper, bringing Stede back to his senses.

He cursed softly, thinking of the war booty he'd buried a stone's throw away, then of the cold fury on General Barrington's face if he ever realized his daughter had killed her own fiancé to save the life of a privateer, especially one known as a n'er-do-well. Missus Llassa's hex didn't give much comfort, either. Stede imagined her lounging in her smoky den of iniquity, clad in a turban and kaftan, smoking opium and chewing snuff by candlelight while surrounded by cards, crystals, pouches of ground bones, herbs and chemical-laced jars that held unspeakably creepy things.

Yes, by now she'd probably made a doll into the spitting image of Stede and was busy pushing pins into it. Or maybe she was in his room above McMulligan's, combing hairs from his straight razor while fixing to boil them in the cauldron she kept out back, behind her shack. Feeling the blood drain from his face, he recalled the story of one poor fellow whose spurned lover had hired Missus Llassa, to teach him a lesson. Rumor had it, his cock never crowed again, so to speak.

Cutting off the horrifying thought, Stede looked at Lucinda and Jonathan. They were star-crossed lovers, all right. And while Stede was within his rights for killing Basil, since Basil had challenged him to the duel, Lucinda could hang for this. And regarding her, Basil's only crime was that he'd threatened to marry her. Hers, of course, was that she'd been born a woman at a time when fathers could tell the gentler sex who to marry.

Once more, Stede sighed, muttering, "Sweet Betsy Ross." Then he slipped his hand over Lucinda's. It was still shaking and her skin was ice-cold. As he took the pistol, his eyes met the other man's. "Get her out of here," he said.

Horses were still approaching through the trees. "General Barrington and some men from town," Jonathan explained. "They were on my tail."

"How many?"

"Ten. Maybe more."

"Take Lucinda and go," Stede repeated. But Jonathan seemed to know the sacrifice Stede was making, and he wavered, questions playing in his eyes. Stede wasn't about to let Lucinda ruin her life, however, not when she'd saved his. Besides, Lucinda was the only one who'd ever encouraged his passion for painting. "Go on," he urged.

Nodding abruptly, Jonathan slipped his arm around Lucinda's shoulders and glanced toward the woods. "If we can, we'll head them off. Unless you want to stay and claim responsibility for…"

Lucinda gasped. "Basil's family might retaliate!"

People would assume Stede had killed Basil, fair and square, and Stede didn't want Lucinda and Jonathan vouching for him, since that would destroy Lucinda's reputation. But she was right. Basil's family might wind up crying foul play to redeem Basil's honor. Even if no one retaliated by killing Stede, the influential family could make Stede's life miserable.

Lucinda broke from Jonathan's grasp and flung herself into Stede's arms. His arms circled her waist instinctively as she kissed his cheek. "I can't let you take the blame for this."

He placed a finger on her lips, silencing her. "You saved my life."

Her gaze darted to Basil's body once more, then she glanced a final time at Stede and turned, whispering one last word as she grasped Jonathan's hand. "Godspeed!"

And then Stede found himself alone in the woods with the body of the man who'd tried to kill him in cold blood. Still holding Lucinda's smoking gun, he hoped Basil hadn't really hired Missus Llassa, the most highly esteemed witch in America.

"If I've got a hex on me," he muttered, "I'd sure like to know what kind." One thing was certain. There would be no asking Basil. And if Stede stuck around much longer, he'd be out of this frying pan and into the fire. Squinting at Basil, he considered his next move. Then, just as the first horse came into view, Stede leaned and grabbed Basil's musket. Shouldering it, he growled, "Sweet Betsy Ross," a final time, then he slipped between the trees and vanished into shadows.

1

"LOOK!" Tanya Taylor blew dust from an old canvas, then sneezed.

"Bless you," called May. The proprietress of Finders Keepers clambered toward Tanya. "What did you unearth, honey?"

"A painting." Propping it on a player piano, beside an oil lamp and brass candlesticks, Tanya stepped back to admire it. "It's of a duel!" she exclaimed, a delighted shiver zipping down her spine.

In a shadowy, grassy clearing, golden, orange and red leaves burst like suns over stately trees. The air looked strange, somehow. "Haunted," she said as May sidled closer. "Mystical." As if a spell had been cast on a fairy glen.

May tugged down a blouse calculated to hide her girth, and as she surveyed the work, she removed a pin from a russet chignon, then stabbed it in again. "If memory serves me, I found it leaning against a trash bin outside a brownstone on Bank Street." She thought a moment. "Yes...it was about forty years ago, around the time I moved to Sag Harbor to open the shop."

"Why would someone throw away a picture that's so..." Tanya searched for a word, as she took in the gilded chipped frame, "...captivating." Everything about it drew her like a magnet, although it wasn't large, only about two by two feet.

"Oh," said May. "You know how rich people are, down in the West Village," she sniffed. "No taste. Maybe somebody died and their family pitched it. Who knows? Anyway, it's been in the attic with things I never tagged."

"It's so real," Tanya said. Soft, liquid mist moved on the same breeze that rustled the tree leaves, and for a second, Tanya could swear she heard skirts swishing in dark hallways, wind chimes, and a foghorn. Between the trees, she glimpsed waters that churned dangerously, frothing with whitecaps, and suddenly, the energy of the current seemed to enter her own bloodstream with the promise of a coming storm.

In the clearing were two men. One was tall, thin, blond, and dressed in white; the other dark. The blonde was running forward, his musket aimed at the darker man. But now Tanya discerned a flash of fire coming from the trees, as if a third party was shooting the darker man's attacker.

"That dude's star quality," said May.

She meant the dark guy. Definitely. There was something off-center about his face; the nose was too pronounced and aquiline, the face too rectangular and drawn, the dust of his mustache and rakish spray of beard too unkempt. Long dark hair was pulled back into a ponytail, and he was dressed in a dark tailored coat worn over tight breeches. His eyes seemed green, but it was hard to tell, since the canvas was dirty, and yet, whatever the color, the eyes had the unnerving quality of always watching the viewer. No matter how Tanya moved, the gaze followed.

"I could use a date with a guy like him," May said.

"Me, too. Next week," Tanya returned, trying not to think about her friend, Izzie's, art opening. Tanya had to go, of course, which meant running into Brad, and since she was still stinging from their breakup, she'd rather stay home. Even worse, a week later, Brad would be reviewing Tanya's own art opening, and she had a sneaking suspicion her ex-lover wouldn't be kind.

Glancing toward a beveled mirror in a corner, she surveyed herself and winced. On impulse, she'd bleached her hair again after the breakup and, as luck would have it, her mother called, so by the time Tanya had managed to rinse, her knotty curls had turned bleach-white. Even Izzie, and their other best friend, Marlo, had agreed that it looked as if Tanya was wearing a shoulder-length wig of cotton balls.

At least she'd been blessed with good skin. But she was so pale that no matter how much mascara and liner she used, she'd never been able to form eyelashes or brows. At any rate, she'd bought dresses, both for her and Izzie's openings, and now she didn't want to wear either one, since they looked too young. Brad's new babe, Sylvia Gray, was one of those sophisticates born in the perfect black dress, and while just two years shy of thirty, Tanya was still wearing platforms, confections such as the jeans skirt she had on, and too many strands of mismatched beads. A lump formed in her throat. Just two months ago, she'd been on top of the world. Brad hadn't been great in bed, and all the boring sex had hammered her self-esteem. Still, she'd thought things were improving, right up until he'd dumped her.

Too bad he'd been the first boyfriend lately to pass muster with her folks. But Brad was gone now, and her paintings still weren't ready. Plus, she'd eaten so much postrelationship chocolate that the new dresses probably no longer fit. Every day, she'd been staring at her canvasses, second-guessing herself, feeling something was missing…

"That aliveness," she whispered now, her heart squeezing tightly. Whoever did this painting had that quality. It was a gift. She was a better painter, technically, but this artist had breathed life into the work.

"He's conceding the duel," she heard May say, "but the guy's going to shoot him anyway, and then somebody shoots from the trees, but we're not sure who."

"Yes," murmured Tanya, stepping closer. The canvas was filthy, the paint chipping, but she could discern shadowy figures in the woods now. A man wearing a cloak, maybe. A woman in white. Or was she a ghost? And who was shooting the blonde? What had happened afterward? Had he died?

This was only a painting, yes. But she could almost swear it was alive. She felt the heat of the dark man's gaze. He was admiring…desiring. Everything Brad hadn't been. Warmth flooded her skin, and her cheeks burned. Beneath her top, her nipples were affected, and while the idea was crazy, she was sure the man was watching her….

"That hottie's all yours for three hundred dollars," said May.

It was more than she could afford. Buying two dresses had left her broke, and her boss, James, had been dropping hints that she needed to leave her apartment above

Treasured Maps, the shop which he owned, and where she worked, so he could renovate. Besides, she did need a better place, if only because her folks kept threatening to visit. After years of living in suburban Short Hills, they'd never comprehend why their daughter was living in an apartment with paint-splattered floors, much less why the shower stall, toilet and bathtub were in separate locations. James charged her next to nothing, however, and she could paint without fear of ruining anything, a luxury she'd never have in another apartment. Besides, the security in the building was top-notch, and she loved working for James, even if showing clients rare maps didn't pay much. Still, she did have to move soon.

"I can't buy it," Tanya forced herself to say. "I just came in to pick up the maps." Months ago, James had wandered in and seen some maps hanging in May's office. Although they weren't valuable, he'd liked them, but May had decided not to sell, saying they were part of her office decor. A few days ago, she'd changed her mind.

"Two-fifty," May countered.

Tanya's gaze drifted over the man, taking in the bunched muscles of his thighs, then she startled. She could swear she'd seen the muscles twitch, just slightly. Shaking her head to clear it of confusion, she blinked. Her throat felt strangely tight. "Two-fifty?"

"I take credit cards, if that helps," said May.

Trying not to think of her balance, Tanya slipped a hand inside her purse, pulled out the card and gave it to May, who headed for the cash register. Gingerly Tanya lifted the picture. It wasn't any more valuable than the maps in May's office, but suddenly, it meant the world to her. To the touch, it was warm, the varnish smooth beneath her fingers, almost like velvet.

"Sorry," May said when Tanya reached the register. "Your card's not going through." Seeing Tanya's stricken expression, she assured, "It's my machine, not your card. I took the number, and I'll complete the transaction later. I met you, and I've met your boss, so I know where to find you two if there's a problem."

The relief flooding Tanya was disproportionate to the situation. "Thank you," she managed. She had no idea what she'd have done if the sale hadn't gone through. Suddenly, she *had* to have the painting.

"TANYA, we're worried." Her mother's voice came over the answering machine, but Tanya barely heard. She was squinting at *Shattered World*, one of the pieces for her exhibit. All the works were of New York landscapes seen from unusual perspectives. To her right, the Empire State building was viewed as if in a fish-eye lens. To her left, was a huge black canvas in which the Jersey skyline could be seen in a tiny, off-center white dot. In *Shattered World*, a fractured skyline was connected by a fine stream of golden light. Light seemed to traverse the whole world of the painting, glowing like a halo.

He'd inspired the light.

She'd been lying in bed, staring at the duel, which she'd hung on the wall that faced her bed, when suddenly, the inspiration had come to her. Now, she was even more convinced the painting she'd bought was special.

"Dad is as worried as I," her mother was saying. "You know how he was hoping to see Brad, but it's been two months since you've brought him for dinner."

"We broke up," Tanya called to the machine.

"Come next week," her mother continued. "And why don't you get voice mail? Your father and I think you might have a machine so you can screen our calls, but we know you wouldn't do that to us."

"Lay on the guilt," Tanya said, stepping back from the canvas as her mother hung up. Yes…it was as if her whole internal world was shattered, but also touched by wild cords of energy and light.

Suddenly she smiled. Even now, she could feel his eyes on her back. Glancing over her shoulder, she sent her mystery admirer an inviting look. Since she was wearing only a half buttoned, paint-splotched smock over panties, she twitched her butt for good measure. She'd learned not to dress when she painted, since she always ruined what she wore. As it was, cobalt-blue streaked across her bare thigh.

Suddenly she frowned and tilted her head. Was someone downstairs? No…it was after hours, and the shop was closed. Wincing, she thought of the upcoming two weeks during which James was closing for vacation. She got creeped out when he left town. "James?" she yelled.

No answer. But something seemed…strange. Off-kilter. As if someone else was here with her. She glanced around. Large by Manhattan standards, her upstairs space was identical in layout to the shop downstairs. Bathed in light from floor-to-ceiling windows, it had cinder-block walls and scarred wood floors. Her bed was in a corner she referred to as the bedroom. Nearby, a Chinese-inspired screen blocked a rack of clothes, obscuring the door leading downstairs, if she was lying in bed. A tiny room with the toilet was in another corner. In the final corner, was a shower stall with a glass door.

Glass…through which she kept feeling watched. Putting down her paintbrush, Tanya headed toward the picture. On impulse, she picked up an old Polaroid camera on the bedside table, snapped a picture of the painting, then chuckled softly, wondering what she was doing. "Are you still watching me?" she teased as the phone rang again.

The answering machine activated. "It's Izzie. Marlo and I want to know what's happened to you. You weren't at yoga. You weren't at dance class. What's his name?"

"Who knows?" Tanya said, smiling. She sidestepped, then danced in front of the picture, toying with a smock button.

"More likely than dating a real man, you're playing with all those sex toys we bought," Izzie teased. "If he is real, however, remember that girlfriends get all the dirty details. You'll be giving them to us tonight…since you haven't forgotten Marlo's anniversary dinner in an hour."

Dinner! Tanya never forgot events like this! It was a year since Marlo's divorce, so they were celebrating. Racing forward, she snatched the phone, but the line was dead. "Maybe everybody's right! I really am falling off the map! And it's your fault." She glared at the man in the painting as she unbuttoned the smock, let it fall to the floor, then shed her panties. The eyes followed her. She'd seen eyes like this in paintings before. But usually such paintings were of religious figures, and they just had a way of making her feel guilty.

Not so, this guy. Heat prickled her nape, and she damned Izzie for mentioning the toy chest at the foot of her bed. After Brad, Izzie and Marlo had insisted that

Tanya buy toys to amuse herself, they'd spent an afternoon laughing, cruising novelty shops. Tanya had bought everything from body paints to ribbed, neon condoms and vibrators, all things she'd never use. The vibrating fingertips, however…

A moment later, the ten tiny sleeves were on her fingers, and when she switched on a wrist pack, each began vibrating gently. Her throat constricted as she traced the skin of her belly, keeping her eyes on the man. Had he been real? Or a figment of imagination? If he was real…what had he been like? Married? Single? What had he done for a living?

Shutting her eyes, she let her head drop back on her neck, working out stiffness and kinks, even though she knew this ridiculous indulgence was going to make her late for dinner. Her pulse quickened as she imagined his fingers touching her. Yes…she was in the picture with him now. He was her lover, and they were alone in the clearing. Already, he'd removed her clothes, and as she lay on her bed, she imagined he was urging her onto soft green grass and parting her legs.

Moments later, she was in ecstasy.

"REMARKABLE," one of James's steady clients, Eduardo, said a few days later. Tanya had brought the painting downstairs, to Treasured Maps, hoping the Weatherby's buyer could suggest someone capable of cleaning it.

"I only want it cleaned," she assured, propping the painting on a fully stocked bar James kept in a corner of the shop. Like James, most of his clients were connoisseurs of more than old maps, so James kept vintage wines and whiskey stored in the basement. "I could never afford restoration," Tanya continued as James joined her and

Eduardo at the bar. "Besides, the painting is only of sentimental value, from a junk store."

"From Finders Keepers," James said to Eduardo.

Tanya's heart quickened when she saw Eduardo's eyes glint with appraisal. Withdrawing manicured hands from the pockets of a gray, custom-made suit, Eduardo thrust them through wavy black hair. He was well over six feet tall and slender. By contrast, sandy-haired James was a short, plump teddy bear of a man.

"When you're finished looking at Tanya's painting," James said, "you must see my new Henry Pople map. It's dated from London in 1733, and…"

His voice trailed off when Eduardo whistled. A magnifier appeared and Eduardo stepped closer. "Remarkable," he murmured once more. "I see a trace of carnelian. Maybe a signature." He glanced at James. "Can you spare the shop today?"

While some of James's clients came by appointment, most didn't, which meant he could close anytime he wished. "Why?"

"So you and Tanya can come to Weatherby's. My restoration team can use infrared and other techniques to show what exists beneath what's visible to our eyes."

Tanya's heart skipped a beat. "You think it might be valuable?"

Eduardo nodded. "I'm sure it's a Stede O'Flannery."

TANYA HAD NEVER heard of Stede O'Flannery, but everyone at Weatherby's had. She glanced around the restoration room of the auction house, glancing up as Eduardo reentered the room, a file tucked beneath his arm.

"Congratulations. There's no signature, but under the paint, our team found a stamp showing the receipt of sale to O'Flannery. He purchased the canvas, and the painting style is his, so we'll be able to sell it as an authenticated masterpiece."

Was he joking? This was every junk store shopper's dream, and the kind of bargain-hunting adventure for which James and Eduardo lived. Izzie and Marlo were going to be green with envy. Suddenly guilt sliced through her. "But the proprietress of Finders Keepers. She'd never have sold it if she'd known…"

Eduardo shot Tanya a long-suffering glance that bespoke years of auction house training. "Finders Keepers. Isn't that the name of her shop? Besides, every junk store owner has sold things undervalue. If rare finds didn't happen occasionally, no one would ever go into second-hand shops. This is what drives their business, Tanya. After we announce your find, their industry will see a surge in business." He glanced at James. "You haven't trained this employee very well."

James winked at Tanya. "We keep searching Tanya's genetic code for the shark gene, but so far, we've yet to find it."

Her mind was still catching up. "You mean this painting is worth something?"

"O'Flannery isn't in a class with Vermeer or Rembrandt, if that's what you mean. He's somewhat unknown because a handful of collectors horde the works, but that will make it easier to sell." Eduardo opened the file. "Most of his paintings came down through the Barrington family. A patroness, Lucinda, was thought to have been his lover, and he may have died, defending her honor. Rumor had it, the guy slept around with other women, too, and a sorceress put a curse on him. In order to break the curse, he needed to fall in love, but he never did."

Tanya couldn't believe any of this was happening. "Love?"

"Lust was more O'Flannery's thing," explained Eduardo. "He was quite the unsavory character. It's said some of the people associated, not just with him, but with his paintings, went stark-raving mad."

"Good reason to sell," she managed.

He patted the file. "We'll copy the background information for you. The main thing is that mystery surrounds the work, and that increases its value for us."

"How much?" Tanya asked.

"The canvas isn't in great shape, but it should be sold, as is. The buyer will want to oversee restoration and treatment." Eduardo shrugged. "With some buzz, and auctioned in the right lot, I'd say you're looking at the one-five range."

Tanya gasped. "Fifteen thousand dollars?"

Eduardo's lips lifted in a smile. "One-point-five *million*," he said slowly. "Maybe two."

She staggered backward, needing to sit. The only thing that had ever made her knees feel this weak was the gaze of the man in the painting. Somehow, her backside found a chair, and she sank into it. Two million? Had he really said that? She thought of her credit card balance and of her need to move, so James could renovate. Then she thought about the magnetic pull she experienced every time she looked at the man in the painting. He'd watched her work all week…watched her touch herself. She knew it was crazy, but it was as if they'd formed some sort of…well, *relationship*.

Eduardo was pushing a piece of paper in her direction. "If you'll just sign here, Tanya," he said, "we can accept possession of the painting now, photograph it for a catalog immediately and begin the process of selling it for you. Within a week, you'll be a millionaire."

"I'm sorry," she heard herself say. "But…can you promise not to tell anyone about this?" When she heard her own voice, it seemed to come from a far-off place, as if someone else was speaking. "I…have to think," she continued. "I can't sell yet."

Vaguely, she was aware she'd just turned down a sale that could generate two million dollars. That's when she knew she'd joined ranks with those people associated with the painting who'd gone stark-raving mad. Still, there was something so very special about the work. She could feel it. And she simply couldn't let it go.

2

AT A CAFÉ across the street from Treasured Maps, an elderly gentleman shrugged out of a polyester jacket, draped it over a chair, then rested a tour guide next to his espresso. He raised an old thirty-five millimeter camera to his eye, trying to look like a tourist. In reality, he knew every inch of Manhattan, including Twenty-Third Street in Chelsea and this view of Treasured Maps. Adjusting the lens, he snapped pictures as if the facade of Tanya Taylor's building was of architectural interest.

And it was. The two-story brownstone had wide steps and curving scrolled handrails that met in a quaint gate. Both levels had floor-to-ceiling windows, decorated with autumnal wreaths, although the weather still felt more like summer. While lovely, the windows were covered with bars, and a computerized keypad on the front door was too complex to disarm. He hadn't dared go inside the downstairs shop during shop hours, in case he was detected by surveillance equipment.

Tanya lived upstairs, and while she opened the blinds, presumably to get better light when she painted, he'd only glimpsed her. She had her own entrance, separate from that of the shop, reached by rickety steps attached to the building's side. Probably, her interior door was equipped with formidable locks, too. Over the past few days, while staking her out, he'd thought he'd learn something about the place, or her, that would tell him how to break in. He supposed he could try to date her, but she didn't go out for drinks much, and when she did, it was with girlfriends. Besides he was too old.

But he needed that painting. As far as he was concerned, it belonged to him. Yes, Tanya had an O'Flannery inside the shop, and not just any O'Flannery, but one he'd sought for years. He hoped she'd taken it upstairs to her apartment, but with his luck, she'd locked it in a safe with her boss's precious maps.

"Of course she did," he muttered. If she wasn't going to protect it, she'd have left it in Weatherby's. She knew what it was worth. But why had she refused to sell? Had she guessed it was…special? Worth more than Weatherby's would ever ask?

He glanced around. Rays of twilight were shining down Twenty-Third Street, and from where he was seated, he could see to the river. Beyond cars streaming down the West Side Highway was the Chelsea Pier. Masts rose into the fading amber sun, and triangular folds of sails flapped in a soft breeze. It was a scene Stede O'Flannery might have painted.

"There she is," he whispered. As she appeared at the side of the building, carefully making her way down the precarious outer steps from her apartment, he tossed bills onto the table. Because he couldn't afford to waste pricey espresso, he downed it even though it scalded his tongue. Then he slung the camera strap over his shoulder and followed Tanya.

"THIS IS MAY at Finders Keepers. I hate to bother you—" the voice came over the answering machine "—but a week's passed, and I forgot to run your card through. I'm running it now."

Waking, Tanya rolled onto her back in bed, staring into the darkness. Had May called just now? But no…the answering machine had awakened Tanya a while ago, as she was drifting off. Last night, she'd worked on her show until dawn, and after taking a shower this afternoon, she'd closed the blinds, taking a nap so she'd be fresh for Izzie's opening tonight. She glanced at the digital clock on the bedside table. Almost seven-thirty. The opening had already started! Suddenly Tanya's heart missed a beat. She heard something…

Downstairs.

Wood creaked. Papers rustled. Her senses went on alert, and scents in the room sharpened. She could smell vanilla from a candle. Jasmine incense mixed with paint varnish. And something sharper still, woods and pine, like a woodsman…

Her hand groped over the bed's edge until she found a platform shoe. It weighed more than a brick. Good. She could bludgeon someone to death with it. Realizing she was holding her breath, she exhaled silently. Gingerly she pushed back the covers, aware she was clad only in a nightshirt. Adrenaline was drying her throat, leaving a metallic taste in her mouth as she got her bearings.

The outer door of her apartment was equipped with four noisy dead bolts. Her phone receiver wasn't in its cradle, but across the room, resting in the brush holder of her easel. Could she reach it without being heard?

Art thieves, she suddenly thought, damning herself for

overriding Eduardo and James's protestations and bringing a masterpiece home. Stunned, Eduardo had told her to bring the painting back when she was ready to sell, then James had left for vacation, closing the shop. She'd been jumpy ever since. No matter where she went, she felt as if someone were watching her. She blew out a sigh. Her heart had started to slow. *It's just your imagination,* she thought. *No one's here.*

Straining, she heard nothing. Sleeping next to a collector's item was crazy-making. So was the series of digital snapshots she'd taken of the work. Whenever she compared them, she could swear the figures had moved. Not much. Only a fraction. The man she admired had turned slightly, as if to run into the woods, and the blond man seemed to advance. Tanya's spine tingled as if spiders were crawling down the ladder formed by her vertebrae.

She didn't dare make her deeper thoughts any more conscious, much less voice them because the notions forming in her mind were crazy. Illogical. Impossible. Still, she sometimes thought the painting was…coming alive.

Another minute passed. She'd been wrong. No one was downstairs. *The security was great,* she reminded herself, still wondering what had come over her in Weatherby's. She'd felt leaving the painting in the auction house would be a…well, *betrayal.* Of him.

But now, lying in the dark, she knew she was only betraying herself. Selling the painting would generate enough money to change her life. Or someone else's. A creak sounded, and her heart hammered again. Was the building settling down? Or had Weatherby's staff leaked information about the rare find? But no. They were professionals. Another minute passed. No more sounds. Good.

Anyone else would have sold, she realized. Would she ever become what her folks would call a "normal" person? The kind with a good job, stable husband, two kids and a dog? Like her younger sister, Brittania?

Somebody coughed, and ice flooded her veins. Her hand froze around the shoe. She thought she heard a shot glass hitting the bar downstairs, and she gulped, realizing the door to the stairs must be open. She started to call out, "James." But he really was on vacation, on the other side of the world. *Oh God,* she thought, her mind racing as she edged off the bed. *Careful. He'll hear you.*

Was there more than one intruder? She cursed herself for shutting the blinds so tightly and leaving her phone on the other side of the room. What if she tripped over something in the dark? Biting back a gasp, she saw the door leading downstairs really was open. Just a fraction. He'd been upstairs, already! In her room! Watching her sleep!

She stifled a whimper. How had he—or he and others—gotten in? Her eyes darted around wildly. She had to close and lock the door between the floors before he heard her and came running.

Her mind raced. What about the alarm? And the computerized keypad? He—or they—must have come in some way. But how? She decided she'd run to the door, slam it shut and once it was locked, she'd grab her phone and call the police.

She could barely steady her hands. As she slowly crept toward the door, an explosive curse sounded. A cry escaped her lips. Then everything went quiet. Too quiet. Knowing it was now or never, that he'd heard her, she fled for the door.

So did he! Footsteps pounded on the stairs. He was coming up! She had to close the door and pull the chain across before he... Grabbing the door's edge, she tried to force it closed, but it caught on something.

"My foot!"

She stared down at a dark boot wedged in the crack. She tried not to panic, but terror consumed her heart. It was racing fast, exploding in her chest. She prayed she sounded stronger than she felt. "Get your foot out of the door!"

"Don't you be tellin' me what to do, miss."

She pushed harder.

He pushed back, and a tug-of-war ensued. It was like arm wrestling, and worse, he was stronger. He was winning. "I already called the police," she lied.

"I would 'a heard you on the..." He paused. "Telephone... That's it."

She barely registered his words. Someone at Weatherby's must have leaked information about the masterpiece, after all. "You can have the painting."

"I should hope so, miss. It's mine."

His? His voice was a barely discernable Irish brogue, the words strangely antiquated. The boot had odd buckles, too, like none she'd ever seen—and if there was one thing Tanya knew about, it was shoes. The boot looked strangely familiar, too, as if she'd seen a picture of it somewhere. And what did he mean when he'd said the painting was his? Had the proprietress of Finders Keepers learned of Eduardo's appraisal, then hired this man to steal the painting, feeling entitled to it?

At least he didn't seem to have accomplices. "Get your foot out of the door!"

"I'll do no such thing."

Instead he pushed again. Harder. Fear paralyzed her as she was forced backward. What if he intended more than theft? People had been killed for less than one-point-five million dollars. Eduardo said the painting might even bring two million. Renewed panic shot through her as the stranger's dark, hulking body crashed through the doorway.

Instinctively she hauled her hand back, swinging the platform. As he yelped, she ducked, glad Izzie and Marlo had coerced her to take dance classes. With practiced agility, she was able to limbo under his elbow. Eluding his grasp with a pirouette, she tumbled downstairs, running hard now, leaping over the bottom five steps.

She hit the floor running. *You've got to get to the front door!* The second it opened, an alarm would sound. Neighbors would come. Cops! But footsteps thundered behind her. She threw the platform to slow him down. He'd turned on the lamp at the bar before, so dim hazy light illuminated her steps. She had no time to wonder what he'd been doing downstairs. She was fifteen feet from the door. Then ten. Then five…

Gratitude filled her as she swept her arm wide, a splayed hand ready to grab the knob. Something pulled her back! A hand grasped her shirt! She lost her footing! Lunged! She couldn't gain traction. He pulled her backward, and viselike arms circled her waist. Turning, she wrenched hard as he brought her down, then gasped as he rolled with her to the floor.

He landed on top. The door was less than five feet away.

Maybe she could still reach it. Punching wildly, she hit his face while he tried to catch her flailing hands. Her pulse skyrocketed as the masculine scent of him filled her lungs. He writhed against her as she squirmed, his weight crushing her. "Get off me!"

"I've met nicer wildcats in the woods," he spat.

She felt dizzy. Faint. And no wonder. The dress for Izzie's opening had no longer fit, and she'd starved herself for days, so she could wear it. But now, her life depended on staying alert. Her nightshirt had risen, bunching around her waist. There was nothing between their bodies but her exposed panties and the thin fabric of his pants. Not jeans, she thought. Maybe cycling slacks. Heat twined through her limbs, feeling taut, like the corded ropes of his sinews.

He was so strong. Suddenly heat flooded her. He had an erection! He was twisting his torso, too, settling more comfortably between her legs. Was the maniac sexually assaulting her? Had she gotten this all wrong? Was his intrusion unrelated to the painting? But no…he'd said it was his. She tried to glimpse his face, her mind reeling, but hair was hanging in his face. If she got away, could she identify him for the police? "If you think you can rape me," she snarled, "you're—"

"Rape!" he exploded, rolling away. In a flash, he rose to his feet, towering over her. "If you ask me, America would be a better place with no women in it to rape a'tall! If it's not Basil Drake accusin' me, it's always somebody else! It's enough to make any man drink himself to death in McMulligan's and never kiss a wench again, much less show her his divining rod, I swear it is!"

Divining rod? What was he talking about? Whatever the

case, she used the advantage to scramble to her feet. She stilled. Indeed, she could only stare, her eyes bugging. The sexiest green-eyed gaze she'd ever seen flickered down her body feeling as hot as a flame. It settled near the throat of her nightshirt, studying cleavage. She became aware of her bare legs, and that fighting him had left her aroused and panting. But that wasn't the worst thing. Her eyes were deceiving her, or the light was too faint to be reliable.

And yet it was him.

The dark man from the painting. His hair was loose now, no longer tied back. Her hands had tangled with the strip of cloth holding it back, and it had fallen to the floor. Still, she'd know those eyes anywhere. The glittering emeralds followed her wherever she went.

"It's like you're seein' a ghost, isn't it?" he ventured.

Suddenly everything made sense. Relief coursed through her. "Where did James find you?" she demanded.

"James?"

She nodded, not about to be fooled. Surely James or Eduardo had found an actor to impersonate the figure in the painting. They were toying with her, since she'd insisted on bringing a masterpiece home. No doubt, they wanted to teach her a lesson and show her how dangerous it was to keep something so valuable in the apartment. Not that she was going to forgive them for the fright they'd given her. Still, she was calming down. At least until she registered the confusion on the man's face, which looked genuine.

"James?" he said again.

Reminding herself that he was probably a professional actor, she vowed she wouldn't get sucked into this. Pragmatically she said, "Or Eduardo. Maybe he hired you."

"Nobody hired me," the actor assured. "Believe you me, miss. I would have taken any job, since I've got but a few dollars in my pocket, leftover from last time I was here, back in the 1960s. I sojourned with a fellow—he went by the name of Julius Royle…. Well, anyway, miss, it's quite a long story, as you can imagine. The main thing is, that witch Missus Llassa must have put a hex on me, just like Lucinda said."

Julius Royle? Why did the name ring a bell? And Lucinda…well, she was reputed to have been Stede O'Flannery's patroness and lover, according to Eduardo. "Stop it," Tanya insisted. "The joke's gone far enough. You scared me to death. I could have had a coronary. And your timing's terrible." She hadn't needed to get this upset before Izzie's opening, since she wanted to look poised when she saw Brad again. She was going to kill James. Or Eduardo. This joke exceeded the bounds of good taste.

Sadness welled in the actor's eyes. "I wish all this 'twere a joke, miss. I figure I keep gettin' stuck in my own painting because of the hex. The last time I popped out was in the 1960s like I said. That's when I met Julius Royle, who took me under his wing."

"Julius Royle?" she echoed, now realizing why the name was familiar. She'd read about him. He was an old-monied heir who'd lived in the Village, on the fringes of the bohemian art scene, and he was reputed to have gone crazy in the sixties. His family had him committed. "This whole thing's getting stranger by the minute," she forced herself to say.

"I popped out once in the fifties, too," he added helpfully. "The 1950s, I mean. I was cramped up somethin' terrible, locked inside a crate when it happened. I've got no bloody idea why—"

Popped out? What was he talking about? Her long-suffering look stopped his chatter. He was a major stud, yes. Probably not dangerous, she decided. And she was absolutely certain James and Eduardo had hired him. Why else would the spitting image of the man in the picture be inside the shop? Ah. That was why the alarm hadn't sounded, too. James had given the man a key. Once she called his bluff, he'd leave and she could dress for Izzie's opening.

"Wait here," Tanya said simply. Pivoting, she strode to the stairs, taking them two at a time. Instead of heeding her, he followed, so he was right behind her when she reached her bedside table, switched on the lamp and stared at the painting.

He wasn't in it.

"He's gone," she whispered, slack-jawed. She stared at the leaves that shined down like sunbursts on the grassy clearing, piercing the surreal mist that looked like fairy dust. The blonde was still racing forward, his musket raised. But his target had vanished.

She stepped close enough to reach out a finger and trace where the dark figure had been, her knees weakening. She felt a quick pang of hunger, reminding her she hadn't eaten and her head swam. Everything faded to gray, although her eyes were open. She forced them open wider, but suddenly, she saw nothing at all. "This can't be happening," she stated in protest.

And then everything went black. In the instant before she fainted, she heard him mutter, "Sweet Betsy Ross. Not this again."

"THIS IS AN EXACT REPEAT of what happened with Lucinda right before the duel," Stede muttered, feeling forced to scoop the wench into his arms and carry her to bed. Using a free hand, he flung back the covers. Judging by the beating she'd given him, this chit was strong, but she was, thankfully, as light as a feather.

Sitting beside her, he released some buttons of her nightshirt. Not that it was restrictive. Nor did she wear a proper corset. Very little of her was covered, in fact. Still, it was better if a woman's chest met with open air when she swooned. Men had been preaching that bit of common wisdom since time immemorial. Only a cynic would say it was because they sought excuses for undressing vulnerable females. "Besides, as Poor Richard always said," Stede murmured, "'The only ones ill-clothed are those bare of virtue.'" And this woman had plenty of virtues, as far as Stede was concerned.

Still, he'd best be careful. Already, she'd cried rape. And as pretty as she was, she was sure to have plenty of male protectors, just as she'd claimed. He shot a worried glance toward the door, hoping Eduardo, James, or other suitors didn't choose tonight to come calling. Then he glanced at her again, steeling himself against the vision of creamy skin that looked as if it had never seen sunlight. She had a dusting of eyebrows and lashes, and heaving bosoms.

Just looking at her made his President Washington stir. He'd been as horny as a rooster downstairs, too. The way she'd writhed beneath him had been more than bothersome. He wasn't proud of his lack of restraint, but he'd nearly climaxed. There was no helping it. It had been too long since he'd last been satisfied. Now he knew he'd go crazy if he didn't have proper relations soon. With her or somebody else, he didn't care who. A faint smile played on his lips. At least this meant Missus Llassa's spell probably hadn't affected his ability to perform. And that had been his greatest worry.

"Now, let's see where she put her salts."

He headed for the kitchen area, where he figured she kept supplies. Probably, she was some sort of serving wench by day, judging by the garret. And a very good painter, he realized, glancing at the works. As the scents of oil and varnish knifed into his lungs, he felt the first surge of hope he'd experienced in quite some time. Centuries, in fact. Vague memories stirred inside him, too. Images as jumbled as those she painted were coming back to him as he rifled through her cabinets.

Being consigned to the horrifying darkness of the painting was strange, indeed. Like living in a netherworld of shadows. Not really living, but not dead, either. Even in his half-sleep, he picked up information from the contraption they called a television. And he could see things, too. Countless images whirled in his mind. He was sure he'd passed centuries in a dusty attic. Yes…it was like he'd wanted to sneeze for a hundred years. He remembered Julius Royle, and wondered if the man was still living. How Stede would love to see his friend again!

Suddenly he inhaled sharply. He remembered more now. Aye…he was watching the woman paint. She'd stopped, sent him an inviting glance over her shoulder, then twitched her backside as if for the benefit of his pleasure. After that, she'd put strange, tiny gloves onto her fingertips…gloves very unlike the type ladies wore to dances.

They didn't even cover her whole hands. Then she'd begun to touch herself lasciviously. She'd lain on the bed naked, slightly parting her legs, so he could see everything....

Swift heat claimed his groin, making blood surge, but he couldn't afford the feelings. He had to keep his mind keen. If he wasn't careful, he was going to wind up as incapacitated as the woman in bed. And where would he be then?

"Back in my own painting," he muttered. Who knew how much time he had before he was imprisoned once more? He had to spend every waking minute discovering the exact nature of Missus Llassa's hex, so he could be set free. He had no time to court a wench. And if he did find time to spare, he'd be better off digging up the war booty he'd left on Manhattan Island and taking his gold to a pawn shop. Last time he was here, Julius Royle had explained that shopkeepers only took new greenbacks now. If he wound up stuck in his own painting again, it might as well be with a pocketful of usable bills.

She moaned. He braced himself against the sound, feeling as faint as she looked. Aye, it was he, not she, who'd soon be needing the salts. She didn't sound like a women in need of vapors, though, but one in the throes of passion. Which was just his own wishful thinking, he reminded himself as he rifled through cabinets with renewed effort.

"Ah," he said, relieved. "Salts."

The blue-wrapped, cylindrical container looked nothing like any salts he'd seen before. A picture on the front depicted a girl in a short yellow dress, carrying an umbrella. She was every bit as bare-legged as the woman in bed. "Morton Iodized Salt," he said, reading the label.

With bare-legged pictures such as this on the labels, he'd bet these salts sold as fast as shots of McMulligan's best whiskey. But Mark McMulligan's pub was gone now....

Sadness threatened to overwhelm him, but he refused to let feelings of mourning in—not of losing his mama, nor his papa, nor Lucinda. Nor of McMulligan's pub, which was lost to history, or how he'd been stuck inside a painting, due to the jealousy of that pretender and no-account rake, Basil Drake.

Shaking the container, he headed to the bed again. Inside, the salts sounded loose. "Guess they keep 'em like gunpowder nowadays. Well, salts are salts," he muttered, sitting on the bed's edge, trying to ignore her scent. It was floral, probably from bottles of perfumes and powders that sat on a nearby chest of drawers.

Fortunately she was still out like taper flame, so he had a moment to catch his breath. After studying the salts box, he slid a nail beneath the silver spout and raised the container to his nose, frowning. "The wonders of new inventions. Salts that don't even smell," he marveled. Now, that was really something. Some genius named Morton must have invented them.

He pored some into his cupped hand. What had Poor Richard always said? "'In success, be moderate,'" he mused, answering his own question. Pinching salts between his thumb and index finger, he wavered a moment, then tossed them at her face, trying to hit the inch-wide spot between her nose and upper lip. The nose twitched. And a fetching nose it was, too. It had the gentle curve of a good saddle.

But she didn't awaken. Hmm. Salts worked better back

when they smelled like ammonia. He poured some more, pinched, then tossed them at her. Now her eyelashes fluttered, so he shook out another portion, this time straight from the container. Tasting them on her lips, she sputtered.

"Good," he murmured. "Yer wakin' up now."

Surely the salts couldn't taste good, but his stomach rumbled. He was starving. It felt like years since he'd eaten, and he realized it had been. Bacon and eggs, he suddenly thought. That's what he'd had before setting off for his duel with Basil. What he wouldn't give to taste just one more of McMulligan's hotcakes! Pushing aside the thought, he leaned and shook the woman's shoulder; the soft sleeve of her nightshirt teased his palm, feeling as silken as her skin looked, and his throat suddenly constricted. Fortunately she was still sputtering, saving him from his own sappy emotions. She abruptly sneezed. Then everything happened quickly.

"What are you doing?" she yelped, scurrying backward in bed, away from him.

She might not want his help, but the salts had worked, so he was on the right track. "Now, let's take off that wig, lass," he soothed. Why such a pretty female would be wearing a man's powdered wig, Stede would never know.

The prettiest blue eyes he'd ever seen were merely staring at him. "Don't look at me as if I'm crazy enough to be boarded onto a ship of fools," he couldn't help but warn.

She still looked faint. "Ship of fools?"

"The *Narrenschiff,*" he clarified. "You know how they used to load vagabonds and criminals and those of deranged mind onto sailin' crafts and let 'em float from town to town?"

She shook her head slowly, as if to clear it of confusion.

"I only sail on privateer vessels," he quickly assured.

She squinted at him. "What did you say about my wig?"

"You look like you belong in a Whig court."

"Wig court?" she said hoarsely. "What?"

He was starting to wonder if she lacked intelligence. It would be unfortunate, but not the worst quality in a woman, of course. "That powdered wig of yours," he explained. Had she been wearing a waistcoat, breeches and boots, she could have passed for one of the founding fathers.

"It's my *hair,* you jerk," she returned succinctly.

Embarrassed, heat flooded his cheeks. Surely that couldn't be. Instinctively he reached, threading salt-dusted fingers into the strands and tugging, but it was her scalp, all right. Her hair was softer than any man's wig, too. Tendrils teased the spaces between his fingers, flowing between them like running water. Still, the hair was strange to look at. Disheveled. As white as snow. Fuzzy curls framed skin as dainty as fancy teacups.

"Sorry, miss," he murmured, his eyes trailing over her face, unsure what he thought of the hair, until he recalled it wasn't the first time he'd seen hair this color. When he'd popped out in the 1960s, Julius had showed him a picture of a courtier named Marilyn Monroe who'd had hair like this.

The young miss was eyeing him warily. "Could I get out of bed?"

Coming to his senses, he stood and backed away a few paces, to give her room.

"Do you mind?" she huffed. Grabbing a pair of pants

from the floor, she shoved long legs into them. He'd seen pants on women, both in the fifties and the sixties, but it still took some getting used to. And until right this second, he'd forgotten all about zippers.

Vaguely he recalled Julius buying him new clothes, which he'd worn for a week. Mostly tie-dyed shirts and what they'd called bell-bottom pants. He'd only put his riding clothes back on when the new clothes needed to be laundered, and that's when…he'd wound up in the painting again.

He frowned. Did Missus Llassa's hex involve a one-week time frame? His pulse quickened. Aye…the last date he remembered in the fifties was July 11, 1956. He'd come out of the painting for one week, exactly. To the minute. Just as in 1969. This time, maybe he'd break the spell.

He stared at what he assumed was a clock. It had no face, just red numbers. He'd seen it as soon as he'd popped out, and it had said seven-fifteen. Would he vanish one week hence, on Friday night, at exactly seven-fifteen?

The woman was studying him. Her eyes were like two liquid blue pools he'd just as soon drown in. He fought the urge to grab her, pull her to the floor and ravish her. Because it had been so long, he'd knew he'd act like a savage, hungrily pushing open her lips with his tongue, exploring the silk of her inner cheeks, plundering every inch of her skin. Generally he tried to be a gentleman, but he hadn't had proper relations for over two hundred years. At least judging by the newspaper he'd taken downstairs, which claimed it was September 10, 2006. Since puberty, he'd scarcely gone a week without relations, and if the truth be told, he wouldn't feel thoroughly safe until he was absolutely positive Missus Llassa hadn't tampered with his male organs. That meant bringing a sexual act to satisfying completion, and not just for himself, but for his partner. After all, pleasing the woman was the mark of a real man's prowess.

"Who are you?" she whispered.

He hoped she'd be as kind as Julius Royle, but that was probably too much to ask. Still, if this woman helped him, even a little bit, maybe he could find Julius. The man had been a real friend.

Before he could answer, she muttered, "That thing can't be real."

He followed her gaze. It was fixed in the proximity of his groin, which made heat rise to his cheeks. Thinking about having relations had aroused him once more, and he felt ashamed of himself. *All those papas were right. You're nothing but a low-down dirty rascal around whom no man's daughter is safe,* he thought. His waistcoat was unbuttoned, and he was straining the strings of his breeches like a randy schoolboy. Still, he wasn't sure whether the woman had been referring to his condition, or his holstered musket, so he settled on saying, "Very real, indeed, miss."

"Who are you?" she repeated, her voice more demanding.

"I go by the name o' Stede O'Flannery."

"Impossible."

He didn't blame her for wishing that was so. Gentling his voice, he said, "I think you know the truth, Tanya."

She sucked a quick breath through small, perfect, very white teeth. "You know my name?"

He hadn't been sure. "Saw it on yer letters." As near as

he could tell, someone named James owned the shop downstairs, from which maps were sold.

She nodded slowly.

"Now, why don't we go back downstairs?" he suggested, his throat feeling dry again, probably because he'd just watched her thrust those shapely legs into pants of stretch material that showed every curve. "I found a bottle of good whiskey, and I could use another shot."

Her eyes darted to the painting once more, and she studied the empty space where Stede had once painted himself into the landscape. It was days after the duel, and he'd been on the deck of a privateer vessel, sailing out of town. He'd wanted to leave a painted account of what had really happened that morning, just for the record. Then, everything had become hazy. At first he thought he'd died. And then he simply felt as if he were…drifting.

Her voice brought him back to the present. "A shot of whiskey?" she said, her voice scarcely audible. Then she added something that was music to his ears. "I think I could use one, too."

3

"MIND IF I POUR?" he asked, once they were downstairs.

"Please do." Tanya managed, nodding as she slid onto a stool at the island-style bar and looked at him. Her hands were shaking, and if she tried to fix their drinks, she knew she'd spill what had turned out to be one of James's prized bottles of aged whiskey. Reading the label, she winced. How was she going to explain the raid on his liquor supply when he got back from vacation? Surely he hadn't told this guy to help himself....

As much as she was determined not to remove her gaze from the intruder, in case he made any sudden moves, she glanced toward the open door leading to the basement James loftily called his wine cellar. When she found her voice again, she murmured dryly, "I see you found James's stash."

She was surprised to find that she hadn't sounded as unsettled as she felt, which was good. In fact, she'd sounded extremely calm. Maybe too calm, since her pulse was ticking like a stopwatch. When her gaze darted through the windows, she relaxed somewhat. Just past the autumnal wreaths she'd helped James put up, she could see people in the street. The outdoor tables at a sidewalk café across from them were packed, and a tourist even had a camera pointed in her direction.

Adrenaline surged through her. She should bolt for the door again, but something kept her on the stool. Maybe the fact that he'd stopped her from running once before. Or maybe curiosity. *Or lust.* That suggestion came unbidden, and she submerged quickly. The important thing was that if she started screaming bloody murder, someone might hear.

He seemed to read her mind. "Don't you be running scared again," he warned.

She tried to look calm and collected. "Is that a threat?"

"A request."

Somehow, she doubted it. Then again, she'd fainted and he hadn't harmed her. Thoughts raged through her mind with the speed of a brushfire, and when her gaze meshed with his, everything felt just as hot, too. When she'd come to, she'd thought an extra button of her shirt had come undone, but that could have happened during their tussle. And he hadn't tried to trap her upstairs, where she'd have been more vulnerable, which gave her some relief. Yes, if he was going to try anything physical, he'd have taken the opportunity already. And if James and Eduardo had hired him, the guy must have had a key to the place. No windows were open, and like the front door, they had alarms.

For a second, upstairs, she'd believed he was really Stede O'Flannery, and that he'd stepped out of one of his own paintings, but now, her head was clearing. James had even told him where to find the whiskey. That's what must have happened. Yes, James knew all about this. So, soon enough, she'd get a reasonable explanation. Biting back a sudden gasp, she wondered if Eduardo had asked one of his restoration experts to produce a facsimile painting, exactly like the one upstairs, *sans* the man standing in front of her.

"A shekel," he said.

"Shekel?"

"For your thoughts."

"I thought it was a penny," she murmured, then raised her voice, assuring, "too many to enumerate." Whatever the case regarding his identity, curiosity was getting the better of her, and she wanted to play along. As least for a few more minutes. Pushing aside a visceral memory of how his warm, strong body had covered hers, trapping her on the floor, she slowly scanned the street—taking in the café, dry cleaner's, and a pretzel vendor—then she studied her strange houseguest again.

In turn, he glanced quickly away, like the proverbial kid with his hand caught in the cookie jar. Maybe he, too, was suddenly remembering the body heat they'd generated. Inhaling sharply, she found herself recalling how hard and inviting he'd felt, with those long, muscular, tight-encased legs trailing between hers. As if reading her thoughts, he made a soft rumbling sound. Ignoring a shot glass he'd already used, he took two highball glasses from a wire rack, then raised the bottle of whiskey and read the label.

"Aye. I found the stash as you call it, indeed," he finally began, speaking in a throaty voice that sent another unwanted vibration careening through her already jangling system. "And this didn't taste too bad a'tall for being so recently bottled."

Was he crazy? "Recently bottled?"

"Nineteen fifteen. The newest bottle I could find." Before

she could respond, he added, "There's nearly as many spirits down in that cellar as I buried in Killman's cave."

Spirits? For a second, her mind was catching at threads again, all of which seemed to be strangely elusive. She'd thought he was chattering about ghosts, since he, himself, might be one. At least if he was really Stede O'Flannery, which he wasn't, she assured herself for the umpteenth time. Then she realized he'd been talking about alcohol, not spirits of the netherworld variety. "Killman's cave?"

"Aye. That's one place where I put some of my own stash. My spirits, and treasures, and paintings, and such." Before she could question him about that, he rushed on, "And James? He'd be your…"

"Employer."

Something unreadable crossed his features. "Not a suitor, then?"

"Uh…no."

"And Eduardo? Is he a'wooin' ya, miss?"

She felt a moment's pique at how he was interrogating her, then almost burst out laughing at the idea of she and Eduardo as a couple. He was a real shark, not one of James's favorite clients. "He's a buyer at Weatherby's."

"The auction house? In London?"

"They have a business in New York, too," she informed him, realizing something was going terribly wrong, since it hadn't been her intention to start a normal conversation.

"Sweet Betsy Ross. So, I really am in New York?"

"Uh…yes." Definitely she needed to regain the upper hand before the odd direction of this encounter moved along much further. She was getting her bearings, and she still wanted to wrest a confession from him, regarding who he really was.

But he pressed on. "So, Eduardo's not a suitor?"

"No," she managed to say. "Um…I think he might be gay, but I'm not really sure."

"I do hope he *is* gay!" the man exclaimed. "It's a world full o' remarkable inventions, and despite my own sad and sorry circumstances, I still count myself as lucky as any four-leaf clover! There's no excuse for a man bein' glum." He paused a split second. "Well, whatever the fellow's disposition, you're not a'courtin'?"

She shook her head, trying to tell herself he didn't look relieved to hear it, but she saw interest in his gaze, and a quick thrill zinged through her, taking her by complete surprise. It was as unwanted as it was undeniable, especially under these bizarre circumstances, but her eyes drifted over his frame again. He seemed to be one of those people who seemed blessed with…a little something extra. Call it what you would, charm, magnetism or charisma.

Due to his looks alone, he shouldn't have been so heartstopping, although he was about six feet tall, with a looselimbed, rangy body that was moving on the other side of the island bar as if his bones had been oiled from within. He was squinting hard in her direction, his dark, bushy eyebrows arched like hoods over sparkling gems of eyes that were fringed by a spray of equally inky eyelashes, and barely visible in the shadowy room. Abruptly, as if he'd just gotten extremely thirsty, he tilted the whiskey bottle and began to pour.

"I see you're no stranger to a bar," she said, anxious to shift the subject from her romantic life.

He took in the excellently appointed countertop, with its high-end corkscrews, crystal glasses and cocktail shakers. "I used to live in a room above such an establishment, went by the name o' McMulligans. Saw it built from the ground up in 1786."

The words carried a ring of veracity, and suddenly, everything seemed as surreal as when she'd first seen the painting. Once more, she visualized it, hanging upstairs, sans the dark figure, and she fought the urge to run up and look again. Surely her eyes had been deceiving her. Maybe she was even dreaming. Besides, the figure had been about three inches tall, the size of a toy soldier. Maybe this man just seemed to be his spitting image, due to the change in scale. Still, every single nuance was the same, right down to the breeches and boots.

Her throat went bone-dry. "Are you going to pour?" she managed, realizing there wasn't enough whiskey in the basement, much less the world, to offset what was happening.

"Quite right. We don't have all day, now, do we? Time's of the essence, especially in my case, miss." Before filling her glass, he lifted his own, downed a healthy gulp of warm whiskey, then prepared to fill both glasses again, giving himself a double portion.

She drew a deep, steadying breath. It was strange enough that he was here, but if he wound up drunk, she'd be in hot water. Worse, a rumble sounded, as if to point out he was imbibing on an empty stomach, too. "Maybe you'd better eat first," she found herself saying, aware that there were countless issues to discuss, and that she was doing her best to avoid them, while secretly deciding what she thought of his odd appearance in her home.

"I am so hungry I could eat pig-slop," he admitted.

"No need to go that far," she managed. "What do you want? I eat mostly vegan."

There was something off-center about his facial features, just as in the painting, she decided. Whatever it was, it added rather than detracted from his good looks. He had high cheekbones, but a tapered chin where one might have expected to find a square jaw, and a prominent nose. A dusting of dark hair served as a mustache and goatee. He was real enough. But there was no way he could be Stede O'Flannery.

He was staring at her. Finally he said, "Virgin?"

She squinted. "Excuse me?"

"You eat virgin?"

She almost choked on her whiskey. "Vegan."

"Meanin'?"

Was he for real? "I don't eat meat or cheese."

He looked confused. "What's left to eat then, other than the plate?"

He looked so appalled that she admitted it was only a passing fad. "I'm watching my cholesterol."

"Yer what?"

This conversation was going nowhere. "Never mind. For you," she promised. "The Atkins Diet."

"Atkins?"

"All meat."

"I'll eat whatever you're having, miss," he conceded politely. "As Poor Richard always says, 'Hunger never saw bad bread.'" With that, he lifted a highball glass, clinked it to hers and vowed, "I'd be happy to eat pure lard on pine wood, I swear I would." He paused. "It's just good to be back in the world."

"Hear, hear," she said, her fingers curling more tightly around her glass. It felt unexpectedly comforting. Cool to the touch. The whiskey was better, tangy on her lips, warm in her mouth, hotter as it traveled down her throat and curled in her belly. For just a second, she shut her eyes, sure she was dreaming. And yet, just now, when he'd said it was good to be back, she was sure she'd seen a tear of gratitude in his eye.

Only when she opened her eyes did she realize she'd been half expecting him to disappear. But he was standing in the same place, dressed in the antiquated outfit. She watched him swirl the amber liquid in his glass, as if mesmerized, then he knocked back another healthy gulp and released a sigh of ecstasy, as if he'd never tasted anything quite so wonderful. "King George the Third never got a taste of this whiskey," he announced with relish.

She wasn't exactly the world's greatest history buff. "I think this was bottled after his time, right?"

"And he never saw a television or a telephone, or all the things Julius Royle showed me," he continued.

"Guess you're one up on King George the Third, then."

Suddenly he grinned, making her heart do crazy flip-flops. His smile was over-the-top. Captivating. Dazzling. His voice was as warm as the whiskey when he said, "Indeed I am, miss!" He sighed deeply. "Despite my misfortune, indeed I am."

She barely heard. With the smile, he'd gone from being

merely charismatic in a bad-boy sort of way, to being down-right dangerous. And she hated guys who looked like this. She always wound up doing far too many old-fashioned girly-girl type things for them, such as cooking, cleaning and laundry. Already, she'd offered to feed him. *'Fess up, Tanya,* she thought. Already, she was on the road to ruin. Upstairs, the paint was drying on work she was supposed to display next week. She had her career to worry about. Very studiously, she forced herself not to smile back at him.

Not that he noticed. "Hope you don't mind my explor-in', miss," he pressed on, sounding as if he hadn't much time. "But I knew you'd not wish to be awakened. Besides the whiskey, I found plenty o' maps, too. I take it this employer of yours, James…he'd be a sailor, then?"

Spinning on the bar stool, she looked behind her, and gasped when she saw James's maps spread on a drafting table. She rose to her feet and strode toward the mess. James might forgive one bottle of whiskey, especially if he'd told the guy he could have it, but any damage to his precious maps would result in an irreparable rift. She'd lose her job and apartment in one fell swoop.

"You didn't get to the ones in the safe, did you?" she asked, anxiety making her heart pound.

"Oh, good. A safe. That means there's more."

"Only for customers," she managed. "This is a map shop."

"Treasured Maps," he agreed. "Saw it printed on the door."

"Rare maps," she added. Buyers came from all over the world just to look at them. Surely he knew that, at least if he knew James. Relief flooded her as she looked down at the drafting table. The top map was undamaged. No rings from a shot glass. No fingerprints. No spittle. After pinching the edges, she carefully carried the map toward a metal cabinet, specially designed to keep large maps flat and dust-free.

"Mind telling me what I've done, miss?"

Miss. She liked that he was calling her that, more than she wanted to admit, but the thought was fleeting. Whatever equilibrium she'd regained, she lost when she returned to the drafting table. "Oh no," she muttered. Under the top map was a glazed lithograph dated 1879. Beneath that was a hand-colored engraving by Elisha Robinson.

"Sorry, miss, but I…"

"These are very valuable." Her heart hammering, she glanced at him, her mind reeling. Those dangerously sexy eyes were sparkling with confusion and emotion that was hard to deny, and the fact that he looked so genuinely sorry made her heart soften. Silently she cursed herself for being so weak when it came to gorgeous men. "They really are collector's items," she added. In case he still didn't understand, she continued, "Some aren't even for sale, and James lends them to museums."

He looked utterly taken aback, and he'd gone a shade paler. "Well, I guess they would be collector's items," he conceded. Tilting his head, he seemed to be doing mental calculations. "Right you are, miss. They'd be years younger than me, and yet they're old. This is all stranger than a cold day in June, now, isn't it? I'd only hoped to adjust my inner compass and get my bearings," he explained. "Since I have a few wee days to undo a hex and retrieve my treasure, as I've been tryin' to tell ya."

Truly, talking to him was unsettling. Disorienting.

"Treasure?" It was the second time he mentioned it. She racked her brain. "The treasure in Killman's cave?"

He nodded quickly, as if pleased to see she was finally getting on page. "War booty mostly. And I've got some more buried near the city wall."

"Good," she managed to return. "Because if you destroy James's maps, you're going to have to pay him for them. And that'll cost you a fortune. For your sake, I hope it's a *lot* of war booty."

"I'd never destroy a man's property and not pay," he assured, looking offended. "What do you take me for? A low-down scoundrel like Basil Drake?"

Rather than answer, she took a very deep breath and simply headed for the whiskey again. Staring at him pointedly, she took a sip, and suddenly, her head swum. For a second, she was sure she'd faint again. Once more, she silently cursed herself for eating so much chocolate after her breakup. Without foregoing food the past few days, she'd never get into the dress she was to wear tonight.

"If I'd o' found one, I would have used one of your televisions to get my bearings," he added helpfully.

Lifting a remote from the bar, she pressed a button. Behind him, a wall partition rolled back to expose a flat-screen television. "There," she said.

He was eyeing the remote, like a boy eyeing candy. Quickly gliding his hand over hers, he took it, and an electric jolt from his touch skated up her arm to her elbow, then fizzled into something warm that exploded in her tummy. Toying with the buttons, he found CNN, stared a moment, then studied the buttons and lowered the sound. "Are ya still in Vietnam?" he asked, making her lips part in surprise.

"Uh…I think the U.S. left there in 1975."

Feeling a definite need to keep moving, if only to escape the gaze that was following her every move, she headed for the small refrigerator behind him and pressed her glass against the ice dispenser.

When ice tumbled down, he uttered another sound of surprise. "Sons of liberty," he murmured. Following suit, he edged her out of the way, pressed his glass against the dispenser, then flinched as the ice came down, as if it might burn him. "Now, this must be new. Julius didn't have one of these."

"An ice dispenser?"

"Ice dispenser," he repeated, as if trying on the words for size.

There wasn't enough whiskey in the world to help her through this bizarre encounter. She skedaddled back to the bar, thinking that James and Eduardo both knew costume designers in the city. The waistcoat didn't look like part of a Broadway costume, though, nor did the musket, or the strange, dusty leather thong the man retrieved from the floor now, to tie back his hair. Her eyes lingered on the strands. She'd felt them brush against her cheek, and even now, her skin was burning from the softest thing she'd ever felt.

"Look," she suddenly said. "I admit it. I've been playing along for the past few minutes. And I really don't understand why James or Eduardo went to such lengths to produce this elaborate ruse, but…"

He looked appalled. "Your employer and the gay man," he said. "Do you think they're somehow foolin' ya, miss?"

The worst thing was, the man looked entirely ready to

defend her honor. "I don't know how the figure who looks like you vanished from the painting upstairs," she began.

"That was me!" he exploded, leaping to his feet.

"Please stop," she said. Already, she could tell this guy was a real steamroller.

His emerald eyes were flashing fire. "I thought you believed me, miss! There's a hex on me! A curse I tell you! And I need your help until I find Julius Royle. He's my only true friend. Unless of course, he's dead, which he might well be!" He paused. "Not that you care a wit, miss!"

He'd said the last as if she were the most heartless woman to ever walk the planet. "Sorry," she began. "I don't want to make you mad, really I don't. But you've got to admit—"

"I admit nothing! I've done nothing!"

"Maybe not, but you're in my apartment—"

"I gave away my fire, but Basil came gunning for me, anyway," he vowed righteously, his wounded gaze piercing hers, imploringly. "The man came to kill me in cold blood, he did!"

The events to which he was referring seemed very present to him, as if they'd happened yesterday. "Gave away your fire?"

"A delope!" he exclaimed, his eyes searching hers as if he believed she might be lacking in intelligence. "What exact part can't you understand, miss?"

"Don't start insulting my mental acumen."

He huffed a sigh. "Sweet sons of liberty, woman! As sure as my name's Stede O'Flannery, I've got but a wee week to reverse the hex Missus Llassa put on me, or I'll be back inside that fool paintin' again. Next Friday night, at seven-fifteen on the dot, I'll…disappear." His voice broke. "Please, miss. It's no fun livin' inside yer own paintin'."

All at once, she realized history really was repeating itself. Her head swam, her knees buckled, her eyes were wide-open, but she saw nothing at all. And then she set her glass quickly on the bar and fainted again.

When she came to, she was lying on the floor once more, stretched on her back, as if for her own wake. She half expected to see even more sexy Irishmen dancing jigs around her, while finishing off the rest of James's aged whiskey. But there was only one. He was hovering over her, wielding a container of Morton Salt.

"Oh, my God," she whispered, her voice sounding strangled to her own ears. "You think that's full of smelling salts, don't you?"

Looking uncertain, he surveyed the container. "They didn't smell like it," he admitted.

Shakily she sat up, pressing her hand to her forehead. Her palm was sweating. And now she felt a trickle of perspiration drip from her nape down her spine. She shivered, then heard him mutter, "Are ya cold, miss?"

Before she could answer, he'd shrugged, divesting himself of the waistcoat and slinging it around her. It was heavy, the fabric like nothing she'd felt before, the buttons seemingly of real silver. Clutching an edge of it, she realized her heart was beating out of control. She still didn't believe him, not really.

"Maybe you'd better start from the beginning and tell me everything," she finally said, barely realizing she'd slipped a hand into his. As he helped her to her feet, she felt that strange, unexpected tingle once more. This one entered her bloodstream and danced a jig of it's own. Still dizzy, she slipped onto the bar stool again.

"I do have some papers about Stede O'Flannery's history that might be of use to you," she found herself continuing, barely able to believe she was saying the words. "Eduardo copied them for me when I took the painting to Weatherby's for appraisal."

He looked mortified. "You have a dossier on me?"

"It doesn't say exactly what the curse is," she defended. She had a fleeting fantasy that James and Eduardo were taping this on the shop's security cameras. Surely they'd jump out from behind the furniture soon, shouting, "Surprise!" But yesterday, she placed a business call to James, and he really had been on vacation, in his hotel. "According to the information Eduardo gave me, Stede O'Flannery has to fall in love in order to end the curse."

He was staring at her as if she was lower than a common earthworm, not that the contemptuous expression did a thing to mar his good looks. "Then what're you standing there for, miss!"

Her lips parted in astonishment. "Excuse me?"

Thrusting back his waistcoat, he placed his hands on his hips and began pacing furiously, drumming his sides with his fingertips. "The dossier, now, miss."

She could merely stare. He'd crashed into her room, removed James's maps from the cabinet and drank the best whiskey in the house. "I don't like the tone you're taking with me."

His eyes blazed brightly. "How would you like being stuck inside a paintin' for two hundred years?"

Once more, something in the gaze wound up softening

her heart. Other parts of her turned to mush. "Wait right here," she said against her better judgment and headed for the stairs. What he'd called the "dossier" was on her bedside table, within easy reach. Grabbing it, she returned downstairs, then felt a twinge of guilt. He hadn't moved a muscle. He was still standing there, hands on his hips, a look in his eyes as expectant as a kid's eyes on Christmas.

"Here," she said.

"I've gotta fall in love?" he muttered grumpily, sounding none too happy about the idea as he set the file on the bar, opened it, and began scanning the contents.

"Are you okay?" she suddenly asked. Because he didn't look it. As he read, his face grew increasingly pale. His fingers began to shake, calling her attention to broad, strong hands. They had long, beautiful, artistic fingers, of just the sort that might produce artworks like the one upstairs. His lips parted in fury, or surprise, or both, and his glittering eyes looked as hard as rocks now.

They were so intent, that it was clear he hoped what he found inside this file could save his life.

4

_____

"I'LL TRY your tiramisu," the watcher said, and as the waiter left to fill the order, he peered over the *New York Times*. Inside Treasured Maps, Tanya Taylor was no longer alone, but the interior was too dark to make out the identity of her visitor. Judging by her guest's comparative size, the person was male, though. In the past two hours, he'd taken his eyes from the front door of Treasured Maps for less than five minutes, so how had he missed seeing someone enter the shop?

Maybe no one *had* entered the shop. His body tensed with anticipation. Had he finally found what he'd sought for the past forty years?

He glanced around. He was still playing the tourist to the hilt. His silver hair had receded on top, but he'd pulled what was left of it back, forming a two-inch ponytail that protruded from beneath a Mets baseball cap he'd bought from a kiosk. The cap went well, he thought, with his T-shirt. It bore a bright red heart and proclaimed, I Love New York.

The waiter returned with the tiramisu. "May I get you anything else, sir?"

"That's all. Thanks."

He'd craved the dessert, but now he kept his eyes fixed on the darkened windows of Treasured Maps. The only illumination came from a dim lamp on what looked to be an island-style bar. Tanya and the man had vanished for a while, presumably upstairs, and after they'd returned, the exchange had gotten heated.

Why were they arguing? Every minute that ticked by felt like eternity. For nearly forty years he'd watched and waited, after all. Years ago, he'd discovered the greatest art find the world would ever know, hadn't he? His mind suddenly had swum with colors, vibrant golds, verdant greens. Never before had he seen canvasses come so alive. Ripe, plump and dusted with frost, grapes in the still life's he'd once collected looked as if they'd been plucked from a vine.

But the paintings were nothing next to Tanya's particular find. It was a key that would unlock all the deepest mysteries of life. "Life," he murmured now. "Death. Limbo. The netherworld." The privileged would pay anything to study the secret Tanya Taylor had unearthed, albeit unwittingly. It had been conjured in a cauldron, by a witch in a New England cottage many years ago.

A movement caught his eye. The larger figure stalked toward the windows, then vanished. A heartbeat later, a bright light snapped on. The watcher's breath caught as a broad-chested man came into view. His white frilly shirt had puffed sleeves, and when the man pivoted, the watcher whispered, "It's him."

At least, he thought it was. But he had to be sure. Had he rediscovered a supernatural secret that would explode the preconceived notions most people lived by? Yes…up would appear down. Black would appear white. Everything would go topsy-turvy. Most people didn't even have minds that could bend this far.

"And maybe that's a blessing," he murmured, his voice now tinged with world-weariness.

After all, if he was right, this man had been in his teens when the revolutionary war ended, traversed time and space and survived centuries. He could tell truths about the American past that were long-buried under seas and soil, or otherwise lost to the whims and conjectures of professional historians.

"Stede O'Flannery," he asked softly. "Is it really you?"

"WHY, IT'S NO WONDER yer so scared of me, miss!" Stede exclaimed, once he'd turned on an overhead light, so he could better read the dossier.

"I'm not scared," she defended.

She looked terrified, though, and he didn't blame her one bit. "Don't you be worrying, lass—" His voice rang with conviction. "I can explain everything."

"Fast, I hope," she said. Despite the questions swimming in her eyes, she glanced at a wall clock. "Because I've got to leave in a half hour. I've got to get to Izzie's party. Lately I feel I've let her down, and…"

As her voice trailed off, he wondered how he'd keep all the people in her life straight. First, there was James and Eduardo, and now… "Izzie?"

"My friend."

His heart squeezed tight. Real friends were hard to come by, so it would be a shame for her to miss this, but attending a shindig tonight was impossible, not that he had the heart to tell her, at least not yet. Not when she was perched on the lip of the stool as if poised to run, still wrapped in his waistcoat, which was swallowing her as surely as waves could overtake a sinking frigate. One hand was clutching the collar of her nightshirt, which she'd rebuttoned all the way to the top; the other was curled around a whiskey glass, as if, next to Izzie, whiskey was her only true friend in the world. It was a sentiment Stede shared completely.

She was watching him through sweet eyes as round as moons. "Why didn't ya tell me about all these lies?" he demanded, trying to keep from losing his patience when his gaze landed on the dossier again. "My paintings might have made ladies a wee bit overexcited," he admitted. "Once or twice, they sneaked into my room above McMulligan's. Came like thieves in the night, they did," he vowed. "Offering their favors and such, but I didn't bed a one of them. You must believe me."

"I didn't accuse you of anything," she said carefully.

Now, that was a pretty lie, too! It was in the shaking of her hands and the tremor of her voice. Just looking at him had made her faint, not once, but twice! He sighed. Given how aroused he got every time their gazes locked, he knew it was better not to keep talking about sexual congress. Still…

Chewing his lower lip, he put his hands on his hips, then forced himself to inhale deeply, and then exhale slowly, hoping his feelings would abate. He needed to keep a clear head. "Now, do ya mind tellin' me where you got this lying dossier, miss?"

"I told you. It's a copy of Weatherby's files." She watched him as if he was a ghost or a phantom, which he supposed he was. "They've sold…some of Stede O'Flannery's paintings."

So, she still didn't believe he was Stede. Still…Julius

had told him his paintings had become collector's items, which made sense. After all, they'd been so in his own time. Not that he took much comfort in the success. The dossier made him sound like a regular Casanova. Like some philandering no-account rake who lived for nothing more than eating, drinking and screwing. So, maybe people hadn't bought his work on the basis of the art alone. "Weatherby's in London is reputable," he countered. "They'd never slander a man's good name."

She thought about that for a moment, but said nothing.

Suddenly he realized he'd been staring at her far too long, and he blinked to break the spell. She was as much of a witch as Missus Llassa! Their gazes had held, and now his heart was racing like the devil. Her eyes were hard to describe, too, as deep as an ocean, as soft as powder, and the color of frost on ice crystals in wintertime. The longer he stared, the more emotion he saw in the irises. He felt as if he was studying two snowflakes that kept changing shape as they warmed up.

Definitely, he was melting. Heat swirled below his belt, as if stirred by a long-handled conjurers spoon, then settled in the aching place between his legs. Why, this woman was turning his belly into a veritable witches cauldron!

"It's not that I don't enjoy all the pleasures of life, mind you, miss," he conceded, hardly wanting to examine his motives for needing to clarify the issue with her. "But I greatly fear this dossier, which has blackened my name, has given you a very wrong impression—"

"I'm trying to keep an open mind," she assured.

"It's lies," he repeated. "Every single word."

"I don't know what to believe," she admitted.

"Of course you don't," he soothed, not that he could concentrate on the truth right now, not when she was right in front of him, smelling like a bed of roses, reminding him that he hadn't had relations in a tragically long time. "Why would you believe a word I say, miss? Yet, I swear I never took undue advantage of a woman."

Abruptly he seated himself on the stool beside her, just inches away, determined to convince her of his version of the tale. The next thing he knew, the whole story about Lucinda and Basil was pouring out, flowing as smoothly as the whiskey that was helping to loosen his tongue.

He started at the beginning, telling how Lucinda's father, General Barrington, had promised her in marriage to the gambling pretender, Basil Drake, and how she'd gotten so upset that she'd threatened to kill herself. "Not that she was really going to," he added. "But the water turned out to be deeper and colder than she'd expected…"

"A drama queen," she suddenly put in, a spark of recognition in her expression. "I know the type."

Despite the trying circumstances, he couldn't help but offer a flicker of a smile. "Drama queen," he repeated. Now that was apt. "She jumped into the Hudson River," he explained.

"And you saved her?"

"Aye. I was passing on my horse and dived in after her. There was no time to waste, so I rode hard to Chestnut Grove. That was what General Barrington called their place, due to the number of chestnut trees on the property. Once I got there, I took her right upstairs, I did."

"The house was empty?"

"Not a soul in sight. No maid to call…"

"And you were found in bed with her?"

He hardly wanted to recall the scene. It was nearly as bad as his dossier made it sound. "She was a' shiverin' something terrible with cold," he explained. "So, we had to get her out of the clothes. She could have gotten pneumonia, and this was before the antibiotics Julius told me about. Lucinda wasn't always a well woman, you know. She was given to faints and such."

She was still studying him cautiously. "Drama queen," she said again, then took a tiny sip of whiskey, merely wetting her lips with amber liquid, then licking away the moisture in a way that brought another pang to his lower regions.

"Aye," he agreed. For a second, he thought *he'd* swoon. One thing was certain. No matter what century, women were bewitching and any sensible man should prepare to brace himself against their many spells. After gritting his teeth a moment, he plunged on, describing the duel in the woods and how he'd shot his musket skyward, to forfeit. "Basil ran forward, intending to kill me, anyway, and he nearly did, too. As it turned out, Lucinda had followed, and she shot Basil from the trees. Because I'd saved her life, she wanted to save mine."

She sucked in an audible breath. "It was Lucinda?"

"Aye. And her true love, a cabinetmaker named Jonathan Wilson, was right on her heels. Which would have been fine, but General Barrington was behind *them.*" Quickly he explained the rest of the situation, including everything Lucinda had said about Missus Llassa's hex. "And that's why I figure I'm stuck in my own painting," he finished. "I've no idea why I pop out when I do, or why I go back. But after tonight, I think I stay for exactly one week."

His face twisted into a grimace. "That means you'll be rid of me soon enough, miss," he found himself adding, knowing she couldn't wait to see him gone. "Not that I blame ya," he muttered. "I can't imagine what I'd do if I'd o' been sittin' quietly before my fire above McMulligan's and had a stranger suddenly appear, expecting to be fed." He glanced at the wall clock. "One week hence, at exactly seven-fifteen, you can expect me to vanish, miss."

"Let me get this right. You were…uh…" She paused as if looking for a word. *"Popped out,"* she emphasized, "before tonight?"

He sighed. It was certainly difficult to explain all this. Nodding, he described his experience in 1956. He'd awakened inside a crate in a locked storage unit at a guarded warehouse. Apparently whoever owned the painting had stored it there. He'd hacked his way out of a crate that had been stuffed with straw to protect the artwork, using the dagger he kept sheathed in his ankle holster, but he hadn't been able to escape the locked unit. After days of yelling, he'd alerted a security guard, who'd come to investigate.

"He almost shot me, and when I saw the shape of his musket, I knew Missus Llassa had conjured some very strange spell, indeed," he explained. "So, I tied up the man, questioned him, found some food and then discovered his television. After that…"

He didn't want to think about it. "Everything…just vanished. Once more, I could only smell sawdust and see squiggly yellow things that I now knew were packing straw."

"You were inside the painting again?"

He was relieved to see that, if nothing else, morbid

curiosity was getting the best of her. "I wish it weren't so, miss, but it was."

"You didn't know you were in another time?"

"Not at first." And when he'd understood, he'd cried like a baby, not that he was going to tell her that part. He just hoped her changing attitude meant she was starting to believe him. "Before that, the last thing I remember is leaving the clearing. It was early morning, in 1791, and—"

"Seventeen ninety-one?"

"Aye. I left Jonathan and Lucinda, rode into town, grabbed my things at McMulligan's, then boarded the American Dreamer. The next thing I knew, I awakened in the crate, in 1956. Then thirteen years passed and I was popped out in the living room of a man named Julius Royle."

"I knew that name rang a bell," she said. "He's from a very old-money family. They're like Rockefellers or Morgans or something, right?"

He nodded once more. "Indeed. And that was lucky for me. But years have passed, and I've no idea why I've popped out again. There's no rhyme or reason to any of it. As I was saying, the last thing I remember was being aboard the American Dreamer. I set to painting on deck, wanting to make a picture showing what happened in the clearing, just for the record. I figured there wouldn't be much action for a while. We had a letter of marque, you see."

"Which is?"

He was taken aback. "I'm a commissioned privateer, miss." The dossier had gotten that much about him right.

"You're a pirate?"

He gasped, never having thought of it quite that way. "We made prize money. If there weren't booty, no man would go to sea, miss." And yet that was a lie. Even now, he recalled the thrilling surge of waves when a well-crafted vessel rolled across swells of the deep. He'd seen sea monsters harpooned, just as he'd seen them swallow men, and storms so wild they created funnels of wind. There was peace, too, more than a land-bound man could imagine. He could almost feel the ship rocking, cradling him gently, like a loving woman holding him in her arms while he drifted to sleep….

Abruptly he cut off the thought. "The *Salem Rattlesnake* once took cargo worth a million British pounds in a single cruise," he forced himself to continue, knowing he'd better not quit talking, since that might give her an opening during which she could protest his presence in her home. "But a privateer's more respectable," he assured. "Why, lass, in the war, it was found that we were better than regular navy crews when it came to stopping the Brit's commercial trade. A letter o' marque, which we carried aboard, proved we were emissaries of a government, you see."

She didn't look convinced. "But the…booty." She paused. "That would be the source of your buried treasure?"

While the skeptical cast of her pink button mouth didn't encourage him, her words did. At least they were settling into a regular conversation. At least as regular as it could be, under the circumstances. "Aye. The map showin' the whereabouts of some of my booty was on yer employer's table, but you put it away. It's buried by a stone wall that protected the southern tip of Manhattan Island. It's in Battery Park now."

Her lips parted in surprise, and he watched as she rose, went to a file cabinet and returned with another dossier. He almost wished she'd quit walking about the room like that. Her form-fitting slacks showed off all the curves he'd admired earlier when she was bare-legged.

"There really was a wall in Battery Park," she said, her voice catching with barely masked excitement as she opened the dossier for him.

"Of course there is." Hadn't he just informed her of it? Edging nearer, his nostrils flared at the scent of her. Now he smelled more than roses...the heat of a female. Exhaling shakily, he peered over her shoulder.

"This is an article from the *New York Times,*" she explained, a tapered finger tracing the text. The nail, alone, was mesmerizing, painted the white-yellow color of a new moon.

Her voice was as smooth as the summer night air, too, and full of throaty catches. "James cut out the article, to show it to customers interested in old maps of the area. It was in the paper last December." She paused, then read. "'Three weeks after the Transportation Authority began digging a subway tunnel under Battery Park, the workers hit a remnant of the original battery that once protected the colonial settlement—'" she scanned downward "'—this is the oldest piece of a fortification in Manhattan and the only one to survive the Revolutionary War period...'"

As he quickly finished reading, she continued. "If you're for real, you're in luck. They're still deciding what to do with the wall, and they unearthed more of it since the article was published. It's considered an archeological find."

Which would make it easier for him to find his booty.

Another wave of encouragement surged inside him. "My first real luck," he said. He could only hope she was going to be his second. "Otherwise, I need help finding Julius Royle," he forced himself to say, even though he hated asking strangers for favors. "If he's still alive, that is. And I need to find out whatever I can about this hex and how to stop it."

"The file…er, dossier," she said, correcting herself. "It says you have to fall in love."

He wished it were that simple. Oh, when he was a wee lad, he'd fall in and out of love ten times a day. But the older he got, the more he wanted a woman with substance. Besides… "Everything in the dossier is a lie, so I don't see why this account of my hex would be true, necessarily…."

His voice trailed off. How could Missus Llassa have put such a terrifying curse on him? He wasn't like a normal man at all. He bit back a shudder. "Julius will help me," he repeated.

Previously, Julius had wanted to use every possible avenue to ensure Stede didn't become trapped again. Stede had never been prone to negative emotions—not anxiety, nor terror, nor anger—at least not in his own time. But once a man was trapped inside a painting, everything changed. Before he thought it through, he grasped her hand impulsively, and as he did, something hit the back of his throat that felt like sawdust and tasted like smoking gunpowder.

She uttered a soft sound he scarcely heard. Beneath his fingers, the lady's palm was like velvet. He had to fight not to moan from the pleasure of it. Gently he rubbed his thumb over the back of the slender hand. Ever so slowly, he lifted it to his mouth, pressing the warmth of his lips to her skin. A tingle entered his bloodstream and didn't stop moving until it fizzled at his toes. Somehow, he brought her hand downward once more, but he wasn't about to release her fingers.

He searched her eyes. Oh, she thought him a liar. Or maybe crazy. He didn't care which, as long as she helped him. He didn't want to get fresh, nor manipulate her, but he needed help, so he lowered his voice to a tone Lucinda always called "seductive silk." "Tanya," he murmured. "I hope you don't mind if I use your Christian name…"

Her eyes widened as he inched closer. "Uh…I guess it's not as weird as the way you keep calling me miss."

"Help me," he urged. "I saw how excited you were when you bought my painting."

At that, her fingers gripped around his, and she squeezed, sending another bolt of white light dancing along his sinews. Her voice shook. "You saw me buy it? What are you talking about?"

He could see her as plain as day, but it was as if he'd been staring down the wrong end of a telescope. "Aye. Indeed I did. 'Twas in a shop crowded with dusty items. I think I was in an attic at one point, maybe for years, and it was so dusty, I felt like sneezing all the time. A red-headed lady named May…"

His voice trailed off when her eyes flashed. When they sparked with violet, he realized his mistake. If he could remember that much, he could remember…

Heat warmed his face as images flooded him. He could see her naked on her duvet, caressing her thighs, tracing circles with a long fingernail, teasing herself before parting her cleft. Arousal threatened to overtake him, and for a second, he went blind with it, recalling how she'd rolled onto her belly, stretching like a cat. She'd moaned and sighed, lifting her gorgeous backside, and he'd imagined he was behind her, as hard as he was getting now, ready to enter… He realized she'd gone as white as a sheet. "Sorry," he murmured.

"You see people while…while you're, uh, in the painting?" she whispered slowly.

He felt torn. This was a way of proving himself, yes. But it put him in an embarrassing predicament, also. Of course, it was she, not he, who'd been parading naked, flaunting herself like a woman in a bawdy house. Taking a deep breath, he forced himself to say, "Aye."

"That's impossible." She abruptly sat up from the stool. Unfortunately they were standing too close, and the front of her body brushed his. His mind went blank. With an unplanned tug, he pulled her to him, and as if by magic, she came so near that he smelled the whiskey on her breath.

It shouldn't have made him want to kiss her, but it did. Instead he murmured, "I saw ya, I did." And now, everything in his body had gone as tight as a hangman's noose. To hell with decorum, he thought. She'd teased him, tempting him more than any wanton wench in McMulligan's ever had. "I saw everything you did since I've been here…"

Color was flooding her chalk-white skin now, and she was flushing scarlet. "Impossible," she repeated, the word barely audible.

"It's like remembering a dream," he offered huskily. "Everything's vague and shadowy. It's as if I've seen everything before, but only in my sleep." He paused, knowing this might make her believe him. "Ya put a spot of cream in yer coffee, miss. And ya never answer yer phone." Not wanting to scare her, he fought the urge to lift a finger to her cheek and stroke. His heart was pounding dangerously hard against his ribs. "Yer mama wants ya to come to New Jersey for dinner, and you hate yer sister, because you think they respect her more than you."

"Oh, no. You remember…"

"Indeed I do, miss." His heart was thundering in warning, but he couldn't heed it when their bellies were brushing the way sails caressed the wind. Fiery waves rolled turbulently and, unable to stop himself, he tilted his hips, locking them to hers, wanting to seduce her. "You…touched yourself, Tanya," he said throatily. *For me.*

"But I didn't know you…"

"Here," he used his hips to caress her. "And here." As his splayed hands pressured her back, he stared at her through eyes glazed with memories and lust. "You were on the bed…" It was getting harder to talk. Any moment, he was sure he'd lose control and simply explode. "Naked," he managed to continue as tight bands wrapped his chest, stealing his breath. He could see her breasts, full and swollen, and once more, she was fondling them. Her hips arched, lifting off the mattress…

"I saw you take your pleasure," he murmured.

At the words, she flung her hands out, to steady herself, grabbing the first thing she reached—his shoulders. Feeling the clutch of her fingers was simply too much. His hands tightened on her delicate back, offering support as hunger surged. Faster than lightning coming up in a summer squall, he pulled her against him as his mouth plunged to her neck.

She tasted of sea salt and reminded him of forbidden alleyways in dangerous port towns. But it was her mouth he wanted most, and as he claimed it, lust took him under, consuming him, engorging his lower body. He was drowning. So was she, and he wasn't surprised that she tilted back her chin, or that her lips were hot when they fused to his, not after what he'd watched her do....

He could have kissed her for eternity. Her lips were soft. Pliable, and as he deepened the kiss, he was swept away by sensations he'd been sure he'd never feel again. Aye. She was tender, her mouth soft against the demanding firmness of his. When his tongue savaged, plundering, diving deep and exploring tiny ridges of teeth, she sank against him, her body molding to his. Testing the silken flesh of her inner cheeks, he realized she'd never satisfy him. He'd always want more.

Thrusting his hands downward, he stroked her backside, pulling her nearer, to where he was bursting, straining the drawstrings of his breeches. When she released a strangled cry of ecstasy, he swallowed the sound with the renewed assault of his mouth. *Bed.* The thought crashed through his building pleasure, and he broke the kiss, intending to swoop his arms under her knees, lift her to his chest and carry her upstairs.

But something blindsided him. Before he realized what it was, he'd stepped back a pace. His jaw went slack. His lips were damp, parted and swollen, and his hand was pressed to his cheek. She'd slapped him! He could feel the imprint of each long, beautiful finger he'd been imagining, only seconds ago, wrapping around choice parts of his anatomy.

"It wasn't as if you weren't liking it, miss," he muttered.

She only stared back in shock. Her face had gone from scarlet to snow-white again, and her blue eyes had turned violet with passion. "Stay right here," she whispered.

"Where are you going?" he demanded, his heart still pounding like thunder, his groin aching.

"Upstairs," she said shakily. "To dress. Because I am now late for Izzie's party."

The party? Just a moment ago, they were about to become lovers. He'd felt the tremble of her heart, the way her hips lifted, seeking his. They'd be good together. He'd satisfy her completely. But she didn't look even a wee bit appreciative.

Her lips were pursed so tightly they could have been sewn shut, and her eyes looked formidable, reminding him of blue star-stones he'd found aboard a ship bound from Africa. "Stay here," she repeated. "And no matter what, don't move."

As she spun around and headed for the stairs, he tried to tell himself she'd return shortly. Maybe she had ideas of her own. Maybe she was getting some of the vibrating treasures he recalled her keeping stored in the pleasure chest at the foot of her bed.

But he had a sneaking suspicion that wasn't the case.

And he knew he was right when he heard the upstairs door slam shut, a dead bolt turn and a chain lock slide into place.

5

AFTER SNATCHING the phone, Tanya sank onto the bed and stared at the painting. Nothing had changed. The musket-wielding blonde was charging toward the opposite side of the lush, green clearing. Was he really Basil Drake? The other man was no longer in the picture, but she was sure she wasn't dreaming.

This just didn't…

"Feel like a dream," she said.

The sensations left in the wake of the phantom man's kiss were real enough, still making her hot and dizzy. She was as disoriented as he'd be feeling if his story were true. Which it wasn't. It couldn't be….

As her tongue traced the perspiration beading above her upper lip, she realized her mouth was swollen. Under-standably, she thought. He'd been…savage. Possessive. So ravenous that he truly might have been the victim of a lover's curse, trapped inside his own painting for years. Yet the kiss was sweet, too, and when she remembered how gallantly he'd lifted her hand to brush searing lips across the tender back of it, her heart filled to bursting.

It had been a gesture from Hollywood movies. Or from some other century. No guys Tanya dated did things like that. Which was why she'd wound up in his embrace, she thought with renewed panic. She hadn't meant to kiss him. After Brad, she'd been trying to get her life on track. With Izzie and Marlo's support, she'd felt more determined than ever to do only reasonable grown-up things. Just like her sister. Yes, just like Brittania, she'd soon settle down with a well-employed man who would buy her a nice house in New Jersey and father their kids.

Instead, hard ridges and tensed muscles of the stranger's body had left imprints on her flesh. She'd been powerless to move. In fact, she'd wanted him to leave indentations all over her, exactly the way any ancient fossil might.

And then she'd come to her senses. Even though she'd been the one to slap him, not the other way around, his hand was still burning her cheek, curving her flesh like something specifically crafted to fit there, pressuring the small of her back.

"Which means the NYPD can dust my spine for his prints."

Lifting the phone, she began punching in 9-1-1, then realized the police would ask questions about the relationship. She'd be forced to admit to the consensual kiss. After that, they wouldn't believe he was an intruder, and things would only worsen if she told them about his bizarre claims.

Besides, what if he wasn't lying? "Absurd," she pronounced. Whoever he was, he was sexy as hell, though. White-hot desire hit her core, soliciting a mind-bending throb. The guy was like something chiseled out of diamonds, not flesh and bone, and below the belt, he'd been as hard as a statue.

"Keep moving," she muttered. Just a moment ago, she'd been sandwiched between rocklike pectorals and hands that had felt like heaven. Or hell, she thought, re-calling the devilish glint in his eyes that no by-the-book gallantry could hide. She quickly punched in Izzie's number. "Pick up," she whispered, glancing toward the locked door. One ring...two...

What if he burst through the door? He was so brawny he could accomplish it. Heaven knew, he kissed like a Neanderthal, albeit a sweet-hearted one, but... "Maybe he's stealing something from the shop!"

...three rings. She counted mentally. Four...

Surely Izzie was already at the party. Probably, she was on the other line of her cell, talking to Marlo, who was still dressing and trying to soothe Izzie's nerves. What was Tanya planning to tell Izzie, anyway? she suddenly wondered. That a revolutionary privateer had popped out of a painting she shouldn't have bought, and was in the shop, drinking James's best whiskey and talking about digging up buried war booty near a subway tunnel?

"Get real, Tanya," she warned, noting that everything in the room was sliding off-kilter. She'd been under stress due to Brad's breakup, her escalating credit card debt, and James wanting her to move. Discovering a painting worth millions had been surreal, too. Maybe she'd gone off the deep end. "Crazy people don't know they're crazy," she admitted.

"Yes, that's what makes crazy people crazy, isn't it?" she continued. "Crazy people think they're sane and everybody else in the world is nuts—except them." She shuddered. Maybe talking with Izzie wasn't such a good idea, after all. Not that Tanya thought Izzie or Marlo would disbelieve her, much less say she was crazy and have her committed to an asylum, but...

"It's just not fair to call the night of her opening," Tanya decided, stabbing the phone's off button. Usually she and her girlfriends shared everything, but maybe this experience was one she'd better keep to herself. Besides, she was already late for the opening, and Izzie deserved her support.

"What now?"

She rose, headed behind the decorative screen that hid her clothes and shucked her pants and nightshirt. As she slid the new dress off a hanger, she realized her hands were shaking.

"Of course they are," she said as she shimmied into the dress, silently berating herself for buying something so lavish, just to entice Brad. She wasn't interested in him, anymore, but only wanted to smooth her own ruffled feathers. Yes, the threads of the dress might as well be unraveling to spell out the words, "pure ego." And if she hadn't been on a spending spree due to the breakup, she'd never have bought the painting, so none of this would be happening.

"Don't forget that it's worth millions," she muttered. Or was it? She gasped. If she did decide to sell it now, and if someone she knew wasn't involved in the events of the past hour, then how was she going to explain the missing figure? Glancing toward the painting again, then the door, she felt her throat tighten. What was the guy downstairs doing? She'd feel better if she could hear something… anything.

She zipped up, tied the sash behind her, then stepped in front of a mirror, fighting dismay. Of midnight-blue silk, the dress had a halter-style bodice that plunged to her waist. A dangerous two-inch stripe of bare flesh separated the fabric swathing her breasts. The boutique owner had vowed the built-in bodysuit beneath was designed to keep her covered, but now she didn't trust it. Wearing the dress without panties, as she'd been instructed, didn't make her feel very secure, either.

The dress looked good, however. Fantastic, really. She quickly wrapped a matching scarf around her neck. It gave the illusion that she was wearing an old-fashioned choker. She strained her ears once more. It was quiet downstairs.

"Uh…" She started to yell his name, but she wasn't ready to concede that he was Stede O'Flannery. She'd never believe that, of course. What else could she call him, though? Sir? Mister? Both seemed too antiquated. So, she yelled "Stede?" Padding to the door, she put her ear against the wood and listened. "You *are* still down there, aren't you?"

Again, no answer.

Torn between investigating and finishing dressing, she whirled, staring into the mirror again. She'd hoped to put on a few layers of mascara. After three or four coatings, she actually looked as if she had eyelashes. Now there wasn't time. Heading for a tiny bathroom that made those on Greyhound buses look lavish, she sandwiched herself between the toilet and sink, and settled for two whimsical passes of liner pencil over her eyebrows.

"And blusher," she whispered, waving bronzer over her cheeks. Then she tossed the cosmetics into an antique shoulder bag made of finely meshed silver metal and slid bare feet into thrift store pumps Marlo called her glass slippers. They were of transparent fabric, outlined by dark-blue beading that created teardrop shapes over her toes then wrapped around to form ankle straps.

The heels were uncomfortably high, but she'd live. On her way to the door, she stopped at the dresser to spritz herself with perfume. Reaching first for Brad's favorite, she changed her mind, then used some Marlo had given her as a gift. Somehow, it seemed fitting that the scent was called Eternity.

At the door, she paused, curling her hand around the knob. Inhaling deeply, she puffed her cheeks to blow, then exhaled slowly as she turned the dead bolt, slid back the chain and headed downstairs.

He was gone!

Surely she was crazy, or dreaming, or her friends were playing a really sick joke. Her heart suddenly stuttered in her chest, and once more she felt drunken—her knees turning to water, her head swimming. Sensations crowded in, pushing around her like an envelope, feeling the way people did on the subway during rush hour. As a current of warmth rushed through her limbs, she felt as if she were suffocating. It was as if those demanding lips were crushing down on hers once more, cutting off her breath— searing, brazen, forbidden. Her back was arching. Hips sought hips. Heat found heat.

Somehow, she regained her voice. "Uh…Stede?"

Not a peep.

At least the front door was shut. Nothing seemed to be missing. The map cabinet's drawers were closed. Wait a minute, she thought. Now she heard something. He was downstairs. "Oh, no," she mouthed. The man was talking to himself now! Maybe he was a lunatic.

Whoever he was, he definitely had the world's worst timing. She *had* to get to Izzie's opening. Cautiously she descended the rickety stairs, teetering on her high heels and being careful not to grip the dusty splintered wooden handrail, since she might snag her dress or ruin her manicure. Snatches of his voice sounded hopelessly seductive, entering her bloodstream, making her want to purr.

"…as I say, I believe she's dressin' for a party."

Who was he talking to? Himself? Someone else? Fear skittered down her spine. Had an accomplice been downstairs, all along? Should she stay up here? Grab the opportunity and lock him in the basement?

Too late now.

Reaching the bottom step, she sighed in relief. He was in the back, nearest the oldest bottles, and he'd brought the portable shop phone down with him, so there was no accomplice, after all. He wasn't having a conversation with himself. At least she assumed someone was on the other end of the line. Had Izzie seen her number on caller ID and called the shop?

When Tanya waved to get the man's attention, he actually turned from her, tweaking her temper. Just who did he think he was, coming in here, acting like he owned the place, opening James's whiskey and using the phone? She swatted away a dangling bubble chain, which was attached to the bald bulb illuminating the room, then she sought his angular face. It was lost to shadows, making him look even more like the proverbial romantic hero. She took in the lace-up shirt, tight white riding pants and calf-clinging black boots. Glancing her way, he squinted, as if to get a better look at her, and she realized two things at once. First, kissing him had been an irreversible mistake, and second, judging by the traitorous tingling that sugar-coated her skin, it was bound to happen again. Every inch of her was heating up.

She forced herself to cue into what he was saying. "You don't say! As Poor Richard always said, 'To honor thy father and mother means to live so as to be *an honor to them!*'" During a brief pause, he lifted a bottle of whiskey from the rack and absently perused the label. "Aye...not a'tall. It's been a pleasure speaking to ya! It has, indeed..."

A longer pause ensued. Tanya wasn't proud of it, but this was her first opportunity to study him more carefully. As she did, something akin to a shiver shook her shoulders then wended down her spine. It may not have been centuries since she'd made love, but it had been a good long while.

"Now, don't you be pulling my leg," he murmured, chuckling. The sound came easily, indicating he probably had a decent sense of humor. He was chatty, too. Intrigued, she realized this nefarious character could work his way around any city cocktail party.

"The weather's warm, so it's a wonderful time for grilling, to be sure," he was enthusing. "Aye. I do like having my meals served to me, as well. I see...indeed. Now that you mention it, I do have an 'open calendar,' as ya call it. I believe I *am* free..."

The pulse starting ticking too fast in her throat again. Who was he talking to? Had he found the phone book? Called Julius Royle? Relief washed over her. While Tanya doubted he really knew Julius Royle—he was from a family of real movers and shakers—the man probably had other friends. Maybe Eduardo or James was on the line. And he'd come downstairs to further inventory the booze, she realized. A choice bottle of Burgundy was freshly dusted and perched on a shelf.

"I'd be honored to visit your estate. As I said, I like to target shoot, hunt and ride."

This information seemed welcome to the other party, who gabbed while he nodded, then he said, "I think myself no braggart, but I will say my facility with bow and arrow has won me more than one wee trophy, and the lodge where you and your husband dine sounds like paradise on earth, it does."

She squinted.

"Somewhere in the neighborhood of a fortnight?" A pause ensued. "I look forward to the honor of meeting you, and I'll be telling her to call you then, ma'am."

The call had been for her, but he hadn't given her the phone? And the other party was a ma'am? "Was that Izzie?" she managed as he pushed the off button.

He shook his head. "Yer mudder."

"My murder?" A chill zipped through her. What had he said? It had sounded like "your *mooder.*" "Oh my God! My *mother?*" He'd been talking to… "Jean Taylor?" she clarified.

"I believe she said her name was Jean, and a pretty name it is," he said agreeably.

Her head reeled as he dropped James's portable phone into the pocket of his waistcoat. "Hunting?" she echoed. "Target practice? Riding?" Things were sinking in fast. "A fortnight?"

He nodded gravely. "I vowed to chaperone your visit."

She nearly choked. The lodge to which he'd been referring was the Short Hills Country Club. "Chaperone?"

He didn't answer. He was still half-hidden by murky shadows, but that did nothing to mask how his eyes glittered in darkness. They lazily spiraled downward, studying her from the top of her head to the tips of her toes. He examined each exposed inch, his eyes moving as slowly as cold molasses until they settled on cleavage.

"Aye," he murmured in a way that made clear he was contemplating her body, not a visit to her folks.

Confusion mixed with anger as she realized her mother must have tried to call while she was calling Izzie or the police. Not knowing James was gone and that Tanya wasn't working during his vacation, her mother must have tried calling the shop. Since this stranger had invited himself to a family dinner, her mother had guessed Brad was history. "Did she say anything about Brad?"

He shook his head.

"You do know who Brad is, don't you?" After all, he claimed to have been privy to her phone conversations while he was still inside the painting. That meant he'd heard every dirty little detail she'd told Izzie and Marlo. He'd know everything from Brad's penis size to the annoying phrases Brad uttered during orgasm, such as, "Go! Go! Go!" That was right up there, next to, "Give it to me, baby."

"He's yer ex-love," he murmured throatily.

James could have told him that. "Right. Did she say anything about Brittania?"

"Your sister?"

"Why ask me?" she couldn't help but respond. "You're the eavesdropper. Not to mention the spy." She couldn't begin to understand how he'd known the things he did, but now she told herself there had to be a reasonable explanation. Before she thought it through, she stalked closer than she should have, close enough to smell his skin. He really did smell as if he'd just stepped out of a clearing full of hardwood trees. "You can't just take my phone calls."

"I was tryin' to be o' use, miss."

"By making plans with my mother?"

"Judging by yer employer's maps, miss, your family lives near the clearing where I fought my duel. I know it's a longshot, indeed I do, but maybe I'll find a clue as to the nature of Missus Llassa's hex."

"Do you know when I'll visit Short Hills with you in tow?" she asked rhetorically. Answering herself, she assured, "When hell freezes over."

He looked thoroughly nonplussed, as if he was accustomed to dealing with difficult women, which only served to further annoy her, since usually, she wasn't the least bit difficult. "You know," she managed to say. "You really don't exactly bring out the best in my personality."

"I won't be arguin' with ya there," he returned.

"The call could have been about my gallery opening," she huffed, ignoring him. "It's in two weeks. Or it could have been Eduardo or James." As it turned out, the reality of the situation was worse, since it had been her mother. "You have to promise me you won't answer any phones again," she said firmly.

"I'll promise no such thing," he countered. "Ya can't expect me to let the contraption ring," he countered, now sounding annoyed, himself. "It jangles my nerves, it does."

She was feeling just as unhinged. "Why don't you just give me the phone, so I can take it back upstairs?" Before he could answer, she added, "And why did you bring it down here, anyway?" Suddenly the blood drained from her face as the probable truth dawned on her. "You didn't want me to hear you talking! You didn't want me to know anyone called!"

Pivoting, she skedaddled upstairs with him on her heels. "Put that phone in its cradle," she commanded over her shoulder. He did as she asked, but the triumphal feeling was short-lived. Long moments ticked by, during which they merely stared at each other.

Suddenly she was remembering the kiss, and how she'd slapped him. How could she forget? And what else could she have done? Nor could she call the police or anyone she knew. She'd never felt so helpless. Glancing at the clock, she gasped. Time sure flew when a man claiming to be a privateer from another century appeared in one's bedroom.

"I swore I'd be at the opening by nine." And she loved Izzie. She'd never forgive herself if she contributed to anything that marred the night for her friend, but it was eight-thirty now. An hour had passed. She had to hurry. On a Friday night, she'd never get a cab, and because she was dressed to the nines, she didn't want to take the subway.

"Would you quit staring at me?" she suddenly asked, exhaling an exasperated breath.

"What do you expect a man to do, miss?" he returned. "You can't be paradin' around wearing that…"

"Dress?"

He didn't look convinced. "Hmm. Is that what it is?"

"What else would it be?"

"In all my born days, I never once saw a dress like that. And you can't be wearing such allurements, nor such scents, and not expect a warm-blooded man not to notice." As if to say words could never do her outfit justice, he pressed a hand over his heart and shook his head in admiration. For a second, she could swear he was considering dropping to his knees and extolling her virtues, or something.

It had the desired effect. "Thanks," she said shortly, wondering how this man had crashed into her life and repaired what Brad had done to her sexual self-esteem with only one stupid look and a compliment. She'd never really believe his story, of course, but whoever he was, he was cute. Extremely cute. Every time she looked at him, she wanted to play along.

And he didn't seem dangerous. He'd been polite to her mother, too. As trying as Jean Taylor was, that said something positive about his character. Still, Tanya had to get to the opening, to support Izzie, and she couldn't allow this stranger to answer the phone, no more than she could leave him in a shop full of priceless maps.

Luckily a lightbulb flashed in her mind. In order to accomplish the only satisfactory solution, she'd have to act fast and be crafty, though. "Look," she said. "I'm sorry…uh, Stede. You seem so smart…." She let her voice trail off long enough for the compliment to sink in.

"Aye?"

She fluttered her eyelashes. After all, it was a gesture that worked for heroines in novels from bygone times. "Surely you can imagine how unnerving all this has been for me," she continued, leaning a hand against the bar as if she might faint again. "So unexpected. I mean, a smart man like you must realize my situation. For a practical, contemporary woman, it's a little hard to accept that a man from another time has stepped out of a painting…." *And kissed me like that.* The words seemed to hang in the air.

"You do believe me, though. Don't you, miss?"

"Of course I do," she soothed. But she had to get to Izzie's party—and soon. "I'll tell you what," she continued. "I think I'd feel more certain if you came upstairs with me. I want to look at that picture again and make sure you're not in it."

He looked relieved, and she had to admit it pulled at her heartstrings. Lines magically erased from his forehead, and the perfectly formed eyebrows that furrowed when he squinted suddenly relaxed into normal positions. He really was handsome. Movie star quality.

"Anything you wish, miss."

"I knew you'd understand," she said, then headed upstairs. So far, so good, she thought. He was right behind her. Standing beside her, and in front of the canvas, his eyes flicked over the masterpiece. "Not a bad paintin', if I do say so, myself," he murmured. "And you're very good."

She braced herself against the compliment. "As an artist?"

"Aye. Yours is a new style, to be sure, and I don't know much about what's happening in the world of art, but I do know what I like when I see it."

She couldn't let his ego-stroking deter her. She had a minute to bolster her nerve, since he was lost in thought now. Sadness crossed his features as his gaze shifted from the trees, to the blond figure, then to the clearing. Stealthily she edged toward the chest at the foot of her bed and tilted open the lid. What she sought was right on top, shiny silver handcuffs covered with purple faux fur. Surreptitiously leaning, she silently lifted them out, then shut the chest and slipped behind the man, rounding the corner of her mattress.

"Oh, dear," she said, raising her voice as she looped a cuff around the iron rail of the bedstead. Coughing, she covered the sound of the lock clicking into place. "You really aren't in the painting, uh, Stede…and…well, it's all so overwhelming, as you can imagine. I think I feel…" She was holding the other cuff open, ready to receive his wrist, so all she had to do now was grab his hand….

"You look pale, miss," he said, sounding concerned.

Relief flooded her. In just a second, he'd be handcuffed to her bed. She'd only be gone an hour or so, and she could deal with him when she returned. Tonight, Izzie wouldn't expect her to stay for the whole party, since she'd be talking to so many other guests.

As he turned toward her, his lips were pursed firmly together as if puckered for another kiss. Quickly she grasped his hand as if she were falling, and as she seated herself on the bed, she twined her fingers with his. The hand lowered with hers, and suddenly, she wished it didn't feel quite so dry and strong, the skin pulsing with aliveness. The cuffs of his shirt were pleated, and the fabric teased her wrist. It was coarse, but of a fine weave, unlike any material she'd ever felt. Abruptly she squeezed his fingers, thrusting them inside the open cuff, then she gasped.

It was too big! But no…with the speed of lightning, he'd flicked his wrist, twisting it. Fingers that felt like velvet now came away from her grasp as if greased.

Then metal clanked.

She, not he, was cuffed to the bed. "Oh, no," she spoke softly.

Although the cuffs were lined with soft fur, that didn't mitigate the horror. She was at his mercy, and she saw new awareness spark in his eyes. Male and predatory, they traveled over her as if she was his quarry. Just as in the painting, the eyes followed her every move, settling where the dress hem had risen on her thighs. He looked at her legs as if he'd never seen a woman wearing a skirt shorter than her ankles.

It was the wrong time to realize she was panting. Due to the stress of the situation, she couldn't regulate the intake of air. The boutique owner had lied, too. Oh, the built-in bodysuit was keeping her breasts covered. Sort of. But the two-inch stripe of cleavage now exposed most of her sloping flesh. The eyes glued to her thighs lifted, then surveyed her breasts, and she could swear she saw the hands at his sides actually tremble.

Oh, yes, he looked as if he was considering doing something incredibly sexual, and as she waited, she realized she was half hoping he would. She exhaled a shaky breath. If Izzie could see this scene, she'd forgive Tanya for being late. Their eyes met. "What are you going to do to me?" she whispered.

"Convince you to do whatever I wish, miss," he assured.

6

"I CAN'T BELIEVE I'm letting you come along," Tanya muttered twenty minutes later. "And with your musket."

Standing in the steamy twilight, Stede shrugged out of the waistcoat in deference to the heat and held open the cab door. Something in her attitude was starting to grate on his nerves. "I'm afraid you didn't have much choice, miss."

"No, I didn't," she huffed.

Watching her use the utmost care to exit the cab, he didn't know which he felt more—annoyance or amusement. Her blue eyes watched him like a hawk, and the way she tugged down her skirt, he could have been a rapist, indeed. When he'd locked her into the handcuffs, it had been tempting to seduce her, and he would have, if attending her friend's opening hadn't seemed so important to her. He wouldn't interfere with that and have her blaming him for it later. Besides, her time pressures reminded him that he didn't have moments to waste. Unless he became convinced Missus Llassa's curse involved him falling in love as Weatherby's dossier indicated....

But Sweet Betsy Ross, how could he find out more? While Tanya was changing, he'd called the operator, but Julius Royle had no listed phone number. Then they'd lost more precious time after Stede had heard her stomach rumble. Questioning her, he'd found out she'd been starving herself so she could wear the dress, and he'd forced her to eat. He still wasn't sure what he thought of the vegetarian burgers.

Pursing his lips grimly, he slammed the livery door. Watching Tanya pay the fare just made things worse. It was a sore reminder he had to unearth his booty soon. No lady, not even one this difficult, had ever paid Stede O'Flannery's way. No sir. It was almost enough to make Stede wish he was stuck inside his own painting again.

"You handcuffed me to a bed," she reminded him as the cab pulled away.

The street was one-way, so the driver had dropped them on a corner, and when she pivoted and started charging up the street, he hung the coat on the hook of his finger, let it drape down his back and followed her.

"You were tryin' to trap me, ya were," he pointed out, thinking she was being a wee bit unreasonable. Of course, that was the name of the game between men and women. He knew it well. She'd slapped him even though she'd wanted his kisses, and then she'd played as unfairly as Basil Drake, using the cunning of a woodsman to lure him upstairs, only to snap cuffs around his wrists. "At least it wasn't thumb screws, miss," he conceded with mock politeness. "Or stockades."

"Aye," she said dryly.

"It was you who wished to trap me, miss," he repeated.

She flashed him a glance. "That was my intention."

"As Poor Richard says, 'The road to hell is paved with them.'"

"You're implying that my company is hell?"

"I'm still deciding."

The truth was, he didn't trust her. Oh...upstairs, after he'd handcuffed her, she'd given a pretty little story, indeed. She'd explained that she and her girlfriends had bought the items in the bedside chest after her liaison with Brad ended, and that she hadn't intended to use the toys. She'd looked so alluring, she could have been a figment conjured by Missus Llassa's spell. Maybe she was even a witch, herself.

"Let me know when you figure out the answer," she said now.

"Things were simpler last time I sojourned here," he admitted, sending her a perturbed sideways glance. He'd landed in the home of Julius Royle, and the fact was, a man could talk to another man. See eye to eye. Knock back aged whiskey and play a round of cards. At least if the fellow wasn't a scoundrel like Basil. Living with a woman was a whole other experience, but if Stede wasn't careful, he'd be out on his sorry behind, a stranger in a strange land.

He stared a half a block away, toward where well-dressed men and women poured onto the sidewalk outside the art opening. It looked like a party devised for the worst kind of hellions, and even from here, Stede could hear the wild beat of the music. He hadn't heard anything like it since native war dances.

He felt a twinge of relief. "They're not lettin' us in?"

"Not everyone, but we'll be on the guest list."

Needing to brace himself before going inside, he stopped in his tracks. "We're by the docks," he said, his heartbeat quickening at the recognition. "And the river." This was an old section of town, the streets wide and cobbled. "Mr. Aaron Burr," he murmured.

She backtracked and stopped in front of him, watching him curiously. "I think this part of the West Village was once his farm property. It's…"

"The meat packing district now," she finished.

"Meatpacking," he echoed, recalling how Julius had told him of the advent of large slaughterhouses when the world's small farms gave way to big industry. Everything was vaguely familiar and he wondered if he'd come here with Julius, but he couldn't recall. Feeling disoriented, he turned, moving in a complete circle, sensations washing over him, including gratitude at experiencing something so simple as cobblestones beneath his boot heels again.

"Look," she began in what seemed to him a complete non sequitur. "I admit it. I liked kissing you. And under other circumstances, I might want to do it again. But I don't believe for a second that you really came from another time in history."

"You don't?"

"No, I don't. And this is my friend Izzie's art opening. I have to finish the work for mine, too. The show has to be perfect, especially since Brad is an art critic. He's going to be here tonight. So, please don't do anything weird, okay?" After a pause, she added, "He's got a new girlfriend."

All at once, she stepped back, and he imagined his near proximity was affecting her, just as hers was affecting him. Right now, he'd rather be in her bedroom experimenting with the handcuffs. Not to mention those tiny little finger gloves that vibrated when she pushed a button.

And for the moment, he knew he had to stick to Miss Priss like a bee on a honeycomb, at least if he wanted to find Julius Royle. He wanted to get her into, then out of, the art opening as quickly as possible. That way, he could further research the hex that was plaguing him. As tempting as she was, saving his own skin had to remain his first goal.

"You're very good-looking," she suddenly said.

He wondered what she was up to now. "So they say."

"And your voice is sexy," she admitted.

Pretty lies and compliments never went to his head, so he merely nodded.

"The accent," she added. "I like it."

"Women often find a hint of brogue titillating," he conceded. It was best when whispered in their ears in bed, but he didn't mention that.

"The outfit's a little odd, but it looks good on you. People will think you're from the East Village, probably."

His chest constricted when she raised her beautiful hands and started unlacing his shirt. "Here. Keep it a little more open," she coached. "And you're going to have to put the jacket on again, to hide the gun."

"Musket," he corrected. The woman was becoming as transparent as her glass slippers.

"Just don't talk too much. People might realize there's…"

Something strange afoot, he finished silently. She had a point there. He offered a quick nod.

"The music's loud. That's good." She glanced over her shoulder toward the people in the street. Even from here, the sound reminded him of metal grating on metal. A far cry from Beethoven, to be sure.

"Just say you're my date."

"Your date?"

"Uh…you know. Paramour. Lover. Person with whom you're trysting. Or liaising. However you need to say it."

Suddenly he wanted her something fierce. The energy of his desire made him think of hungry mountain lions, or native braves dressed in feather headdresses, beads and war paint, or ships sailing across swells of wild, storm-tossed seas. But he wasn't a painter for nothing. He was getting the picture. "You want me to make Brad jealous?" he guessed.

"That would be nice."

"That won't help you get a good review," he pointed out.

"Actually it will," she countered. "Brad always values what he thinks he can't have."

"That's the sign of a scoundrel and rake."

"He was," she agreed.

Given the faint snatches of conversation he recalled hearing about the relationship, he didn't doubt it. "And so you wish me to squire you around."

Now, she didn't look so sure. "What does that mean to you?"

"Gettin' ya drinks and such."

"Perfect."

"I can definitely make another man turn green with envy," he assured. "But in the case of Basil Drake, that nearly got me killed. So, it's no small thing yer askin'."

She looked incredulous. "Really," she said. "I think it will be okay. I mean, I don't think Brad will challenge you to a duel or anything."

He wasn't so sure. His life experiences had proven otherwise. And anyway, his services didn't come cheap. No sir. He was getting tired of her demanding attitude. "On one condition, miss."

As she tilted her head upward once more to get a better look at him, he felt as if he'd been punched low in the belly. When he inhaled, he brought a scent like freshly laundered bedsheets hung on a line to dry in the spring air. She smelled so soft and floral. And she was as pretty as a flower, her face almost round, the chin smooth and calling to his fingers, promising to be as silken as a flower petal. Already, he could envision how smooth her thighs would feel beneath his palms, how he'd glide them upward, as if on water.

Aye…gently, he'd part her legs, lap the cream, and he'd do what Brad never had, silencing all the complaints he'd heard her make to her girlfriends. It was vague in his mind, of course, coming to him as if in a far-off dream, but he knew the other man hadn't satisfied her. "You don't care for him, miss," he couldn't help but murmur. "Why do ya care if he's a bit jealous?"

"I just do," she said. "It's not as if it's that big a favor," she added. "All you have to do is stand there and be good-looking."

He fought the urge to smile. "I believe I can manage that."

Everything in her eyes said she agreed.

"On one condition," he repeated.

"What?"

"Kiss me again."

Her lips parted in annoyance. But she wanted to. He could tell by the darkening blue irises of her eyes. "Oh, okay," she agreed on a peeved sigh, placing both hands on his shoulders and puckering her mouth as she rose to her tiptoes. She'd meant to give a quick peck, but he angled his head downward, circled her back with an arm, then swept her against him. His hips connected with hers as his mouth covered hers. Increasing the pressure and heat, he withheld his tongue, making her crave more. He clung, waited, let blistering heat find her belly.

Against his chest, he felt her nipples constrict, growing taut and erect, and he had to fight the urge to bare her breasts to his mouth and suckle. His heart pounding, he broke the kiss abruptly. For a second, he wasn't sure why he'd pulled away, but then he turned, hearing something behind them.

She squinted. "What?"

"I felt like someone was watchin' us."

"I've felt that way all week."

He frowned, glancing at her, trying not to notice how breathless she was from the kiss. "Ya have?" He lifted a finger and trailed it down her cheek. His voice turned husky. "I would imagine you have, miss."

This time, he meant by him. Color burst inside her pale cheeks. As much as he wanted to kiss her again, he glanced over his shoulder once more, but he saw no one, only the dimly lit cobbled alleyway behind old facades of meat-packing buildings.

"Do me another favor," she said throatily.

He sent her an inquiring glance. "Aye?"

"Kiss me like that when Brad's watching."

He wasn't thrilled about being used this way. But then, he'd had the misfortune of getting stuck inside a painting, so he figured he'd best make his peace with whatever she wished. Besides, kissing her was hardly the worst fate. "As Poor Richard always said," he murmured, "'Love well, whip well.'"

"Meaning?"

"I'll make the yellow-bellied fellow as mad as a hornet."

When she laughed, he realized he liked the sound of it, and not just because he hadn't heard the sound of a woman's laughter for so long. Suddenly he wasn't sure which was stranger, losing so much of his life to the netherworld of a witch's curse, or finding himself in a new reality with such a beautiful woman.

"Yer a lovely lass, you know," he murmured.

She merely rolled her eyes. "Only because you haven't seen one for centuries," she assured, clearly still not really believing him.

His finger dropped from her chin to her bare shoulder, and he traced an absent circle. "Ya must o' been studying sailin' knots."

"How's that?"

He couldn't help but smile. "You've tied up my insides." Before she could answer, he glanced over his shoulder again, and this time, he thought he saw something flash in the darkness of an alley.

"Are you okay?" she asked when he turned around again.

Of course he wasn't, he thought. The trauma of the duel was with him as if it had happened yesterday. Still, for a man who'd been to hell and back—quite literally—who was in a world full of new contraptions, including vegetarian burgers, and who had just kissed a woman for the second time in centuries, Stede thought he was holding up rather well.

"Miss," he murmured in admission. "Every time you kiss me, I feel like the key in Ben Franklin's jar when he captured electricity."

Her voice was husky. "Now, that's a compliment."

His arm was still around her, and suddenly, the night seemed perfect. Strange, but perfect. As if he should never ask for anything more. Every breath of a man's life was a gift, and even if he wound up back in his painting forever, he should be grateful for this moment. "There was a pirate named Chin Yi," he found himself saying throatily. "He controlled the Chinese coastline from Kwangtung Province…"

"And?"

"We captured one of his vessels." Flatting his palms, he glided them downward on her arms. "And when we boarded, we found silk. I never felt anything like it until tonight, miss, when I touched yer skin."

The compliment caught her off guard. He saw the moment she caught her breath, the startled look in her eyes, the uncertain parting of her lips, as if she wanted to speak but wasn't quite sure what to say. So, he merely kissed her again.

When he drew back, he glanced past her shoulder. He could see all the way to the river, and now, he turned her toward the horizon and pointed. It was cloudless. Light shimmered on the water, meeting the sky with a color that wasn't quite orange, or red, or peach, but that faded into lemon-yellow before it met powder-blue that drifted into the stars and midnight. At the end of the road was the river and a pier. "Now, there's a paintin', lass," he said.

He could see her throat work as she swallowed. "Look. Why don't you call me Tanya?"

That made him smile. So did how she hooked her arm through the crook of his. As they began walking, he sent her a sideways glance, his eyes twinkling with devilment. "Because I think ya like it when I call you miss."

"I think I do," she returned.

And then, once more, Stede thought he heard something. He turned, but there was nothing. Only his lost life, the empty span of centuries. Ghosts.

JUMPING BACK into shadows, the watcher nearly toppled a trash can, unsettling something dark that darted past his foot. "A rat."

There were probably more. While the meatpacking district was trendy, full of galleries and boutiques, much of the city's produce still came through the neighborhood, which meant it attracted rodents. Cursing, he edged away from the trash cans. For a second, he was sure Stede—or the man he thought was Stede—had seen him, but apparently not.

Otherwise, he would have confronted him. Now Tanya and her date waited while a doorman checked through pages on a clipboard. Seemingly he found their names, and they bypassed the line of waiting guests and went inside. When the two came out, he'd get closer. He'd double-check just once more, to make sure his eyes hadn't been deceiving him.

And then he'd make his move.

7

"HE'S LUSCIOUS," Izzie shouted over the music, nodding toward Stede, her fingers curling around a champagne flute.

"No wonder you haven't been around lately," Marlo added breathlessly, adjusting a strap of her cocktail dress. As she swung her head to get a better look at Stede, dark, shoulder-length hair cascaded over her bare shoulders.

Izzie raised her voice. "Where did he come from?"

Good question. "Out of the blue!" Tanya, too, was trying to get a better look at Stede, but couldn't. People were packed into the trendy gallery as tightly as sardines, and he was half hidden by a column, talking to someone Tanya couldn't see. "It's a long story."

"I can't believe he dressed like that for you!" enthused Izzie. "He looks like a storybook knight. And I love what you're wearing. The metal handbag…the choker…the glass slippers…" She paused. "You both look like you're visiting from another time. Brad never would have done this!"

So true. But then, Tanya's date hadn't, either. At least not intentionally.

"Anyway, you can feel free to leave now. I still have to talk to a few critics and dealers, and you must be dying from the heat." Izzie shot Tanya an appraising glance, smiling. "It looks like you've got something better to do tonight."

"Nothing could be better than your opening," Tanya assured. "What time is it?" she asked, lifting Izzie's wrist to glimpse her watch. "Midnight!" Despite the hour, she felt wide-awake.

"Have you two…uh, *done* anything yet?" Marlo shouted.

Tanya had fainted, tussled with him, attempted to handcuff him… "Kissed!"

"Yum!" yelled Izzie.

Once more, the man's hungry mouth was clamping onto hers as if to devour her, making Tanya want to talk about what was happening, at least as much as she could without sounding crazy, but this wasn't the time. Music was beating a pulse-pounding tattoo inside her skull, and how things looked under the wild strobe lights was giving her a headache. Besides, it was Izzie's special night. She tugged the airy sleeve of Izzie's dress. "You look fabulous!"

"Thanks!"

Marlo's cheeks were glowing with the heat of the room and excitement. "Izzie's selling a ton of work!"

"I can't believe it!" seconded Izzie.

Next week, if Tanya had half Izzie's luck, she'd be on her way, too, careerwise. Lifting her voice, she shouted, "Isn't it like a dream?"

"Pinch me!" yelled Izzie. "I know you're going to have this kind of turnout next week!"

Tanya hoped so. She couldn't help but imagine the look on her sister's face. She didn't envy Brittania, not really. But for just one night, she'd like to play the role of golden girl. Because she hadn't focused on creating a suburban life like Brittania's, her sister never gave her credit for things she did achieve, such as a gallery show. Suddenly her lips compressed grimly. Had the visitor really told Tanya's mother he'd escort her to the club for a family dinner? She'd better call before her mother made the reservation and say the plans were a mistake.

"He really is a dream machine," Izzie shouted now. "What's he do for a living?"

All Tanya had to go on was the assumption he was Stede O'Flannery. "Uh…he's a painter."

"Houses or pictures?" yelled Marlo.

"Pictures."

Marlo's eyes searched the crowd. "What's his name?"

Tanya pretended not to hear. Since her girlfriends knew she'd bought the picture Eduardo had appraised for a fortune, she couldn't offer the name Stede O'Flannery. Izzie saved her. "Being secretive, are you? I don't blame you. Keep him to yourself as long as you can!" She frowned. "*If* you can."

"The barracuda," announced Marlo.

Stede had edged from behind the column and now they could see that he'd been talking to Brad's new girlfriend, Sylvia Gray. Somehow, the name suited her. Maybe because she always gave the impression of being encased in silver and black. She had razor-straight hair, as dark as her dress, and she kept it precision cut, aligned with sharp jaw bones.

Earlier, Tanya had been thrilled to watch Stede work the room. He'd done exactly as promised, squiring her on his arm, fetching drinks, murmuring sweet nothings and hanging onto her every word as if she were the most interesting woman he'd ever met. Tanya suspected it wasn't entirely a game. The way his eyes kept drifting over her body, she knew he was thinking about pure, unadulterated sex….

Now she tried to tell herself she was being hopelessly romantic, more attracted to the sexual fantasy of him than the reality which, in truth, she knew nothing about. It was the exact mistake she'd made with Brad. *Get a grip!* she thought, reining in her thoughts. Still, when he'd kissed her in the street, it was as if the man had discovered some secret, vacant, untouched room inside her. His kiss was a light summer's breeze ruffling musty curtains, allowing light to shine inside. Only he had the key to unlock the room again, and thinking of his doing so turned every inch of her body into an erogenous zone.

Too bad Sylvia Gray was coming on to him. But what woman wouldn't? So much for Sylvia's hot and heavy relationship with Brad, Tanya couldn't help but think with vindication. Maybe he was as lukewarm in the sack with Sylvia as he'd been with her.

"Oh, no," shouted Marlo.

Suddenly Tanya felt as if a trap door had opened under her feet. All at once, Brad stepped between Sylvia and Stede, and in a breathless second, it was clear an altercation was heating up fast. A stocky, bearded doorman caught scent of trouble and started toward the trio, but he was having difficulty reaching them because of the crowd.

"Mind holding this?" Tanya managed.

Thrusting her champagne glass at Marlo, who accepted it without question, Tanya lowered her head and plunged through the people, moving her arms as if she were breast-stroking. Maybe she could swim through the sea of people before Stede unsheathed the knife he kept strapped inside his boot, or unholstered the musket. Up ahead, Brad's blond head bobbed above the crowd like a white buoy in dark waters. An ex-high-school linebacker, he was good-looking, blue-eyed, and well-built, but he'd be no match for Stede.

As she moved, the scent of sweating, heavily perfumed bodies and alcohol assaulted Tanya's nostrils, making her feel faintly nauseated. Everything was threatening to pull her under, and for a moment, she felt she was drowning. She kept the forward momentum, though, using her elbows to push people away. She should have known the evening wouldn't come off without a hitch.

About an hour ago, Brad had appeared out of nowhere, moseying next to her as soon as Stede left to get drinks. "It didn't take you long to find someone else," he'd remarked. Nodding at Stede, he'd shot her a smile calculated to undercut his insinuating tone.

Her jaw had slackened. It was as if she, not he, had broken up. "I think it was mutual," she'd managed to say politely, nodding toward Sylvia. "We both needed to move on."

"Given how busy you are, it must be difficult to finish preparations for your own show next week," he'd returned, implying it wouldn't be up to snuff.

"Not at all."

"I'll have to review it as I see fit," he'd informed her.

"I'm sure it will be wonderful. So many people have enjoyed the individual pieces, already," she'd managed to say airily, relieved to see Stede returning.

"I wish you luck with it," Brad had said when Stede was a pace away, but his tone was insincere. As much as she hated to admit it, his review could make or break her future. Predictably, he'd vanished just as Stede reappeared, avoiding an introduction.

A rake, she'd thought. It was an apt word for Brad. Not

that it mattered now. As she neared the melee, her eyes drifted over Stede, and she realized the altercation had gotten ugly. Sylvia was stepping back a pace, looking all innocent. Brad was stepping forward, his chest puffed out. Stede, who'd put his waistcoat back on, to hide the musket just as she'd requested, had unbuttoned it once more. Now he pushed back the fabric to expose the weapon.

"…and I overheard what you said about the review of Miss Taylor's show, sir," he was saying.

"This has nothing to do with reviews," Brad shouted over the music, glancing at Sylvia. "And you know it."

"Are you implying I spoke improperly to your woman?"

"She's not my woman," Brad assured imperiously. "She's a free agent, and the second I stepped away from her, you—"

"Must I remind you? You left Miss Gray without a chaperone, sir!"

"Why are you talking like that? And why are you wearing those clothes?" Looking at Tanya, Brad added, "Where'd you find this guy?"

Stede looked thoroughly repulsed, so she grabbed his arm to subdue him. Jerking his sleeve, she pulled him downward. A spark ignited as her lips hit his ear, but she ignored it and yelled, "You've got to be nice to him, remember?"

He yanked his head back, just far enough to shoot her a stunned sideways glance. "That was before I met this scoundrel, miss. You won't be tellin' me what to do now."

For an instant, their eyes fused and she was mesmerized. He didn't look the least bit rattled, and probably, the tone he was taking with Brad was mostly for show. Still, he looked determined to fight. In other circumstances, she might have been amused, but her show was too important. Her folks and Brittania would be there, and it had to be perfect. Keeping his ear pressed to her lips, she yelled, "If you want to win wars, you have to pick battles."

"Aye. Defending your honor is one I pick, miss."

He was impossible. She watched in horror as, with a sweeping arc of his arm, he withdrew the musket from the holster and pointed it toward the ceiling. The crowd fell back, and given its size, a stampede felt immanent.

Her heart raced. "Let's get out of here before it's too late!"

His blazing eyes fixed on Brad. "Prepare to defend yourself, sir!"

Brad's lips parted in surprise. "Is this guy for real?"

Stede tossed the musket. It flew high in the air, maybe ten feet, spinning until it reached the apex of its trajectory and came back down, tumbling barrel over grip. A thud sounded as the barrel smacked into Stede's waiting palm, sending tiny shivers through her whole system. It was like something out of a movie. He'd repositioned the gun in his hands without ending his and Brad's staring contest.

"Does this appear like fantasy to you, sir? A mere mirage of smoke and mirrors? A wee bit of mumbo-jumbo? Perhaps you think I'm Missus Llassa, herself!"

He was about to pistol whip Brad! Tanya twisted her head, glancing around wildly, relieved to see the burly doorman had almost reached them. Maybe he'd put an end to this insanity. Or not. Metal flashed under the black light strobe, and as if in slow motion, she watched in horror as Stede hauled back his fist and attacked. A crack sounded as the grip made contact. For a second, she thought it was a bullet, then realized it was Brad's jawbone.

Registering relief when she saw no blood, she grabbed Stede's arm. "Let's go!" Thankfully Brad was skimming his jaw with his fingers, seemingly not that badly hurt, so she pulled harder, tugging Stede toward the door just as the doorman lunged. She'd never know what happened next, only that she never let go of Stede. She was half running, half pushing through stifling heat before she wrenched around. The doorman was talking to Brad now, but she and Stede were almost to the door. But no…

"The doorman's following us!"

Stede glanced over his shoulder. "Run!"

The pressing, sweating bodies of the crowd propelled her, so her feet didn't seem to touch the ground. The door seemed miles away, but once they reached it, the crowd spit them out, sending her and Stede tumbling down the steps. She staggered as she hit the street, a high heel stabbing between cobbles. Worse, the doorman had caught up and was now bringing up the rear.

"You two wait here," he commanded furiously from the top of the steps. "We're calling the cops if anyone wants to press charges."

As the doorman disappeared into the crowd, she yelled, "Let go of me!" Somehow, her grip on Stede's sleeve had been lost and now he was the one manhandling her. He all but dragged her along the cobbles, moving toward the river.

"Run," Stede urged gruffly.

"The doorman said to stay."

"So we've got to run before he returns, miss."

"You could have killed Brad."

"Indeed I could have," he muttered, as if to say he'd deserved it, which didn't give her much comfort. "Now, come along. The doorman, as you call him, will surely follow."

"Brad might press charges!"

"Exactly. And I don't have time to be muddlin' with officers of the law tonight."

He was right about that. What on earth would she tell the police? Did the man she was with carry a wallet? Have identification on him? Who was he really? If they got arrested, she'd find out, she realized. Somehow, the thought made her start to trot over the cobbles. No, she wasn't ready for tonight's strange fantasy to end....

She glanced behind her. The doorman was storming down the steps of the gallery as if to give chase, and that ignited fire beneath her feet.

"Quit yer tarrying!" Stede urged once more.

She took off like a shot, but heard the doorman's voice sound from behind them. "I told you to wait!"

They were running fast now, and Stede was beside her, meeting her long legs, stride for stride. His palm was cupped around her elbow, sending an electric current pulsing through her. Steps pounded behind them, probably the doorman's, but she barely noticed. *Just run,* she thought, her feet flying, her eyes studying the cobbles in front of her.

Her senses heightened. Night had fallen and the air smelled smoky. Just ahead was one of the newly developed piers. A wide, dark expanse of river and sky was beyond that. She could see masts and billowing sails of docked boats. Beside her, she glimpsed rock-hard thighs straining under the white fabric of tight pants, and she looked away, her eyes riveting to the ground. Suddenly she gasped. The spike of a heel caught in the stones again, and she lunged, hands out, sprawling.

A strong hand caught her. Without breaking stride, he leaned, lifted her and set her aright. Nearer the river, they hit concrete, and she could run better. The traffic lights on West End Avenue were red, so they kept going, crossing the intersection. Her lungs burning, she twisted to look behind her for the doorman again, but saw no one. Pain sliced into her side, and for a second, she wanted to double, feeling as if her appendix might burst.

"Helluva workout," she muttered, relieved that the doorman had given up chase and gone back to the party. Or had he? Behind them, she was sure she saw a shadow. Inhaling sharply, she felt the tidewaters' salty air knife to her lungs as her eyes set on the end of the pier. She glanced beside her, aware of his sexy, labored breathing and those enticing straining thighs. Sailboats were docked on both sides of the pier, and in the middle, on the pier itself, was a miniature golf course and a children's playground, complete with swing-sets, ping-pong tables, a jungle gym, and a system of large red tubes kids could crawl through.

At the pier's end, she wrapped her fingers around the safety rail and doubled, panting. To her left, another marina housed private yachts; to her right, masts rose toward the stars and sails flapped in the breeze. Beneath, water lapped the seawall and barnacles cleaved to dock posts. For a second, she watched murky water eddy against them. Further out, swooping gulls were mere flashes of white, as incandescent as the one cloud that raced across the sky and vanished, leaving a clear inky landscape.

A warm hand settled on her back. "There," he soothed, concerned. "Are ya faint again?"

"You sure change your tone," she commented, feeling a surge of anger. Just a minute ago, he'd sounded furious, and now he didn't even have the decency to sound winded. He wasn't being particularly courteous regarding her personal space, either. The most intimate part of him felt more than bothersome, pressing against her backside. She heaved a frustrated sigh. He'd really hit Brad, even after she'd told him about the importance of the review.

Before she thought it through, she whirled and clocked him. Sort of. The side of her fist grazed silken stubble on his jaw, anyway. The small victory was short-lived, though, because he caught her fist in his own, curling hopelessly artistic fingers over hers. He was close—chest to chest, belly to belly, and the warmth of his breath hit her like a freight train. With their hips brushing, she could feel the length of him, the size and heat.

His eyes lasered into hers, and she parted her lips to offer some sort of generalized protest, but no sound came out, and just looking at him, she felt torn in half. She wanted him. But she had no idea who he was. "No more fun and games," she panted.

His voice was husky. "I never was playin'."

When his eyes slipped from hers, traveling downward, everything inside her froze. *Oh, no.* Running had shifted the built-in cups of the dress, and the already suggestive two-inch strip of exposed cleavage had broadened considerably, just as it had upstairs when he'd handcuffed her. Now it was more like four inches wide. Whether from the heat of his gaze, or because her nerves were jangling from running, everything that had frozen a moment ago now turned to water. Her tummy felt hot. Her head swam.

Her nipples constricted then, as surely as if she'd plunged over the pier into the cool water, and he noticed. His breath caught audibly, then his lips pressed firmly together as if he were bracing himself against sensations; the glint in his gaze seemed to say it was hopeless, though, especially when he stared where silk edged against her nipples. Her lungs emptied of air as she registered how they ached, pert and chafing against the fabric. She imagined the soothing coolness of his mouth, then gasped as tingling prickles coated her groin.

They were still standing there, exactly as they'd been a moment ago, with his hand wrapped around hers, but she felt like they'd traversed oceans. Her dress was hanging by a thread. If he pulled the sash behind her, they'd be lost. Suddenly his fist felt less like a fist, and more like sheer velvet. He was panting now, in tandem with her, but it wasn't from running.

"Yer hell-bent on hittin' me, aren't you, miss?" he accused softly, his words labored.

"You hit Brad," she returned, scooting her backside against the rail, hoping to escape their contact, something he only took as further invitation, pressing closer. Blood danced in her limbs, and she tried to shift away once more, now intending to better cover her breasts, but he moved with her.

"Brad's going to review my show in a week."

"And I beg yer pardon for the trouble."

But he wasn't even contrite, not really. His voice a rasping sound. Everything seemed to still. She was overly aware of every sound. Her own breathing sounded forced, harsh. Somewhere, far off, a sliver of half moon tipped in a sky pierced with bright white stars, and boats were rocking as if the river were a cradle.

Nearer, towering masts sent long shadows over his face, so she could barely see his eyes, but she could feel heat in them, searing her cleavage again. He was staring down at her, through half-lidded eyes, his gaze lingering where silk rimmed the constricted tips. She thrust out her chest inadvertently, trying to steady her breath, but he mistook the gesture when the fabric shifted another fraction.

"Oh, miss," he murmured simply, his eyes trailing from her neck to her waist as if he wanted to tear off every inch of fabric with his teeth.

She wasn't wearing panties.

It was the wrong time to remember that crucial fact. She felt as tipsy as the ships in the water, so her fingers gripped the rail more tightly. Her other hand was still trapped in his fist, and she gently twisted her wrist to disengage it. "Let me go."

Her voice had sounded too husky, too suggestive. And he considered a very long moment before he released her. Not that being free helped. She was still breathless, from both running and his proximity. Hot yearning had seized her. She cast a glance around wildly, half wishing the doorman really would show up. Hadn't he been chasing them? "You can't just…" Her voice trailed off when she realized her mouth was cottony.

He was merely watching her, seemingly curious as to what she'd do next.

"Crash into my house," she forced herself to continue.

"Take James's maps out of the drawers. Ruin Izzie's opening. Pull a gun at a party and hit my ex-boyfriend." Quickly she darted out her tongue and licked her lips.

His eyes followed the movement, fixing steadfastly to the pink, pointed spear. When he spoke, his voice was throaty. "How can I make up for it?"

Staring into his eyes, she could think of countless ways. But she slowly reached her hand, aware his eyes were studying every move, and grasped the bodice silk. As she pulled it more securely over the slopes of her breasts, one of her fingers brushed a painfully sensitized nipple.

A soft, unmistakable grunt of male longing sounded.

"You can't…" she began again.

"Arouse you like this?" he muttered softly.

Her heart stuttered as a huge hand circled her neck. Leaning, he kissed her. Slowly, wetly, thoroughly. Then he leaned back an inch, watching her face as his fingers splayed on her collarbone, then pranced downward, bridging the space between the breasts she'd tried to cover. She'd barely succeeded. Even now, her fingers clutched the dress, but as he teased the cleavage, the nails of his wide hands nearly scraped distended nipples, too, missing them by a hair's breadth.

He was teasing her mercilessly, making her want to cry out. "I don't know who you are."

"I'd be the man who's doing this to you."

He slid a hand over the back of hers where it still clutched the dress, and suddenly, roughly, he pushed the fabric back so his fingers could slip under the built-in bodysuit. He pushed that away, too, exposing her, his eyes half shut as a thumb and finger found an excited tip. Her core melted as he pinched and tugged. She couldn't let a stranger do this, yet it was part of the allure.

When his hand stilled, she whimpered, begging him to further arouse her, and he did, capturing her mouth, his tongue stroking open her lips. Hers responded, meshing and teasing, as he simultaneously deepened the kiss and fondled, squeezing the mound of her breast, over and over until she gasped, crying out when his hips rocked against hers, creating a thread of heat between her breast and pelvis that felt like a streak of lightning. He was hard now. Very hard. Hers.

Sensing the tide of frustrated desire rising inside her, he licked his tongue down her neck in languid, fiery loops, leading her toward oblivion, then just as suddenly, his mouth descended in scalding heat that exploded on a peaking nipple. Her head jerked, lolled on her neck, and she felt her eyes rolling back.

Everything inside her turned as dark as the night sky. She pleaded mindlessly as he swirled the tongue around the ever-tightening tip, feeling close to shattering as he drew her between firm lips, suckling hard. She wished he had another mouth. Ten mouths. She needed that mouth everywhere. Suckling her breasts, salting her belly, exploring between her legs.

Thrusting splayed hands into his hair, she ripped out the tie that held the ponytail. Loose hair ran in rivulets between her fingers while a darker current flooded her veins, racing toward a breaking dam. Climbing as he suckled harder, she sighed in ecstasy as he thrust his stiffened tongue against her, and she guided his head, urging him to trace more mind-bending patterns, arching her hips for the hard crush of his. Up, down and around one nipple…he licked and licked until the other ached. Her belly felt swollen now. She was throbbing with unstoppable pleasure. She wanted…needed…

"More," she whispered raggedly. She needed just one touch. Pressure. Wanted him to get down on his knees, push up her dress and put his mouth on her—

"Let's do it here," she whispered. Why not? Outside. On the pier. Untangling her hands from his hair, she flattened them, ran them down his thighs, clasped the bunched muscles. Flesh leaped beneath the thin fabric, and she knew just how to convince him to give her more.

There! A strangled cry tore from his throat as her hand caressed the front of the breeches. Heat poured through the fabric, and he was steely against the taut drawstring laces. Gasping, she grasped him, her fingers curling around the thick ridge. When she squeezed, his tongue went wild on her breast, and she sobbed something senseless. Quickly his hand came roughly between their bodies, gliding over hers and staying it.

His head reared back, leaving her breast exposed. The night breeze hit her hot wet flesh. "Don't stop," she muttered, stunned.

In the shadows, his lips were slack and wet, his eyes glazed. She glanced around, taking in her breasts that were now exposed for his greedy eyes. She glanced over his shoulder, taking in the recreational red tubes made for kids to play in, then the swing-sets, then the boats. Where could they go?

When he opened his mouth, she had no doubt he was going to ask her opinion. Inside the tubes? On the deck of an unattended sailboat?

Instead he grabbed the sides of her dress and yanked them over breasts still wet with his saliva. Panting hard, he said, "Wait right here, miss."

Then he pivoted, strode toward the children's playground, ducked under a nautical rope and vanished.

SENSING HER BEHIND him, Stede turned, but he couldn't really see her. He bit back a curse. If she didn't stay put, they could both be killed. Someone had followed them, after all. He was sure of it now, but his mind felt as foggy as a morning lagoon and he was still blind with passion. He needed her in bed, not to be on her hands and knees in some sort of strange tunnel built for dwarves or trolls. If he wasn't careful, his broad shoulders were going to get stuck, too. "A bloody, impossible woman," he exploded under his breath, sexual frustration pushing him to the edge.

He glanced over his shoulder. "I asked you to remain, so that I might spy whoever it 'tis. Now we'll have to hide here."

She giggled breathlessly.

How could a man protect a woman so hell-bent on getting into trouble? She was worse than Lucinda! "I can't believe ya really plunged inside this strange tunnel wearing that dress."

"You're the one who started crawling through a tunnel built for children to play in."

So that was the purpose of the round tubes. Still glancing over his shoulder, he took in the dress. Or what was left of it. It wasn't decent. Women were made for man's pleasure, to be sure. But not without some wooing. Not that she'd seemed to mind. Clearly, Tanya Taylor could go from knocking a man senseless, to taking her pleasure without missing a heartbeat.

Pressing a finger to his lips, he felt an unexpected rush of fury. What had just happened? All he'd wanted to do was find Julius Royle tonight! For all he knew, this wench was part of the curse. Had Missus Llassa put her in his path to slow him down? He'd already wasted hours at the opening, and if he didn't stop making love to her, he'd never find out why he kept landing back in his own painting.

At the other end of the play tube, he stayed crouched down, getting his bearings. His senses sharp, he glanced around, glad she was staying quiet, at least. She squinted back in the dark. Even in the shadows cast by the far-off lamp, he could see she was moony-eyed, and he wanted nothing more than to draw her into his embrace again.

"Go back to the end of the pier," he whispered, his voice hoarse with need.

"Why?" she mouthed.

Couldn't the woman take anything at face value? "Somebody followed us." And whoever it was had gotten an eyeful.

She was crouched down beside him now, at the lip of the tunnel. Her voice was barely audible. "The doorman?"

"Aye." He paused, keeping his voice low. "Well…I don't know, miss. Maybe."

A rattle sounded nearby. His eyes darted to the shadows, flitting like a phantom. "Wait a minute," he began, "let me circle behind him, then you make a wee bit of noise."

Her lips were still red and wet, crushed from his kisses, but she looked appalled. "You want to use me as bait?"

He nodded. If she stayed here to lure the other man toward her, he could attack from behind. "Aye."

She considered, looking none too thrilled. "Okay."

He could feel her eyes on his back as he crept stealthily

around the play area, his movements silent. Fear snaked into his veins, not that he particularly heeded it, but Tanya had said she'd felt followed before tonight, and earlier, when he'd kissed her in the street, he'd sensed another presence. Walking the way an Apache had once taught him, he traced his fingertips along the ground for balance, ducking behind a dinosaur statue near a sign that said, Miniature Golf.

Leaning back, he tried to catch his breath, but he couldn't, not when images of her body were still in his mind—the pale slopes of her breasts, the taut ruddy nipples he'd savaged with the heat of his moist mouth.

He heard her cough. Then a stealthy footstep. And another. It was definitely a man, not a woman. Already, Stede was almost behind him. He was by the gaming tables. She coughed again, and the person realized her exact location and started advancing toward the tube. The footsteps picked up pace, as Stede inched toward the stranger with nothing covering him now except shadows.

Hopefully the other man would be so intent on the noise that he wouldn't turn around and see Stede. A soft banging sounded. She'd hit the side of the tube. He just hoped she didn't disregard him and step outside, into the open. She'd be less protected, easier to grab. Stede had to move fast now. If the plan backfired, the man would get to Tanya before Stede could tackle him. The man was only ten feet from the tube where Tanya was now. Nine. Eight…

His shadow was clearly visible. It wasn't the doorman. A long gray ponytail protruded from beneath a cap, and the fellow wore farm pants with a short-sleeved shirt. Stede speeded to a crouching run just as Tanya loosed a war cry. She appeared from the tube now, raising shoes that looked more lethal than muskets above her head. Realizing it no longer mattered if the man heard him, Stede ran the last steps full-out, his boots pounding.

As the man whirled toward Stede, Stede grabbed the back of his belt. With a swipe, he pulled the man down to the concrete, tackling him. Too late, he realized that the man's looks had been deceiving. He was an elderly gentleman. A grunt sounded. Then a sickening thud. *The man's head.* Stede hadn't meant for it to hit the ground. He'd meant to attack the man, not kill him, but now, when he looked beneath him, blood was trickling from under the man.

Shades of Basil Drake, Stede thought. In a flash, he was back in the clearing, standing over the dead man, his musket in hand.

"Sweet Betsy Ross," he muttered, quickly rolling away and rising to a crouch. What had he done? Gripping the shoulder of the man, he turned him over, and his heart nearly broke. Somehow, he was glad Tanya was next to him. She was down on her haunches, too, the lovely fingers of her slender hands curled around both shoes, as if she intended to use them as weapons again. "Oh, no," she whispered. "Did we kill him?"

For the second time in his life, Stede was kneeling between a man who might be dead and a sweet-hearted woman who was too sensitive to witness such events. Worse, the man's face was so lifeless he really might be dead. "Perhaps, miss," he said, fighting an urge to pull her into his embrace, bury his head between her breasts and simply fall asleep for all eternity.

"I wonder who it is?" she asked worriedly.

As he reached to check the man's pulse, Stede felt his

GET FREE BOOKS and FREE GIFTS
WHEN YOU PLAY THE...

Lucky 7

SLOT MACHINE GAME!

Just scratch off the silver box with a coin. Then check below to see the gifts you get!

YES!

I have scratched off the silver box. Please send me the 2 free Harlequin® Blaze® books and 2 free gifts for which I qualify. I understand I am under no obligation to purchase any books, as explained on the back of this card.

351 HDL EF42   **151 HDL EF4Q**

FIRST NAME   LAST NAME

ADDRESS

APT.#   CITY

STATE/ PROV.   ZIP/POSTAL CODE

7	7	7	**Worth TWO FREE BOOKS** plus 2 BONUS Mystery Gifts!
🍒	🍒	🍒	**Worth TWO FREE BOOKS!**
♣	♣	♣	**Worth ONE FREE BOOK!**
🔔	🔔	🍒	**TRY AGAIN!**

www.eHarlequin.com

(H-B-10/06)

Offer limited to one per household and not valid to current Harlequin® Blaze® subscribers.

Your Privacy - Harlequin Books is committed to protecting your privacy. Our Privacy Policy is available online at www.eHarlequin.com or upon request from the Harlequin Reader Service. From time to time we make our lists of customers available to reputable firms who may have a product or service of interest to you. If you would prefer for us not to share your name and address, please check here ☐.

The Harlequin Reader Service® — Here's how it works:

Accepting your 2 free books and 2 free mystery gifts places you under no obligation to buy anything. You may keep the books and gifts and return the shipping statement marked "cancel." If you do not cancel, about a month later we'll send you 6 additional books and bill you just $3.99 each in the U.S., or $4.47 each in Canada, plus 25¢ shipping & handling per book and applicable taxes if any.* That's the complete price and — compared to cover prices of $4.75 each in the U.S. and $5.75 each in Canada — it's quite a bargain! You may cancel at any time, but if you choose to continue, every month we'll send you 6 more books, which you may either purchase at the discount price or return to us and cancel your subscription.

*Terms and prices subject to change without notice. Sales tax applicable in N.Y. Canadian residents will be charged applicable provincial taxes and GST. All orders subject to approval. Credit or debit balances in a customer's account(s) may be offset by any other outstanding balance owed by or to the customer. Please allow 4 to 6 weeks for delivery.

very last hope ebb away. So many years had passed that he'd scarcely recognized the person. "This, miss," he said, "is Julius Royle."

8

"STEDE, dear fellow, you haven't changed a bit!" Suddenly Julius Royle rolled. Jumping spryly to his feet with a chuckle, he clamped his friend's shoulder, squeezing hard as he pulled an old camera from the pavement. "I'm sorry to say I think you cracked the lens. The old camera hit the ground hard, and now I'm bleeding profusely from where your lady friend stabbed me with her shoes. Come along, anyway," he prattled, wrapping a handkerchief around his arm to staunch the bleeding as he jogged toward a busy street, the urgency of his voice forcing Tanya and Stede to follow. "We've got to hurry! We haven't much time! We've got to lift this hex on you, old boy, and we've only got a week! I've been waiting for the day you might turn up again! You can introduce me to your lady friend in the cab. As you're soon to find out, it's a good thing you've met someone already."

What was he talking about? "Good thing?" Tanya echoed, shoving her feet back into her shoes as she ran, surprised by the turn of events and fighting embarrassment over the passion the man must have witnessed.

"To lift the hex," Julius said quickly.

"But what have I got to do with—"

"Sweet Betsy Ross!" Stede interrupted, looking

shocked, his eyes roving over the other man's face as he jogged to keep up. "You're all right then, Julius?"

"As right as rain."

For a moment, both spoke at once, then Stede said, "I thought I'd killed you, and—"

"No such luck, my lad," Julius interjected in the hyperbolic tone that seemed to undercut all his words even as he spoke them. "You may be a rough-and-tumble sort, but it would take more than a privateer from the 1700s to kill old Julius Royle. I'm a survivor. I even survived the last stock market crash before my siblings tried to take me down. You gave me quite the conk on the noggin, though."

"Sorry," Tanya uttered. For a second, she teetered on the high heels since her legs were turning rubbery again. She was starting to feel as if *she'd* gotten trapped inside a painting, instead of Stede coming out of one.

"Rest assured," Julius returned dryly. "When you're as old as I am, a few more stab wounds are hardly even noticeable." He laughed as he moved swiftly toward the road. "At least it wasn't my heart, dear lady. And if it had been, you would hardly be the first to do it mortal damage."

"What are ya doin' here?" asked Stede, who was thinking along his own track. "And are ya still at that fancy town house, Julius? 'Twas on Bank Street?"

"That's where May found the painting," Tanya put in quickly, her heart racing, her mind barely able to keep pace. Blinking, she surveyed Julius and realized he did look familiar. But was he who he claimed? She could swear she recognized him from photographs in a biography she'd read about artistic types who had lived in the Village in the sixties. Still, everything happening seemed impossible, so she said, "Are you really Julius Royle?"

"Of course I'm Julius Royle!"

"He is, indeed," said Stede.

"Who else would I be?" Julius continued in a tone that suggested he wasn't accustomed to having to explain himself. "Why is no one listening to me? We haven't much time, I tell you!" Then he added, "Who's May?"

"She's got a secondhand store called Finders Keepers in Sag Harbor," Tanya explained. "She found…the painting that, uh…" Pausing, she didn't think she could force herself to say it, but she did, anyway. "That…uh…Stede was…you know, stuck inside."

Fortunately Julius didn't seem to find what she'd said the least bit odd. "Well, that explains a lot! The movers must have misplaced the painting when my siblings hired them to move my things!"

He was a strange man, Tanya decided. Nothing about him should have given the impression of wealth—he was dressed in inexpensive clothes, just jeans, a T-shirt, and cap, and he was prattling like a schoolmarm—yet he projected a manner-born quality that was hard to define. His brown eyes were more watchful than his speech patterns might suggest, and his voice was cultured, the words all spoken in a slightly dry, cynical tone, as if to say she should take nothing he said at face value. It was as if all was spoken in hyperbole, with a wink behind it, and while she usually didn't like people who had such a manner, she found herself liking Julius immensely. Clearly, he'd evolved layers of defense against other human beings, probably from living a life in which he'd found no one to trust.

Stede was staring at him. "You left your manse?"

Before Julius could answer, Tanya jumped in again, returning to the conversation she'd initiated, glad they'd almost reached the end of the pier. "May found the painting on Bank Street, near a Dumpster, then she kept it in storage for years. Right after she brought it into her shop to sell, I discovered it."

"That does explain a lot," Julius repeated. "But like I said, we haven't much time. I'll explain everything in the cab."

Motioning to them as if he were starting to feel winded, Julius continued jogging toward the West Side highway. Curiouser and curiouser, Tanya thought, clutching her bodice as she ran. After what had just happened with Stede, she no longer really trusted the dress; one tug and she'd find herself naked in the street if she wasn't careful. She blew out a sigh.

Tanya definitely felt as if she'd stepped through a looking glass or slid down a rabbit hole. Not for the first time since the strange evening began, she felt the whole world sliding off-kilter, spinning on its axis into some new, indefinable direction that would take her places totally beyond her control.

Time seemed to bend. It was late, but she felt rested, and yet a thread of paranoia was weaving through her thoughts, too. Was any of this really happening? How long had Julius Royle been following her? And he *was* Julius Royle. She was increasingly positive that she recognized him.

"Taxi!" he shouted, waving his arm as soon as they approached the West Side Highway.

A yellow cab maneuvered across three lanes of traffic, screeched to the curb, and they slid in. "Twenty-Nine West Eleventh Street," ordered Julius.

Squeezed between the two men, Tanya concentrated on catching her breath. Just when she thought it might steady, the widely splayed fingers of Stede's hand landed on her thigh, glided toward her knee and curled around the cap. He started rubbing sensual circles that made her want to ask the driver to turn the car around, so she could take Stede home with her, instead of wherever they were going. As the two men talked, she looked between them, her head bouncing from side to side, as if she were at Wimbledon.

"Why did ya leave home?" Stede was asking, looking stunned. "Ya loved those things, Julius. The antique furniture, those beautiful lanterns, yer paintin's and such. It was a museum, it was!"

"It's quite a tale," assured Julius, adjusting his cap, then pulling down a T-shirt sporting a logo that read I Love New York. Glancing up front, Julius seemed to realize the driver couldn't hear them through the Plexiglas separating the seats, so he plunged into the story. "Well, you know my siblings always wanted to control the money I was dispensing to them," he began. "I was the main heir to the fortune, a considerable sum, if I do say so myself." He glanced at Tanya. "We made money in railroads, then bought into communications systems." He paused, his expression becoming veiled, as if he had no idea how to proceed.

Stede gasped. "I caused you trouble, didn't I?"

Tanya could see Julius's throat work as he swallowed. "No, no. Of course not." He took a deep breath. "Well, all right…I mean, yes you did, Stede, but…" Julius shook his head as if trying to set his thoughts straight. "What I'm trying to say, dear fellow, is that having you come into my life was an experience for which I wouldn't trade the world, so even though it did cause difficulty, I couldn't care less. And I found out a great deal about my family and how untrustworthy they are, you see, which is good information for any man to have."

The hand on her knee tightened, sending delightful chills up her thigh as Julius plunged on. "Being raised as I was, a boy has everything handed to him on a platter, you know. A cliché, to be sure. But in my case it was true, just as I told you in the past, when you stayed with me, Stede. Every whim was indulged. Every taste and desire. I had horses, boats, cars, women. Houses wherever I wanted them. And my family has lived that way for generations."

"Sons of liberty," Stede interjected, now talking to Tanya. "You should see this man's home! Ya must have an even fancier one, today."

"Actually I don't. But meeting you," Julius continued. "Now, that was truly special. Something money could never buy. And it set me on a very different life course." Leaning his head back, he seemed to be contemplating sweet memories. "Of course, after you vanished, I was foolish enough to tell my brother and sister how you'd popped out the week before, right into my living room where I was sitting by the fire, watching television."

"You told them?"

"Indeed, I did. As soon as you got popped back in. At that point, I had to trust somebody and get some advice."

"I know how you feel," murmured Tanya, registering that some of Julius's phrases sounded almost as antiquated as Stede's, probably the legacy of his high-born family.

"Neither of us knew why this was happening to you," Julius continued, talking to Stede. "And others you'd met in the past, such as the security guard in the warehouse in 1956, weren't so friendly to you, as you'll recall—"

"Oh, Julius! How I've missed you," interjected Stede, and now, when his grip on her knee tightened, it felt less sensual, almost painful. Thankfully it loosened as he continued. "You believed in me! In every word!"

"Of course I did," assured Julius. "And I thought my siblings would be as interested as I. You hold the key to time, my lad. Life and death. Immortality of a certain sort. You're living proof in mystery and miracles, hexes and curses. Magic of all kinds. I thought they'd want to help do whatever possible to bring you back from the horrifying netherworld you described to me. I wanted to use whatever resources the Royle family fortunes could provide."

"Certainly I don't wish to return," Stede said gratefully.

Julius's eyes darkened, looking sad. "You were living…and yet not quite living. Seeing your surroundings at a remove, as if in a dream, through haze and fog. It was important to release you from that, and while it would be wrong to publicize your story, since it could only endanger you, you might clarify points in history, help us discover the past." His voice turned bitter. "But my brother and sister didn't care about that. They started commitment proceedings."

Tanya inhaled sharply as the pieces began to fall into place. "They thought you were crazy?"

He shook his head. "Not really. They know better. But as soon as I began talking about having a man pop out of a painting, they took the opportunity." He suddenly did a double-take, looking at Tanya. "You *have* heard all of Stede's story?"

She inclined her chin in response, her heart still beating too hard. Julius Royle was making the strangest events sound so normal. He had been somewhat famous as an art collector, at least that's what she remembered, and he'd had the exact same experience she'd had with Stede. "I…uh…woke up and found…uh, Stede downstairs," she explained.

Once more, Julius nodded as if that were the most ordinary thing in the world. "I can imagine how it happened. I'm just glad I found you. I used to buy quite a lot of art, you know, and I always liked Stede's paintings. I still have loyal spies at Weatherby's."

"Somebody from Weatherby's told you I'd found the painting? Eduardo?"

Julius shook his head. "Eduardo and I go way back, but he never tells me a thing, nor do I give up my contacts."

So it could have been Eduardo, she deduced. Once more, doubt niggled. This meant Eduardo and James could have talked Julius into playing along with some charade, to fool her. But deep down, she knew that wasn't the truth. Besides, had he talked to Eduardo, he'd have known where the painting came from. "Your contact didn't mention May?"

Julius shook his head. "The person only knew that the O'Flannery painting I sought had been brought in for correct identification, then taken to Treasured Maps." Pausing, he shook his head in disgust. "Even after my brother and sister used my obsession with Stede and his work to have me declared incompetent and committed to a mental hospital, I kept trying to find the painting." He laughed. "My sister keeps your other works that I owned in storage. Anyway, the hospital wasn't a bad one," he assured Stede. "I'll give my loving siblings that much. They never lacked taste. They incarcerated me in a place with lovely landscaped grounds, a decent chef, cute nurses and a rehabilitation program with amazing computers and plenty of Internet access."

"But a prison, nonetheless!" protested Stede, stunned by the injustice. "I brought you bad luck, I did. What could a man like me do to make it up to ya?"

"Not a thing," Julius assured, then pointed at a brick walk-up building as the cab pulled to a curb. "Your pretty friend can pay the cab fare, however. You've probably got even less money than me, and I spent quite a bit standing outside, watching the map store. It cost me a pretty penny in coffee and dessert fees."

Inside, Tanya's mind was turning like a series of interlocking wheels. "You were watching me from the café across the street?" she asked, thrusting bills at the driver as Julius got out of the cab.

"Yes, I was."

That further explained why she'd felt watched all week. "Why didn't you just approach me?" she asked, getting out of the cab with Stede right behind her, relieved to see this was a street she knew well. She figured the chance of something dangerous happening on such a nice block was next to nil.

"Approach you? And say what?" Julius queried as he opened the front door of an apartment building and started leading them upstairs. "That I thought a man might pop out of a painting you'd bought?" He shot her a grin. "And bought for well under market value, I hear. Good girl."

Given that his own family had used his story to lock him in a mental hospital and presumably take his fortune, she could see why he'd decided not to march to her doorstep and repeat the same information. "I can see why you'd wait," she admitted, climbing stairs that already seemed never ending. They were covered with worn carpet of an indiscriminate color. Stopping, she tried to catch her breath. "Which floor?"

"Eighth. Almost there," he assured.

"You must have seen me before now," Stede said. "Were you in the alleyway when we went into the party?"

"Yes. That was me. But I had to be sure it was you. Inside the map store, it was too dark. I thought it was you, but I wanted to see you up close. In the alley, I knew. I was about to approach you then, but then you two…"

Started kissing.

A brief, embarrassed silence ensued, during which Tanya realized how winded she was. As far as that went, Stede could still be kissing her. Grasping the rail, she filled her lungs and kept climbing. The only saving grace was that, as she climbed, she could feel Stede right behind her, and she was pretty sure his eyes were riveted to her backside, which brought another rush of pleasure.

"I waited," Julius was saying. "Thinking I'd approach you when you came outside the gallery party, but when you did, you were running, so I followed you to the river."

Thankfully they'd reached the apartment door, and neither she, nor Stede, felt compelled to recount how he'd protected her honor at the party, nor to discuss their near lovemaking. Briefly she thought of how this was going to affect her career chances, then squelched the thought. Julius was right. What was happening tonight was much more significant. Time was bending, all right, and the kiss on the pier had been otherworldly.

"Cozy," she noted once they were ushered inside and Julius snapped on two authentic-looking Tiffany lamps that gave off dim light.

Not looking nearly as convinced as she, Stede began pacing as Julius rattled about in a makeshift kitchen that was set up in a corner. He clanked pots and pans until he found a tin teakettle and put on water for coffee. She glanced over the setup, her eyes lingering on an old, huge refrigerator with a first generation microwave perched on top, then a hotplate that served as his oven.

"How long have you been livin' here?" Stede exploded.

"Eleven years, since I left the Happy Acres."

"Surely it wasn't really called Happy Acres," she said.

"Of course it wasn't," Julius said with a laugh, then glanced at Stede. "Don't fret. I agreed to stop managing my brother and sister's finances, as per our parents' will, in exchange for my freedom. Now, they manage the money and refuse to dole any out to me. Still, I assure you, every moment of freedom has been worth it."

Stede's eyes caught hers. "He lived in a palace before, he did," he muttered, sounding thoroughly disgusted.

Given what she knew of Julius's background, she could only imagine. This wasn't a particularly small room—maybe twelve-by-twelve feet—yet that's all it was, just a room, and it was brimming with clutter. Stacks of books, magazines and newspapers littered every surface. It had high ceilings, and gilded picture frames were on a high shelf, probably leftovers from when Julius could afford to buy pictures to fill them. Impressive windows with deep-set sills were strewn with dusty pillows, and like the rest of the place, the ornate molding had seen better days. What were once blue, painted walls had faded to gray.

"That settles it. Tomorrow we'll dig up my treasure, we will," Stede suddenly vowed as if the solution couldn't be clearer. "Making you a rich man again is the least I can do, Julius."

"Couldn't allow it," assured Julius, coming into the living area with three steaming cups on a tarnished silver tray. "At least not until we're sure you won't be going back into…" His voice trailed off.

The painting.

The words hung suspended in the air. "No, you'd better leave your treasure where you can find it in the future."

Her heart suddenly stretched to breaking. Could this man really return to a painting, then reappear in yet another time? Would he use a buried treasure to generate income long after she, herself, was dead? The thoughts took hold, and she didn't hear the rest of what was said. Spying framed newspaper articles on a far wall, she moved toward them, her eyes widening. One headline proclaimed, Heir To Royle Fortune Declared Insane. Quickly she scanned the article, which talked about family infighting between Julius and his siblings after their parents died. Apparently, Julius was to administer all funds to his brother and sister, a situation they hadn't been happy with.

"It's really you," she whispered, her eyes returning to the photograph. The resemblance was unmistakable. Their host really was Julius Royle, but he was years older now. As the last vestiges of doubt fell away, she felt as if she were going into shock all over again, as stunned as when she'd first seen Stede. So, everything was true. And that meant…

"What did you mean by saying it was a good thing Stede had already met me?" she asked, speaking more sharply than she'd intended. After whirling around to get a better look at Julius, she headed toward a musty futon to rest her aching feet. Meanwhile, Stede gave up on pacing and seated himself right beside her, close enough that the warmth from his thigh seeped into her own.

"Well…" Julius was rummaging in the freezer compartment of the huge fridge, rattling ice trays. "It took some doing, but I managed to find and buy Lucinda's diary."

"Lucinda's diary?" Stede asked.

Surprise and pain were in his tone, and when Tanya looked at him, there was such hurt in his eyes that she wondered about his relationship with the other woman, if he'd loved her. He'd said he hadn't, but…

"Here we go," said Julius, bringing a book from the freezer. It was wrapped in countless layers of plastic and crusted with ice.

She squinted. "You keep it in the freezer?"

As he seated himself in the only chair, a regal, hand-carved piece with a slatted back and faded needlepoint seat cover, he caught her eye. "No file cabinets," he explained, unwinding masking tape he'd wrapped around the protective plastic, then extracted a very old-looking diary with a cracked leather cover. "No security system, either. Besides, the refrigerator is fireproof, and the cold helps keep antiquities safe. Like Southern belles, they wither in the heat." He winked at Tanya. "As luck would have it, this place has a fridge big enough to store mink coats. When apartment houses burn down, the fridge is usually all that's left."

He was definitely living in a firetrap, though it was on a very nice block.

"The refrigerator is an amazing invention," agreed Stede. "But you say that's Lucinda's diary?"

Carefully Julius turned pages, found what he wanted, then handed the book to Stede. "She talks about the hex, my lad. Some of it's written before your duel in the clearing, some after. She asked around town, to find out anything she could, then the brave girl even paid Missus Llassa more than Basil Drake did, to tell her what she'd done. Beyond that, Missus Llassa refused to let Lucinda pay her to reverse the curse, saying her reputation would be destroyed."

Stede was clearly stunned. "Where did you find the diary?"

"A library in New England. It was handed down in the well-preserved papers of the Barrington family. As it turns out, Lucinda did marry Jonathan Wilson. During the happily ever after, they had eleven children, nine of whom survived. Most of the descendants are situated in Maine now. I may not have money, but I bought art for so many years that I still have contacts. Not to mention years of skill in tracking such works."

"How did you pay for it?" Tanya couldn't help but ask, curious. "A diary this old must be worth a small fortune in its own right."

Julius laughed. "It was. But I visited my dear sister's country house and filched a tiny Egyptian fetish I didn't think she'd ever miss. It brought me enough on the black market to buy the diary and afford some concerts and lectures, which I enjoy." Once more, he chuckled. "My sister did miss the fetish, though, and she suspects me. But then, she feels so guilty about having stolen my position and fortune that she kindly let me get away with the theft and didn't call in the police."

"I've never met a man more reconciled to a sad fate as you, my friend," said Stede, shaking his head. "I take inspiration from you, I do."

Julius clapped him on the shoulder, then winked at Tanya again. "I don't know which is better, having been rich…or getting to watch my self-centered siblings live overly indulgent lives they can't enjoy."

"Can't enjoy?" Tanya prompted.

"Nope. They're too eaten with guilt." Julius sighed with genuine satisfaction. "Well, I could talk about my situation for days on end," he promised, "but there are more pressing matters. As I said, I used my contacts to find whatever might help you, Stede, in case you ever came back." All at once, his brown eyes turned liquid, looking teary. "I hoped I'd still be living, but I was no longer at my brownstone on Bank Street, so I feared you wouldn't find me…."

"I called information, just the way you taught me last time I was here, but you weren't listed."

"That's news to me. Oh, Stede, I'm so sorry."

Clearly the two men had formed a real bond, and it spoke well for both of them. Tanya drew a deep breath as Stede's hand tightened on her knee again, the touch less sensual than an appeal for support. His voice was gruff. "There's not enough treasure in the world to repay you," Stede said helplessly.

Julius's eyes met the other man's, and they gazed at each other a long moment. "Your friendship's quite enough."

"You're a true gentleman," returned Stede hoarsely.

"The only of my siblings to do our family honor," agreed Julius. "But do look at the book, my lad, while I find a spot of whiskey with which to lace our coffee."

He rose, then returned from the kitchen area with a bottle, splashing a drop into his and Stede's mugs after Tanya declined, taking cream instead. Sipping the coffee, she found it surprisingly good, tasting mildly of vanilla and nuts. She shut her eyes, basking in the warmth of it, which matched the autumnal night. "Excellent," she said.

"One of my many specialties," said Julius.

She didn't doubt he had others. "So Missus Llassa admitted to puttin' this hex on me," Stede murmured as he read. "And she did it after the duel, which explains why I was aboard the *American Dreamer* when I got stuck in my own paintin'."

Julius leaned, turning a page for Stede, having clearly memorized and dissected the entire work. "See? Here's the curse, itself. He read the first lines. "'In your own painting you will be, perchance for all eternity…'"

Inching closer to Stede, Tanya felt her breath catching when she saw the words written so long ago by a woman's delicate hand. "'Awakened through the centuries until love's currency does free,'" she continued, picking up where Julius had left off. Then she squinted, unable to read the text. "'…something about 'you and thee,'" she murmured, frustrated. "I can't read it. The ink's too faded. Then it says, 'you must say you…'" She squinted even harder, but it was no use. Words were missing. "Then the word 'me' appears." Her heart sank. But what had she expected? The diary was over two hundred years old.

"It's all I could find," apologized Julius.

"And enough it is," Stede assured quickly.

"Not really," disagreed Julius. "It's a start, however. And—" Leaning once more, he turned the page, his liver-spotted hand suddenly shaking, seemingly less from age than excitement.

"When Lucinda spoke with Missus Llassa, the old witch explained that you have to fall in love in a week. Otherwise you'll find yourself in the painting again."

"The two times I've popped out, I've been here a week," marveled Stede. "I'd begun to think time was part of the hex."

"The third time's the charm," Tanya tried to assure, but she realized this meant Stede really could vanish next Friday at… "What time did you, uh, pop out?"

"Seven-fifteen," he said promptly.

"All you have to do is fall in love," Julius said. "The words of the hex suggest it, and that's what Missus Llassa told Lucinda. The only thing we don't have is the key to whatever makes you pop out. I mean, why in those specific years, but not others?"

"If we knew that…" Tanya's voice trailed off. "Well, if he did wind up back in the picture…"

"We'd know how to get him out again," finished Julius.

She could feel the chase taking hold, the internal need to see the mystery solved. "What could it be?" she murmured.

Julius shook his head. "I've been over and over it in my mind. I bought the painting from a woman named Susannah Billings."

"Of Billings Candy?" Tanya guessed, recognizing the name from news articles. A flighty candy-store heiress and reputed wild child, she'd dated a number of

Hollywood bad boys. "Billings," she repeated, her lips parting in surprise.

Julius nodded. "Unlike many of Stede's paintings, this one was handed down through an ancestor of Jonathan Wilson's who later sold it to the Billings."

"So, somehow Stede's painting made it back to Lucinda after she married Jonathan Wilson?"

Julius nodded once more. "She was a known collector of his work. The Wilson family has remained furniture makers to this day, just as the Billings have been in candy. I met Susannah on the West Coast. It was the sixties," Julius reminded. "She'd been protesting, and not just the war, but everything else in life, as near as I could tell. She'd claimed her parents were—" Pausing, he searched his mind for the phrase. "Establishment pigs. Oppressors. When I met her, she'd changed her name to Moon Beam. Two words," he clarified. "Her first and last name. She was as broke as I am today, without a pot to piss in, as the saying goes. And she was selling the few heirlooms she had left, wanting to divest herself of her family roots."

"What's wrong?" Tanya suddenly murmured, realizing Stede was merely staring at the diary, shaking his head.

He shrugged, and when he lifted his gaze, the depth of feeling tugged all her heartstrings. "Just seeing Lucinda's handwriting after so many years…" he began simply.

Once more, she wondered at the relationship. He'd claimed only to be friends with the woman, and that spoke well of him, too, she decided. Some men never did learn how to be friends with women. How would she feel, she wondered, if she saw two-hundred-year-old handwriting of someone she loved? Of one of her family members?

Suddenly her heart ached. Surely Stede was taking in that his friends were long gone. She blinked, realizing her eyes had settled on Julius. For the first time, she realized he looked tired. She was, too. It was late.

"Maybe you should get some sleep," she said. After all, Julius had to be nearly seventy. His movements were spry, and earlier, he'd seemed unstoppable, but he wasn't a young man. He must have changed a great deal since Stede had last seen him. In the sixties, he would have looked as he did in the newspaper picture. She swallowed hard, unable to really put a name to the emotions coursing through her. If this was what she was feeling, how much more was Stede undergoing?

She glanced around once more, taking in Julius's relatively impoverished circumstances. Her own weren't much better, since she didn't exactly have a guest room, but she could offer more space. "Stede can stay with me," she said, avoiding his gaze when she felt a sudden rush of heat tunneling through her.

"You must take the diary," Julius returned, nodding toward where it lay in Stede's large hands. "You'll both want to read it."

She haggled for a moment, protesting, then ended by saying, "It was expensive. I couldn't."

But it was a fait accompli. "Treasured Maps has better security than me, anyway," Julius pointed out. "I should know. I cased the joint long enough."

"We'll return on the morrow," Stede said gruffly.

Julius cracked a smile. "If you really intend to dig up your treasure, count me out. Like I said, I think you should leave it buried just in case. But you might want to talk to

Moon Beam, which is something you'll want to do without me in tow, too." He handed Tanya a piece of paper with Moon Beam's address. "I've spoken to her before, but you might want to, also. I couldn't get any information that seemed useful to me." Pausing, he shook his head. "Maybe she'll say something to you that…"

"Would give us the key to why Stede pops out," Tanya finished.

"Meantime—" Julius glanced between her and Stede, then settled his gaze where Stede's hand was absently fondling her knee. "You two have plenty of work to do."

She squinted. "Work?"

Julius leaned forward, and quickly, his brown eyes sharpened, turning so dark they looked almost black in the dim light. "Yes, indeed, my dear. We may not know why Stede gets popped out of the picture, but we do know how he can keep from going back inside."

"He's got to fall in love…" she murmured.

"And there's only one way to a man's heart," Julius said succinctly. "And it's not food."

Not food? What was he saying? What was he suggesting? Once more, she'd gone through the looking glass, or down the rabbit hole, and nothing was making sense. "You're saying I should…"

"Make him fall in love with you," Julius finished. "As pretty as you are, my dear, it should be a snap." He gave two quick, encouraging taps on her spare knee.

She could only stare. Was Julius Royle really suggesting that sex with her would save Stede from spending eternity in a dreamlike haze? She pulled her gaze away from Julius's, then drifted her eyes from Stede's silken hair, to his broad shoulders, to the tangle of chest hair visible at the neck of a frilly blouse that didn't make him look the least bit unmasculine. Finally she took in the outlines of the bunched muscles barely concealed by his white breeches.

"I'd sure hate to see anything bad happen to him," she admitted shakily. Lifting her chin, she found herself looking deeply into the hottest green eyes she'd ever encountered. The next thing she knew, she'd added, "I'll do whatever I can to help, of course. You can count on me, Stede."

9

STEDE HADN'T HAD SEX in over two hundred years, and under normal circumstances, he'd hop into a female's bed faster than a rooster could say cockadoodledo. He'd come up behind the woman as quick as a summer squall with the mast of his boat high, then he'd cover her like a storm cloud. Instead he strode across the scarred wood floor of Tanya's apartment as soon as they were inside, politely asking, "Do ya think ya could spare this blanket and pillow tonight, miss?"

Before she could answer, he lifted both from the bed, managed to brush past her without making bodily contact, then found the most comfortable spot furthest from the bed, nearest the kitchen area and paintings. Even without turning around, he could feel the surprise in her eyes when she realized he didn't intend to share a mattress.

"Sure," she said uncertainly.

Against his will, her voice made him turn, pulling him like a compass to the North Star. Just looking at her made every inch of him ache, but he was Stede O'Flannery, and that meant he was no woman's pity case, no matter how pretty she was. No sir. He wasn't having relations with a woman just because he was rowing down this dark, deep, unfathomable river of trouble without a paddle.

But then, maybe he should reconsider.

Everything about her bespoke a port where a hungry man would want to dock. She was standing near the bed, her pale blue eyes searching his expectantly. Even from here, the spicy scent of her fogged his brain while everything else begged for his fingertips—the skin he knew was smoother than the silk of her dress, and the fluffy cloud of white hair that, even now, he couldn't believe was real. It was as strange as this unearthly night, puffy on top, thinner at the bottom, the curls wound so tight that they looked like peach fuzz.

His eyes swept her breasts, and when he recalled the tips stiffening, turning into ripe, turgid peaks as he'd plucked at them, his manhood betrayed him once more, the arousal stealing his breath. He bit back a long-suffering grunt of frustration, wondering what he was supposed to do now. Even the sirens the ancient poet, Homer, discovered while on seafaring adventures couldn't do this woman justice. His annoyance only increased when she smiled as if to say she understood exactly what he was thinking when he knew she didn't.

"Ah," she guessed. "You want a shower, don't you?"

Her smile was dazzling, striking him like whatever brilliance had created all the new inventions around him. Even now, he was marveling at those Julius had mentioned, the microwave oven, something called an iPod, and electrical lights that switched on whenever a man clapped his hands. Because Julius had verified his story, Tanya believed him now, and for the first time, she looked unguarded, which only made her that much more irresistible.

Stede tried to catch his breath, but he couldn't. Her seeming willingness to have proper relations was doing very strange things to his ability to think, or walk, or talk like an ordinary man. So, he simply stared at her lips with an intensity he usually reserved for the most complicated sea charts. He considered the lips' dampness, then their glossy pink paleness, then the flash of small, straight, very white teeth. Her smile was lighting up the room like the bedside lamp she'd switched on, but it flickered into his blood just like an old-fashioned candle flame. Just as his internal thermometer climbed to a temperature he'd expect in the Amazon, another pang of arousal threatened to disorganize his thoughts once more.

"Are you all right?"

"Indeed. Now, why wouldn't I be?"

"I don't know, I just…"

Tearing his gaze from her mouth, he took in the glass door of a shower stall that was visible from any vantage point in the room. Fortunately he'd showered at Julius's years ago, right before vanishing into the painting again, so he did feel clean, although when he rubbed his jaw, he could tell his whiskers were starting to grow again. By morning, he might well have a beard.

As he considered the shower stall door, vague images of her naked body assaulted him, coming through a smoky haze—how she'd look with her creamy arms raised high above her head, her breasts thrust out, her flat belly covered with white bubbles. As if from the other side of the world, he saw the suds rinsing into pubic hair the color of yellow straw under morning sunlight, and when his eyes returned to her lips, one of Poor Richard's aphorisms came to him. "Keep your mouth wet and your feet dry."

If the truth be told, it was the only of Poor Richard's sayings that had never made sense to Stede. But it did so now. "Thank ya for asking, miss," he said, shaking his head. "But I'll be keepin' my feet dry tonight and bedding down."

Feeling hot water dance on his skin would have been like heaven, though. He well remembered the remarkable invention called a shower. It had been one of his favorites, right up there with the automobile. It was tempting to parade around as naked as a jaybird for the benefit of Tanya's heart-stopping eyes, too, but Stede didn't feel up to it, not after the way she and Julius had all but planned some kind of wedding night for the two of them. What did they think he was? A common stud horse for hire?

But Stede O'Flannery was not that easy.

Six days, he suddenly thought. Hadn't he already wasted much of the first? He quickly arranged the blanket on the floor like a bedroll, then tossed down the pillow, unbuckled his boots and kicked them off, removed his waistcoat, then laid on the hardwood floor, pulling the blanket up to his chin. It was as uncomfortable as waking to face a mad papa's shotgun after a night of pleasure. Even though he shut his eyes tightly, he was aware that the prettiest woman in the world was still standing by the bed staring at him.

So be it.

It had been too horrible a night for any man to contemplate, even a seafarer. So bad that Stede almost wished he'd never popped out of his painting at all! Once upon a time, he might have been one of the richest privateers on Manhattan Island, but he was overwhelmed by the fear he'd go back inside the painting and simply live in semidarkness forever. Or maybe he'd get lucky, end the curse and be stuck in a time other than his own with all these new things to learn about. Not that he wouldn't survive. He was an adventurer who'd seen many strange lands, after all. How much stranger could America be, in the year 2006?

Something else struck him. What if he fell out of love later? Would he vanish again? Nowadays, people got divorces. His mind felt so muddled. Which was why flinty anger curled inside him when her soft, gentle hand rested on his back. He'd been so preoccupied, he hadn't heard her cross the room.

Without opening his eyes, he could feel her crouching in front of him. A little tuft of sweet breath, laced with champagne and coffee, poofed against his ear, making it tingle. "Are you all right?"

Sons of liberty! Of course he wasn't. Her voice was husky and suggestive and his John Hancock was getting stiff. Narrowly opening his eyes, he shot her a perturbed look, to communicate that what she was offering didn't interest him in the least. But it was a lie. Her dress hem had risen, and when he caught her scent, it wasn't perfume, but something headier. She was still wearing those intriguing glass slippers.

"I'm sleeping."

"Look," she murmured, her breath sounding short.

How could he help but look? She leaned, and the bodice shifted, exposing the sheer built-in undergarment and sending his senses whirling. Her eyes brimmed with concern, and she fluttered sandy, nonexistent eyelashes. "I know you're nervous." She paused, adding, "Stede." She said his name as if she couldn't really believe he was here.

He didn't believe it, either. But what was she talking about? "I beg your pardon, miss?"

"Nervous," she repeated. "About having sex."

His lips parted in mortification. He tossed off the blanket and was on his feet in a flash. "I've never been nervous about having relations in my life," he fumed. "And if you were a man," he added, just to make sure she got the point, "I might even challenge ya to a duel for what you've just said."

"I didn't mean to be offensive."

"I may be in a world of trouble," he added, shrugging off a hand that settled on his shoulder. "But I assure you I'm no charity case."

The worst thing was, she actually looked amused, for some reason. Pink was flooding into her snow-dusted cheeks, and she was pursing those shiny pink kissable lips. Hell's fire! He could have been a clown in a dance hall, given the way she was looking at him. "Charity case?" she echoed.

"No O'Flannery's ever taken charity," he assured gruffly, and that went doubly for taking female favors under such strange circumstances. "You won't see me starting now," he vowed. "Not even to save my life! My mama and papa are rolling over in their graves this very moment, I assure you they are! And quit squintin' at me like you've just seen a whale swimmin' in two feet of water, if you please, or I'm going to vanish downstairs and spend the night with the whiskey."

Her lips twitched. Everything he had below the waistband

twitched in tandem. "You know it's not a problem to let you stay here," she said, her voice quavering with seduction.

Now she was pretending not to know what he was talking about! Now, that was salt in the wound, indeed! Even worse, her pretty hands landed flatly on his pectorals, so his nipples hardened. Suddenly he wanted her rubbing him, and pinching him, and teasing him with her pretty pink tongue. Warmth settled in his lower belly, but he wasn't backing down. "Don't pretend you don't know what I mean," he bit out hoarsely. His hand covered hers, intending to remove it, but letting them lay.

At least she had the decency to blush. He could see her throat working as she swallowed, and the little tick in her neck betrayed her racing pulse. "Charity case," she said. "I, uh…think that would be a little extreme."

Now she was contradicting him! Her fingers curled, and the nails dug into his chest, feeling maddening. "You don't understand," he found himself blurting out to her, his heart tugging. "You can't. Julius…"

Her eyes clouded. "Looks different?"

"Changed, miss," he suddenly said. "He was a young man the last time I saw him. Just like me. Now his skin's all wrinkled. It hangs on him like an old sack, and his eyes are watery." Bitterness twisted his words. "His fortune's gone. As much as I'd like to remove this hex on me, I've—"

"We'll visit Moon Beam," she said quickly. "And I'll get more information from Eduardo."

So, she wanted to help him. He shook his head. "First I've got to dig up my treasure, and restore poor Julius's fortune. His hair's the shiny silver of new coins, and—"

His voice broke off. How could he even begin to explain what it had been like, to see a friend's handwriting after two hundred years? "Lucinda's gone," he muttered. "Just like my mama and papa. And Jonathan Wilson. General Barrington. McMulligan's."

His eyes stung, feeling gritty, and all at once, he felt as close to tears as he ever had. "Please, miss," he said roughly. "You must leave me be now."

But the fool wench didn't move, of course, since women were impossible in every century. She was intentionally infuriating him, scraping those nails all the way down his shirt as if she'd been born and bred for one purpose—to shred the last thread of sanity!

"All the loss must be so hard to take."

He didn't know which was worse, that her words were kind or her voice so thick with desire. Despite his distraught state, he was aware of every nuance. He'd already discovered how easy it was to remove her dress. And the bed was only a few feet away. His itching fingertips were nearly touching hair as white and soft as clouds.

And she did understand. He blew out a sigh, just wishing she'd quit bothering him with her hands. His emotions were so tangled he couldn't hope to sort them out, but he didn't want sympathy, no more than to have her to undress him out of pity for his horrible situation. She was right, though. He hated all the loss. And he dreaded experiencing any more. Anger coiled inside him like a cobra about to strike. Maybe at her, maybe at the whole world.

"Leave me be," he whispered more adamantly.

She only tossed her head, the gesture reminding him of how wild stallions moved in the woods. Her splayed fingers had moved down to his belly, and when they settled on his waistband, he realized he was pressuring the drawstring in a way that was painful now, his erection burgeoning. Heat washed over his skin. He wanted… "Stop," he muttered.

"You're afraid," she said softly.

"Stop saying that," he returned.

His hands covered hers, staying them from going lower on his breeches, but then he recalled her fingers cupping the hard length of him earlier tonight, and he felt fidgety. As rattled as a cricket in a cage. He wanted to get down on his knees. Follow her to the bed. Rip off her dress. Do anything…

He kept his hands steady, ignoring how delicate hers felt beneath. He could feel the tension, how they strained to glide over his hips, and already, he was anticipating the relief of them. Soft where he was hard. Cool where he was burning. Slender where he was thick. "I'm not a stud in a barnyard," he muttered, the words carrying less conviction.

"You have to fall in love," she pointed out.

"And you, miss?" he prodded raspily, his hand suddenly jerking, forcing hers lower, so it molded the hip she'd sought. "Do you want to fall in love?"

"The hex is on you, not me."

"True enough."

Her fingers were a heartbeat from where he wanted her most. Her eyes had widened, the blue irises sparking like taper flame. "Did I do something wrong?"

"Not a thing."

She blew out a peeved sigh. "Look. After we left Julius's, you didn't even, uh, touch me. I mean, earlier, you had your hand on my knee in the cab. And your hand on my knee at Julius's. Earlier, you didn't seem to mind..."

But things were different now. He brought his lips nearer, too near he realized, then fought an urge to capture her earlobe between his teeth. His voice was as rusty as an unused anchor. "And you'll do that for me, will ya, miss? You'll love me all week. Show me the toys I know you keep in your own treasure chest. Show me every secret."

Her voice was scarcely audible. "That was the idea."

He jerked back his head, surveyed her eyes. "And you'll be doin' me this grand service..."

Her voice was so low he had to lean even closer, straining to hear. "To help you."

"To help me," he repeated.

She nodded.

Once more, he leaned away, so they were eye to eye. Nose to nose. He stared at her so intently that, for a fraction of a second, he forgot that he held her hands in the vise of his. They were inches from an erection that was making him feel like a chained bull seeing red. "That's mighty kind of ya, miss."

She looked stung.

"But like I said," he continued succinctly. "O'Flannery's don't take charity." He paused. "Especially not in the bedroom."

Her chest was heaving with such exertion now that they might as well have been in bed. "Let me see," she said, crimson turning her cheeks red and white, like mixed roses. "What would a woman have told you in 1791?" She pretended to think a moment, then she returned, just as succinctly, "You're a horse's ass, Stede O'Flannery."

She was riled, and it almost made him smile. He'd bet she'd been thinking about being alone with him all night. "You're not the first woman to mention it," he assured.

"I *was* trying to help you," she explained.

"Save charity for the collection plate at yer local church," he suggested kindly.

She stepped back and he felt bereft, but pleased at her strong will. She was beautiful, maybe the most beautiful woman he'd ever known, in fact. But he hated simpering types, and at first, she *had* fainted a bit more than most women did. Now that Julius had identified him, however, she'd gotten her sea legs. It was just too bad his own mind was crumbling. If Julius was right, all he had to do was fall in love, then he'd be free. But he didn't want Tanya Taylor under these conditions, not even to save his life.

What was wrong with him?

He knew he'd gone stir-crazy as he watched her sashay to the bed. He felt like a fellow trapped aboard a schooner for months. His eyes traversed delicate shoulders, then the curve of her bare back and landed on her sash at the exact moment she reached behind herself and untied it. Slender fingers appeared near her neck and she untied the bodice, too. When the dress fell, it pooled like blue water around her high heeled shoes, and he realized she hadn't worn a stitch beneath all night. He took in her shapely legs and backside, and his groin wrenched again, nearly bringing him to his knees.

Then she turned around and stepped away from the dress, wearing nothing but her scintillating shoes. His arousal burned. Ached. Threatened to burst through the fabric of his breeches. At least that's how it felt. When he tried to find his voice, he couldn't. Everything was as he remembered it from the netherworld, her bare breasts ripe and full, her belly flat, her curls the color of straw.

"See you in the morning!" she said brightly, seemingly enjoying his shock.

"I beg your pardon?" he asked hoarsely.

"Red sky at night, sailor's delight!"

Leaning, she caught the bubble chain of the lamp between her fingers. Shadows danced across her skin, the way shadows of trees danced on snow in the wilds.

"You're a work of art, ya are, Tanya Taylor," he returned as the light went out. Everything went utterly silent. Black. Still. He waited to hear her tucking herself into her bed, but he didn't. Then he became conscious of his labored breath. His heart was pounding wildly. In the absence of the light, desire claimed him totally.

Then the light snapped back on.

She was standing there, just as a moment ago, looking even more beautiful, if that were possible. She arched a brow. "Did you say something else?"

He hadn't, of course. "I said I could see ya from the paintin'," he began, determined not to let her get the best of him. "And so I know ya usually wear nightshirts to bed, Tanya Taylor."

"It's a bit warm this evening."

She was the most maddening woman. "Very."

"And you quit calling me miss," she pointed out.

He'd liked the sound of the name, Tanya, in his mouth, too. "Under the circumstances," he managed a singsong, "using yer more familiar name didn't seem entirely inappropriate."

She shot him an innocent glance, but even from here,

he could see she was panting with excitement. "What circumstances would those be?"

"That yer naked as a jaybird, wench."

She considered a long moment. "Is wench a nice word for a woman? I mean, in your time?"

"I don't mind it," he said.

"Well, no man would," she returned. All at once, she didn't look quite so confident. "It's not charity," she suddenly said, her voice quivering as if she'd only now realized she was naked. She crossed her hands under her breasts.

Unfortunately it only served to lift them for his gaze. It was his turn to arch a brow. "Not charity?"

She puffed her lips in a pout. "I want you, Stede."

He tilted his head, pretending to consider.

"Okay," she muttered. "Think of it as a favor to me."

He actually laughed. The sound took him by surprise, since it had been so long. Then it tempered to a chuckle and a smile, a real smile that warmed his cheeks as much as his heart. "You want me," he repeated, his eyes capturing hers. "Do you, lass?"

She nodded slowly.

Inclining his chin, he gazed at her from beneath lowered eyelids. "Just so ya know—miss, or lass, or Tanya Taylor, or whatever you like to be called in bed— I already guessed that."

"I want you to know," she returned, her own lips curving, "you're a very competitive man."

"I never take weapons to bed," he assured.

"If you ever *go* to bed," she countered.

He'd never remember crossing the room, or that he grasped the hem of his own shirt, pulling it over his head, or yanked the string of his pants, gasping when the fly opened, relieving the agonizing pressure he'd endured all night. Splayed fingers of both hands circled her neck, slid upward and thrust into her hair. He brought her face to his and covered her mouth, crushing their lips together.

She tasted of nuts, vanilla and coffee, but beneath was something hotter. Primal fire ignited between them every time they touched. It was what had possessed her not to throw him into the street, the way any rational woman would have. And it was what was possessing him to push his tongue deep, thrusting it and shuddering when she responded.

When her breasts cushioned against his hard chest, her nipples hardened. So did his. Lower, hips sought hips, and when she felt his arousal, it was she who turned the kiss wild. He leaned, ramming her pelvic bone, maybe too hard, he thought, as rigid heat settled between her parting thighs.

Just as he gasped at the blissful relief of contact, her knees hit the mattress and she dropped. He stared where she was sitting naked on the edge of the bed now, then watched as she scooted back, her scissoring legs exposing glimpses of a glistening sex that made him feel crazy with lust. Reaching, he grabbed his pants and jerked them down on thighs coated with dark hair. She paled.

"Ya look lovely," he murmured, his eyes roving over skin the rose color of a sailor's dawn. She was trembling, those powdery eyes fixed on his maleness. He'd seen enough men aboard ships to know he was impressive, so he didn't need her validation. He was as hard as he was ever going to get, too, a drop of moisture visible on his flesh. Still, it did his ego good to see her seem so stunned. "It's been a good long time since I've seen a woman lookin' at me this way, Tanya."

"Glad to be of service," she whispered.

He stepped all the way out of the pants, and when his gaze landed on eyes as glazed as his own, he said, "There's only one thing I gotta ask ya, Tanya."

"Anything."

He squinted hard. "Are ya a witch?"

"Uh…no," she promised.

"And you know nothing more about Missus Llassa?"

She shook her head.

Abruptly he nodded, then he leaned over the bed, his hands shaking as he cupped her knees. At the first touch of skin, breath left his lungs. His hands turned damp and he started panting. Any thoughts of witchery flitted from his mind completely.

"Show me," he rasped.

He didn't need his hands to ease apart her knees. She spread them immediately, and his mouth turned to sawdust. His release came dangerously near when he viewed her there, as delicate as a flower. Rosy and pink. So open and wet that a low dark sound was torn from his throat.

"I'm gonna pleasure ya now, Tanya Taylor," he whispered.

Already his mind was blank, and she was reaching upward, grasping his shoulders to pull him on top of her. Instead of going down, he brought a hand between her legs, crooked a finger and flicked it to the nub of her desire. Arching, she tightened her hold on his shoulders, releasing soft sounds.

"Inside me," she whispered.

Her urgency pushed him toward the brink. One touch, and he'd come. Or she would. She was burning hot, and when he splayed a hand on her belly, her skin was feverish with perspiration.

Once more, she pulled him down. This time, he slid on top, groaning when he felt the brush of bellies and chests. His nipples constricted, seared by hers, and when his hard sex found her, and the tip nestled against soft, damp curls, he realized his control had been destroyed.

He hovered, anyway. Or tried. He was a big man and women always liked him to take his time, but he felt how hot she was and knew he was completely powerless.

Her lips parted. His closed over them just as his hands found her hips. Suddenly his eyes slammed shut. All his senses dimmed, shattering as he suddenly thrust inside. Their mouths locked as he ripped right through her. She gave a stunned cry, but her legs parted to better take him. A second later, they wrapped his back, then each of her internal ridges was stroking and milking him.

He muttered senseless nothings as he pounded into her again and again, moving like a starved animal, surprised when she dragged him closer as if she liked it. As if she wanted more. Her nails, her spike heels, dug into his flesh. The fact that she still had on her shoes made his desire climb. He was back in the netherworld again, but now she was with him, touching everywhere at once. Licking his nipples. Fondling his testicles. He was floating and everything was fading to black.

Then he was thrusting again. His hips moving fast, furiously. He was wanting. Needing. Demanding. He was barely aware of her beneath him, only that she was drenched and hot, sweating and clutching him, riding him hard, and he came forcefully, his mind and body exploding in tandem.

Consciousness ceased. Hands ran through her hair, his lips rained kisses on her cheeks. "Hell's fire," he muttered against her lips. "Hell's fire." It was all he could think to say. His heart was hammering like a racehorse's, and against his chest, hers was doing the same.

"Please forgive me, miss…" He hated himself for it, but even though he'd come, he still rocked against her, burying himself deeper.

Had he really taken this gorgeous woman like a teen boy in short pants buying a whore? He urged her further onto the mattress, then rolled with her, pulling her into his embrace again, not about to withdraw from her warmth, hoping to use their closeness to continue to arouse her. She was breathless, brushing fingers through locks of his dark hair, then sweeping kisses across his mouth.

"I doubt ya felt much pleasure a'tall," he murmured.

"Oh, I did," she whispered breathlessly.

"I want to touch every inch," he countered, wanting to please her the way he knew her last lover hadn't. "Lick my tongue into every little itty bitty spot." Instead he wreathed his hands around her back. Then he simply splayed his fingers, examining each inch as he stroked down to the satiny flesh of her buttocks, roving over curves and valleys before bringing her beneath him again. Using his knee, he opened her, parting her more, then he began grinding his hips until she surged, arching and shuddering. "That's the way, miss," he encouraged her, getting hard again, driven wild by scents of her perspiration mingling with his.

She sucked a breath through clenched teeth as he angled

his head down, caught an earlobe between his teeth and bit, teasing her. Sponging the rim with his tongue, he dipped inside, dampened the area, then blew out a hot breath. Her head rolled back on the pillow, exposing more of her neck. She was so beautiful. Astonishing, really. He suckled hard, suddenly wanted to leave a mark, something large and red that would still be there…

…after he was gone.

Pushing aside the thought, he reversed the direction of his hips, pushing his weight against her in circles until she released soft, sweet whinnies. She was catching the rhythm, her hips begging for more, and she was panting, too, her breath sharp and jagged. "It's been…been a while for you, I guess…"

He was basking in the slick heat of her that suckled all around him. He was as hard as a rock now. His desire strong, and he was stunned. Any moment now, he could come again. He'd never get enough of this woman. "A long…long time, indeed, miss."

"Let's make up for lost time," she said in a rush.

He ducked his head for a kiss with a lot of tongue. Her body burned as he flexed, but he wouldn't stop until she was writhing, brazen, losing herself.

"Did you learn these moves in pirate school?"

She'd seen nothing yet, but he shook his head, his green eyes blazing into hers. "Privateer school," he corrected, blood engorging him.

Her voice turned urgent. "Show me more."

She wasn't a virgin, but she wasn't a practiced lover, either, and he decided he liked that, too, as he leaned away, just far enough to explore the slopes of her breasts.

"Oh, Stede," she cried as he feathered the aching tips with his lips, soothing the nipples, licking and swirling until he could feel her creaming.

"Come for me," he whispered huskily, gliding a hand between their bodies, thrusting his hips while he found her clitoris and stroked. He tried to hold back, but he gasped with her. She was so slick there. Swollen. He strummed the slippery knob, then covered her with a thumb and kept it there, applying pressure as he flexed his hips once more, going even deeper, to the hilt.

"The light," she whispered.

It was hot, bright, intimate.

His eyes were riveted to her face. The hand between them quickened as her head moved from side to side on the pillow. Her eyes shut, as if against the light, but it was really her pleasure she was trying to hide. "Let me watch you, Tanya," he urged.

At the words, her hands tightened on his shoulders, and he grunted when they dug into his skin, raking down to his buttocks. Quickening his fingers, he pushed her further, rubbing, strumming, circling. She was putty in his hands now. Drenched with sweat. Feverish. Slick beyond what he'd ever felt. His own eyes rolled backward.

"Come," he suddenly said.

She was teetering. On the brink. She just didn't know him well enough. Was aware he was watching her face. "You're beautiful," he murmured, his own pleasure threatening to take him first, but he couldn't let that happen again.

Suddenly she arched. A solitary cry sounded. She'd hung on so long that the orgasm was strong, powerful, and he moaned, exploding, shooting inside her and gushing, the release washing over them both like a wave. She was the hottest, wettest woman he'd ever made love to, and as he withdrew the hand from between them and relaxed his weight, he, burying his head into the hollow of her shoulder, thrusting deeper as he shivered with satisfaction, both hers and his. His hands found her cloudlike hair and he smoothed the strands.

For a long moment, they lay there. He could hear her breath slowly steadying, her heartbeat becoming more regular. She lifted an arm, found the pull chain of the lamp and tugged, putting out the light. He only chuckled, turning it on again.

She was breathless. "Are you always this difficult?"

"Aye," he said easily. Somewhere, in the far reaches of his mind, he knew he only had a few days to remove the hex and save his skin. But just for a moment, he wanted to stop and smell the roses as if he was a free man. "For once, we've proved Poor Richard wrong," he murmured, still stroking her hair.

Her voice was husky. "How's that?"

"He said, 'He who lives carnally won't live eternally.'"

Her soft chuckle was a delight to his ears. "But living carnally may lead to your salvation."

"Aye. A conundrum, if I do say so myself."

When she spoke again, something sweet came into her voice, something strangely innocent. "Do you want to try to fall in love with me, Stede?"

What choice did he have? That was his first thought. His second was that, already, this felt like bliss. "How do you propose ta capture my heart, then?"

"Well…this is a start. And I could take you to New York's most romantic places."

"Only after you help me unearth my treasure tomorrow."

He felt her smile against his chest. "So, you do want to try to fall in love?"

"At this moment, I believe I already am, miss."

"Again," she said. "Good answer."

"I went to privateer school," he reminded.

"The things you say sound more like the kind of things a guy learns in port towns. Near the docks," she clarified. "Near where they serve up booze and women."

He chuckled. "And a sense of humor you've got, too."

She seemed pleased he noticed. A long silence fell. Even now, he was experiencing the ebbing palpitations of her orgasm, and damn if they weren't threatening to arouse him yet another time. "If I don't wind up back in my own painting, it's you, lass, who're goin' to be the death of me," he declared.

"Miss," she whispered back.

He was absently stroking her hair. "Aye?"

"Miss. I think that's the name I like best in bed."

He released another throaty chuckle. Then he shook his head once more, shutting his eyes as he muttered, "Sons of liberty, what a night we've just had, Tanya Taylor."

A second later he started snoring.

10

"QUIT LOOKING at me like that," Tanya warned late the next night, as they stepped from the subway into unseasonably warm air and headed for Battery Park.

"And how would that be, miss?"

She merely smirked because Stede O'Flannery knew exactly what she'd meant. Glancing up from a subway map, he shot an appraising glance over what she'd called her cat burglar outfit, the dark slacks and shirt she'd worn to help dig up his treasure. He looked as if he wanted to make love to her right now, just as he had countless times last night, then even more times today. Color seeped into her cheeks, and she bit back laughter. "Like *that*," she said again, her lips twitching.

"I best quit lookin' then, miss," he promised, his green eyes sparkling in the twilight shadows. "And start doing."

She only laughed harder, recalling how she'd awakened yesterday to see the clueless man tossing Morton salt at her nose. "Make sure you bring your smelling salts," she suggested.

He merely winked. "You'll need them," he promised. Leaning, he delivered a quick kiss, then he drew away. "But then, maybe I like my women better knocked out cold. They're more agreeable."

She swatted him. "Liar."

"Careful, or I shall challenge you to a duel," he warned.

"If you dare."

"We'll be meetin' in your dwelling place then," he said, taking the bait.

"You're on."

As they continued walking, he smiled at her in silent promise, his eyes gleaming, and she realized she couldn't wait to be in bed with him again. So far today, they'd gone out for meals, letting him try new foods and old, then she phoned Julius who refused to see them, saying they needed time alone, so they could fall in love and end the hex. As it turned out, Saturday wasn't the best day for following leads, so when Tanya called Moon Beam and introduced herself as an old friend of Julius's, Moon Beam offered an appointment Monday, saying she could make no other time. She'd invited them to her midtown office, giving instructions to refer to her as Susannah Billings, since that's how she was known at work.

Eduardo was unreachable, but Tanya had left a message, asking for any further information about the painting she'd bought, then she and Stede spent hours reviewing his experiences, trying to understand what determined whether he'd pop out or not. Julius had been right. Other than the diary, which indicated that Stede needed to fall in love, this missing piece to the puzzle had to be found, but Tanya could think of nothing different happening on the evening Stede had appeared. She'd been sleeping soundly; it had been just one more normal, uneventful night.

Moon Beam, aka Susannah Billings's, response had been disappointing. So was not being able to track down

Eduardo. When they'd come downtown earlier this morning to case Battery Park, find the probable location of Stede's treasure and list supplies they'd need to dig, she and Stede visited historic sites, including St. Paul's.

She'd never visited the old church before, the great spire of which was visible from their vantage point now, circling the tip of the island. The church was of Georgian Classic-Revival architecture, the oldest public building in continual use in Manhattan and the only remaining colonial church. Inside, it was pink and blue, surprisingly reminiscent of a baby's room, and the original chandeliers were still hanging. One of the closest buildings to the World Trade Towers, St. Paul's had survived, just as it had a fire in 1750. George Washington's pew was in the north aisle still, and he'd worshiped there before the country's capital had moved from New York to Philadelphia.

Stede had been inside the church in his own time, and when he saw how it had been transformed into a help center during the 9/11 attack, he'd been moved, taking in the decorative banners sent from around the world, which hung from the high ceilings, and displays depicting photographs of the area before the tragedy. Pausing beside George Washington's pew, he'd stared in surprise, realizing it had been transformed into a podiatrist's office during the 9/11 aftermath and used to heal the feet of weary relief workers. With a ring of conviction, Stede had told Tanya how he'd met the man once, and he'd said he was absolutely certain the president would approve of how his pew had been occupied.

Already, he'd stolen her heart. There was something free about Stede O'Flannery. Kind and quite simply put, good. And strangely, where she would have expected chauvinism, he was more accepting of women than her other male peers. Yes…he was different from men of the age. Or maybe he'd been so in his own time, too. She'd never know which was the truth. Either way, he wanted a partnership relationship that no man had ever offered her. With him, she felt more herself than she ever had with men she'd dated.

He looked good in modern clothes, too. After she'd shown him Wall Street, because it was the oldest part of the island and still contained places he remembered, they'd stopped in Century Twenty-One and bought slacks, T-shirts and some new bands for his hair. She'd suggested sneakers, but he was deeply attached to his scuffed-up boots, as it turned out. When he'd put on the tight black jeans and zip-up, white, short-sleeved shirt he was wearing now, he'd looked so good that Tanya hadn't given a rat's behind about using her credit card. "The sky's the limit," she'd assured. Let Saks, Barney's and Bergdorf's sue her. She was a little sorry about getting him the electric razor, though, since she liked him with a little stubble.

Now, as she looked at him, she couldn't help but feel he was too good to be true. He was a phantom, after all. A mirage. A shadow. For the first time, she realized that she should watch her heart. He really might vanish. He could be gone in an instant. What if they were wrong about him having a week to spend with her?

She cut off the thoughts, hardly wanting to imagine her dream lover trapped inside a painting forever, then she forced her attention onto the matter at hand as they finished circling the tip of Battery Park. "Luck's on our side. A lot of tourists are gone."

He stopped walking and peered through the darkness at the water and the Statue of Liberty, the ferry boats, and Staten Island. "It's an amazing world, eh?"

She nodded, as he lowered his chin, seeking another kiss. Their lips clung a long moment, then he hugged her to his side as they stared across the water. Colored lights—gold, red and yellow—shimmered on the surface, in tandem with ripples left by the wake of boats.

"We'd better get moving," she said, knowing she'd be happy to stand here like this for a good long while. He winked as they began walking again, passing the few remaining tourists viewing the war memorial and Fort Clinton. "If officers approach," he assured, "we'll pretend we're kissing."

Heat threatened to pull her back under, since she'd discovered he loved with his whole being, in a way she'd never experienced before. "Pretend?"

"Aye."

"If that was a rehearsal, you're a good actor."

"My," he said, laughing, "I do like foolin' ya then, Tanya Taylor."

Her heart warming, they walked in silence until they reached the site and slipped beneath yellow tape that cordoned the area. A moment later, he hopped into a muddy trench, dropped his black bag, unzipped it and pulled out a small shovel. "Here we go. Please stand watch. I'll dig."

"In the twenty-first century, the weaker sex can dig, you know," she said.

"Now, there's an improvement," he returned agreeably.

Stepping out of the trench, he thrust the shovel into her hands, then seated himself on a rock and stared studiously at his nails. When he glanced up and took in the look on her face, his shoulders shook with merriment.

"Be that as it may." Her lips curled into a smile as she handed him the shovel again.

His throaty chuckle thrilled her blood. "That's what I thought," he said, kissing her again before he began digging.

She looked over her shoulder. Only one person was in view now—he was down by the river—and while she couldn't tell, he could be a parks policeman. Through the trees, the Hudson glimmered. Nearer, she was astonished to see the colonial wall, just as earlier today. It was just an ordinary wall, as it turned out, made of brownish stones, but it was special nevertheless, if only by virtue of being so old.

If Izzie and Marlo could only see me now, she thought. Not to mention her sister, Brittania. Was she really doing an illegal archeological dig at a city-owned site where taxpayers were funding the excavation of a new subway and an old colonial wall? Coming downtown on the crowded six train wearing their black shoulder packs had felt adventurous, but now, reality was sinking in. She glanced at his bag, which had contained the entrenching tools. Hers— a flexible case specially made to carry a case of prize wine—was empty. At least for the moment. She dropped it to the ground.

"They have security cameras everywhere, Stede," she suddenly said. Since the phenomenon was before his time, she added, "In the trees. On top of buildings. They show ongoing movies. You know movies, right?"

"Is the wench, Marilyn Monroe, in any of them?"

Laughing, he climbed out of the trench long enough to deliver yet another kiss. "There, miss. We just made you the star."

"Doesn't anything bother you?" she remarked as he returned to digging.

He thought a moment. "Not much."

"A good quality in a man," she decided.

"Having proper relations improves my mood," he confessed. He glanced up, scanning the terrain, then his twinkling eyes settled where her tight black slacks hugged her hips. He had a way of making a women feel like a woman. Every time he looked at her, she felt as if she was just a little bit more of everything—smarter, sexier, funnier, more creative. Everything seemed to brighten. It was as if nothing bad could happen and she could conquer the whole world.

"Now…how were ya sayin' I look?"

She considered. "Happy."

"I've been released from my own paintin,' miss," he said with a throaty sigh as he dug. "And I've had a night to remember. A mornin,' too. What more could I want?"

She sobered. "To know more about the hex. And anyway," she added, the thought suddenly occurring to her. "How will we know if you're really in love?"

"So we'll be positive I won't vanish again?"

She nodded.

"It's a feelin,' miss," he said, without looking up. "A man can't mistake it."

"But what if you fall out of love?" she pressed on. In the cold light of day, she only knew she wanted to get to know him. Definitely sleep with him. But when she considered that he had no identification cards, or birth certificate, and how he might fit in with her life, her parents, her friends, James…

He glanced up. "What's wrong, miss?"

She stared where he was driving the small spade at the bottom of the wall, clearing dirt from beneath the stones and creating a pile of rubble. "Well…I mean, if things don't work out, and…"

"We start fightin'? I've already thought of that," he said with confidence. "And it's bound to happen. But by then we'll have talked to Miss Moon Beam, or Miss Susannah Billings, as she now likes to be called. And we'll have read through Lucinda's diary again. That fellow from Weatherby's, Eduardo, will call. Surely we'll find some…"

"Clue?"

"Aye." He paused. "It's a good thing I came back during this time, indeed."

She could see what he meant. She was afraid to flick on her pocket flashlight, so as not to draw attention, but squinting into the trench, she could see how much of the old, revolutionary wall was already visible.

"The way the world's been changing," he remarked, "my treasure might not have been here in another year."

"If there is treasure here," she agreed, feeling a rush of nervousness. "You'd better get it out now."

"You still don't believe me, miss?"

She wasn't sure. Seeing the treasure would just make everything more real. "Are you sure it's at this exact spot?"

Stede stopped digging, reached into his jeans pocket, pulled out a compass, then nodded. "Indeed."

"You're sure?"

"I know where I put my own treasure, miss," he said, starting to look offended.

"Sorry," she murmured.

He started to come out of the trench again, this time for a conciliatory kiss, but she pushed him and the shovel back in. "Dig. Before someone takes an interest in us, and we have to explain you're a privateer looking for treasure."

Chuckling, he crooned, "Yer all the treasure I'll ever need, Tanya Taylor."

"No wonder you're rumored to have made so many women swoon."

"Lies," he assured.

There wasn't much light, just from the moon and lamps that stood like sentinels on iron stands near the river. The lone figure was still pacing on the sidewalk. "Hurry," she murmured as Stede continued working, her eyes studying muscles rippling under his tight shirt. They seemed to shimmer, reminding her of the light on the water.

"Wait a minute," she suddenly said. "When I met you, didn't you say you buried treasure in Killman's cave?"

He kept digging, but glanced up as he did, sending her a long look. "You didn't think this was my only treasure, did ya?"

"How many treasures does a man need?" she returned dryly.

He chided her. "'Great talkers, little doers.'"

"Let me guess. Poor Richard."

He merely chuckled and kept digging. Enough time passed that she'd seen a few yachts and pleasure boats pass. The lone figure near the water had looked away, as if uninterested in them. At that moment, a metallic ring sounded. Sucking in a breath, she gave up her watch and jumped into the trench beside him, peering into the darkness. "Did you find something?"

"Aye."

Using cloth from the pack he'd carried, he rubbed at some metal wedged under the wall until she could see silver. Working more carefully, he began dislodging packed dirt, and when he could get a handhold, he thrust both hands under the wall. "If I could find the blasted handles," he muttered. Tugging, he pulled upward, but nothing came. Leaning back, he took a deep breath, wiping sweat from his forehead with a sleeve, then he gripped the handles and pulled once more.

"Can I help?" He was too close to the trunk for her to see around him.

"Right kind of you, but I've got it, miss."

Inhaling sharply, he gripped the handles, yanked once more, and she gasped as a trunk appeared from the ground, just as surely as he, himself, had popped out of the painting. She had no idea what she'd expected, but the trunk was small, only about a foot square, and not very flashy, but made of dull, dirt-encrusted silver metal. It was definitely a trunk, though. "I can't believe this," she whispered.

He merely shook his head. "Oh ye of little faith."

"Well, it is extraordinary," she muttered.

"At your abode, I'm going to blindfold you, lass," he promised, as she helped slip the treasure chest into the wine carrier. Since the bag she'd brought was made to carry crates that were approximately the same size, the chest fit perfectly.

"Awesome," she pronounced, then looked at him as

they each gripped a handle and climbed out, now using cinder blocks the construction crew had left behind for steps. "But what's this about a blindfold?"

"To teach you to trust. You're the most suspicious wench I've ever met," he bantered as they began walking toward the subway.

Ignoring that, she couldn't help but say, "One, two, three. This was as easy as pie. Do I get to see what's in it?"

He considered. "Not tonight."

"Now who's not trusting who?"

"Ya can blindfold me, too."

"If you're lucky," she promised, thinking of the silk sashes in her pleasure chest.

Before he could offer a comeback, a voice broke through the night. "Hold it right there!"

Turning to look over her shoulder, she blinked as a flashlight shined in her face. When her eyes adjusted, she realized it was a parks policeman, after all, probably the man she'd been watching. Stede tensed beside her. "Fabulous! Wonderful to see you!" she improvised, reaching into her back pocket. Forcing Stede closer, she enthused, "I'm Annie Evans, and I just moved here, to work for Import Wines. My boss is a wine collector, and he's expecting this delivery on a yacht at the yacht club."

Thankfully the officer was young and didn't seem to possess anything near Tanya's own suspicious nature. He jerked his thumb northward. "The yacht club's that way."

She tilted her chin east. "We thought it was that way. Thanks."

With that, she and Stede started moving along the circuitous sidewalk in the direction the officer had indicated. Minutes passed, and they'd put good distance between themselves and the trench, when the man suddenly shouted. "Hey! Wait a minute. What's this bag doing here, and did you use this shovel?"

"Run," Stede said simply.

Just as her feet took flight, Tanya realized the chest had started to feel heavier. Her arms were aching. With every step, the contents jangled. Definitely, both of them needed to carry the weight, if they were running. They took the subway steps downward, two at a time.

"Here." The chest left her hand and Stede shouldered it as he jumped the turnstile. She followed him over it just as a whistle sounded and a headlight shined on the track. She gripped a side of the black carrier bag again, once she'd hit the platform. "C'mon," she pleaded, praying the train arrived before the cop made it to the station.

Suddenly it dawned on her. "The parks police carry radios. He can call the train." So far, she was turning out to be a lousy criminal. But then, with Stede around it was hard to think straight. In fact, it would be hard to think in the company of any man who was digging up buried treasure.

He glanced around, not looking the least bit worried, then he said, "Follow me, miss." When she merely stood there, holding the carrier's handle, he added, "See what I mean? Trust."

She raised her free hand, palm out. "I know, I know," she said, her feet moving in the direction he indicated. "You're a master at running from the law. Privateer school."

"You'd be a slow learner," he teased. "But I'm beginnin' to think there's hope for ya, Tanya Taylor."

She found herself laughing as they entered a long, dark

subway tunnel. "Does this mean we don't get to work on my trust issues?"

"With the blindfold?" he asked as they plunged into darkness.

"Aye," she returned.

"You'll still be needing that lesson," he promised.

"Now, I KNOW you're crazy," Tanya murmured hours later, her cheeks warming as Stede's hard, warm body pressed against her back.

"Crazy as a fox," he assured in raspy seduction, slipping a red silk sash over her eyes. As he used his mouth and nose to nuzzle her neck, her pulse ratcheted. Her heart beat double time as he knotted the sash at the back of her head.

Definitely this was more exciting than their walk in the subway tunnel and emerging to hail a cab. Already, she felt herself getting excited as he withdrew, his steps away from her barely discernible, almost silent. "Where are you now?"

His voice sounded from the other side of the room. "Here."

How had he gotten so far away? Her voice hitched as she imagined his plans for her tonight. "You just want to take my mind off your treasure." She'd put the chest inside James's safe, and she'd shown Stede the combination, because she really did trust him. "Are you going somewhere?"

"No, miss." Now his voice was dangerously close, and her heart thudded when the length of his body pressured her back again. "I'm preparin' to acquaint ya with some of my other treasures."

Feeling his broad chest, she sank backward into his waiting arms, and felt a moment's weightlessness before they caught her. "Pleased to meet you," she murmured. Arms as strong as vise grips squeezed her sides, pulling her closer, when she felt his erection pressing into her behind. "We might not be falling in love," she whispered shakily, "but lust is definite. Do you think that will work just as well?"

"You tell me," he whispered. Liquid fingers were undoing her blouse, moving like feathers in wind, so at first, she didn't even feel them. Then the tails of the blouse came free and air hit bare skin. Fingers danced up her ribs, leaving a rippling wake of prickles, as if spiders were prancing there. "Ya won't be seein' me, miss," he murmured, his voice turning dark. "Not until I've been seein' every bare inch of you."

Fingers dipped inside the cup of her bra, tracing the whole area around her nipples, but never really touching until she thought she'd go mad. She'd changed into the sexiest underwire she owned. It was of prissy white lace stitched with black that traced the taut peaks his every touch was making ache even more. She pushed out her chest.

"Touch me," she urged, reaching behind her instinctively, grasping the sides of his thighs, climbing higher still when she felt the impossibly tight muscles flexing beneath her palms. "Nice muscles."

"Horseback riding," he explained as she slipped a hand behind her and between them and caressed his fly, panting when she felt him, rigid and straining. His strangled cry sounded twice as loud in the silence, and it satisfied her even more than his touch when he pushed her hand away. He wanted her, and she felt her heart singing with the knowledge of it. "Thought you wanted to show me your treasures," she whispered.

"Perhaps it's your pleasure chest I'm thinkin' of now, miss," he taunted, the burning spear of his tongue against her ear as he slipped her blouse from her shoulders. When his hands found her breasts again and the front catch of the bra gave, she came free of the confining fabric. He moaned in approval as he worked the straps down her arms, then he was behind her again, his arms wrapping her bare waist so tightly that they almost lifted her.

His skin was work-roughened, either from the past or digging. Either way, it produced mind-shattering friction, like his whiskers, as he flattened hands on her ribs, then pushed upward, catching her breasts from beneath and lifting them. A second later, huge hands covered her completely, squeezing hard enough that she cried out, but with pleasure.

Already, everything was growing dimmer, leaving only his touch. "I want ya as excited for me," he murmured, "as ya are when you're alone."

"That can be arranged," she replied as he massaged more deeply, kneading her breasts until she was sure she'd come from nothing more than this. Her own voice sounded as otherworldly to her ears as his touch. "Which of my toys did you like best?" she asked, wanting to tease him as he was teasing her, dangling him by a thread until they were both overcome with lust.

"All of them," he muttered. Stepping back a fraction, he broke the connection between their lower bodies and rubbed palms over the waiting tips of her breasts. Nothing else touched. Only callused palms roughening her nipples. They constricted further, and she was aware of how much she wanted his mouth on them, wanted him inside her.

"You're what we call a breast man," she whispered, perspiration tingling her skin. "Definitely."

"There's plenty of other parts of you that I like, too."

She thought of the vibrating gloves she'd bought, the silicone dildo, handcuffs and whip, but they were games for another day. Ready, she turned in his arms. Or she tried, but he held her fast, dragging her against him, this time with force. She was aware of the strength in him then, the bulging biceps, the corded forearms. At some point, he'd removed his waistcoat and shirt. She hadn't even noticed. Chest hair bristled on her bare back. Heat flooded her as his erection slammed her backside. She was a captive to pleasure, shanghaied into his embrace, like some maiden kidnapped during one of his ocean voyages. Her thighs shook, the flesh quivering as he unsnapped her pants, arrowing his hand downward, dipping under the waistband of her pants and panties.

When he caught her lower curls in his fingers and tugged, her mouth went dry. He pulled again, lifting skin and moving his hand in circles…squares…up and down. Even as she arched, the hand around her waist tightened, as if she'd try to escape.

Then a finger stroked between her lower lips, parting the cleft to test her wetness. She didn't disappoint, and she felt him shuddering as he registered her arousal, his hand shaking as he pushed strong fingers inside. One of them. Two. Three. Thick male fingers roughened from work were opening the slick, waiting part of her body, and once buried deep, he cupped her, curving the rest of his hand over her mound perfectly. "Yes," she whispered, arching as he thrust a strong finger deeper still, the heat of his hand warming her like a fire, making her crave. Her heart pounding, she opened her eyes, straining to see, but only registered darkness.

HIS FINGERS massaged inside, drawing out every last drop of pleasure. Twisting his wrist, he turned his fingers into pure heaven, making her spiral and leap. With a hard thrust, she climbed, jumped, spun. Pin prickles fell over her back like a shower. She was drenching his hand. "Please," she begged urgently.

Shuddering, she let him finish pushing her slacks down her thighs. She drew her legs tight together as he pushed the fabric to her calves, caressing her skin. Even if the lights weren't so dim, she wouldn't have been able to see a thing as she stepped from the pants. The blindfold was tight against her eyes, and when he left her again, she felt as if she was in a vacuum. "Where did you go?"

No answer. Damn him. She was completely naked now and she felt utterly bereft. When they'd arrived, she'd turned on music, but he'd turned it off again. Now there was only silence. Her breathing. His breathing.

Then nothing.

"You're so quiet," she said.

No answer.

His voice was on the other side of the room again. "An Indian brave taught me how to move without making a sound," he said, the reassuring huskiness of his voice suggesting that Native Americans were the last thing on his mind. "Sailed with him to England and back."

Was she really standing there, in the middle of the room, naked and blindfolded, having a conversation about Indian braves? "Are you looking at me?"

A choked, hoarse laugh sounded. "Now, what do you think, Miss Tanya Taylor?"

Her heart warmed with pleasure. Everything else was already white-hot with need. "Am I driving you crazy?"

"I'll be on a ship of fools, I will," he muttered.

He'd mentioned such ships before, filled with passengers thought to be insane. They'd sailed from shore to shore, since many communities didn't want such people in their midst. "No need for that. Let's get crazy together."

"You'll let me on your ship of fools, you will?"

"We'll sail away all night."

A tantalizing finger traced her knee. She gasped. He'd crossed the room again! She parted for him, widening her stance and felt something soft flickered against her inner thigh. A paintbrush that curled and looped on her belly. He drew long painterly strokes down her legs and circled around her back…sweeping her buttocks. Definitely he was making her crazy enough for a ship of fools….

When the brush's feathery touch painted the tips of her nipples, she felt as if her whole body was falling backward into a cloud, and it wasn't just his ministrations bringing her closer to the edge, but the fact that it was him.

He was doing this to her. Stede O'Flannery. Time traveler. Painter. Privateer. He was big, dark and swarthy, and he had a sense of humor, too. Even though she'd never watched him paint, he was an artist, both in and out of the bedroom. *He* was painting down her arms now, the bristles arousing her beyond any point of return. Gently lifting her feet, one by one, he traced the instep before tossing aside the brush and drawing her big toe between his lips.

His mouth was hot, wet. Losing her balance, she reached wildly, but found nothing to hold onto. He caught her hand as she spread her legs to brace herself, her heart hammering. Now she wanted to rip the stupid sash from her eyes, but she brought a hand to his shoulders.

Another followed, settling on his other shoulder. She felt roundness, the smoothness, the raw power, and knew without the support, she'd sink to the floor. Hands glided up the outsides of her legs, then molded her hips from below, not stopping until they settled on her waist. She could feel his eyes burning into her. Feel his breath blowing softly against where she was so hot for him.

His lips pressed against her belly in what wasn't really a kiss, just pressure, making her stagger. His breath when he drew away quivered on her skin, feeling more exciting than if he'd taken her by a storm. Yes…this was more remarkable than being devoured. The quickness of his response on their first night had given way to excruciating patience.

Or torture. Tension spiked as his tongue circled her navel, dipping inside. Her back curved into an arc as the tongue taunted and teased, going lower still, turning hotter and wetter with each stroke, until it poured over her like a boiling river, reaching the zone. When his mouth settled where his hand had already caressed, it was searing, scalding, hopelessly wet. She didn't know where it ended and she began, and she was blinded, not by the sash now, but by dark, practiced ministrations of the tongue flickering against her clitoris.

"Please," she sobbed, her knees nearly buckling. She wanted to lie back, but his hands were half stroking, half spanking her backside, hauling her to his lips, his tongue wild. She grasped his hair in fistfuls, clutching it as she shattered.

Then the world went topsy-turvy. He'd lifted her into his arms, cradled her against his chest, and was carrying her to bed. He was naked, too. She had no idea when he'd removed the pants, but she sighed as she sank into the luxury of the mattress. With a flick of his wrist, the blindfold came off, and her heart stuttered when she saw him.

Dressed, he was mind-numbing. Without clothes, he had the kind of body that would leave any woman speechless. He was a foot from the bed, and as her eyes took in the excited rise and fall of a chest covered with dark hair, she blew out another shaky sigh. She was still feeling her orgasm when her gaze found the powerful, dusky looking erection nestled in jet curls. She felt as if she'd been a ribbon on a present that had just come undone. Once more, she wondered when he'd taken off his clothes. How? She'd been so lost to ecstasy that she hadn't known. Or else he was that silent. "Must have been some Indian," she whispered hoarsely.

"Apache." Dazed dark eyes found hers. "And that's not all he taught me."

"Scalping?" she managed to guess. "How to make arrowheads?"

He took the few steps toward her with his chin low, studying her from under the heavy lids of eyes charged with hot sexuality. Given the intensity of the gaze, he might as well have been wearing war paint. He shook his head. "He taught me how to treat a woman in bed."

She liked how he laid on top of her, without fanfare, in an easy, matter-of-fact way that said he wanted to get down to business. Just as easily, she pulled him into her arms. "How, sailor?" she asked, lifting a hand, palm out. And then she added, "I think I would have liked that Apache."

11

TANYA WOKE with a start, then rolled onto her back, dragging the duvet with her, so she could better squint at Stede. He was on the phone, and he looked good, wearing nothing but a sheet wrapped around him like a shawl. Against the white of it, his skin looked dark and enticing, and her heart skipped a hopeful beat. Maybe Moon Beam, aka Susannah Billings, had thought of something else and called, Tanya decided.

The trip to the woman's office on Monday had rendered nothing useful, except a confession that the heiress had stolen the painting from her parents. They'd forgiven her later, she'd said, but only after she'd ended her life as a flower child, gotten a business degree and a job, then stopped calling herself Moon Beam. Now a tall, statuesque beauty in her late fifties, it was hard to imagine her as the hippie she'd been when Julius Royle had bought the painting from her; at least until her conservative navy dress had risen on her thigh, exposing a rose tattoo.

She'd been kind enough to recount how she'd been living in the sixties, "crashing in a squat," as she'd explained it. "I never should have stolen the painting," she'd continued, "but my boyfriend talked me into taking it off the wall of my parents' living room. They didn't care much about it. After they'd bought it from someone in the Wilson family, they'd left it in a crate, only taking possession after it was almost stolen. Anyway, my boyfriend told me my parents were, as he put it, 'bourgeois pigs,' and when Julius offered to buy the picture and take it back east, I was thrilled. Back then, he was living on the fringes of the hippie scene, too, but he was more of a seeker. An explorer in human consciousness.

"After my parents realized I'd stolen the painting, they decided to forgive and forget. Julius had paid for it, you know. And by then, his brother and sister were trying to lock him in a mental ward." Her eyes had sharpened with concern, and she'd lowered her voice. "I heard Julius kept claiming one of the figures in the painting came to life. Back then, we all thought he'd taken too many drugs or something. But his family just thought he was crazy. How's he doing now?"

"Great," Tanya had ensured.

"Julius doesn't take drugs," Stede had put in, offended.

"Then he must have gone mad, like his siblings said."

Just as Tanya had grabbed Stede's hand, so he wouldn't correct Susannah, she'd continued. "The painting wasn't worth nearly what it is today, and to be honest, my parents had quit collecting paintings. As I said, that particular one had been stored in a crate of straw until the Wilsons sold it. I think the story was that Lucinda Barrington retrieved it from a ship called the *American Dreamer* and left it to her husband in her will. Art was a passing fad for my mother, though. By the time I'd taken the piece from my folks and Julius was locked up, Mom started learning to fly and was talking my father into buying her an airplane."

"An airplane?" Tanya had echoed, hardly able to imagine the Billings's lifestyle. Still, she was sorry no clue had emerged regarding why Stede might have popped out of the painting when he did. Not that they'd told Susannah about Julius's experience with the picture, nor Tanya's. Even someone as liberal as Susannah, aka Moon Beam, wouldn't be able to take in the reality of what had happened. Still, Tanya and Stede had wondered if Jonathan Wilson hadn't meant to hand down the legend associated with the painting, too, as a way of safeguarding Stede by keeping it in the family. It had been with the Wilsons for years.

Whatever the case, it would probably remain a mystery, and since Monday, when she wasn't making love to Stede, Tanya had racked her brain, studying Lucinda's diary, but still nothing made sense. The only unique element in Susannah's story was that she'd stolen the work, intending to hawk it, so she and her boyfriend could afford to fly to the Woodstock concert in upstate New York in 1969.

Now it was Thursday morning. Her show was Saturday night, the day after Stede might disappear. She pushed aside the thought. Fortunately, Stede had convinced her she was more ready than she'd imagined. And surely he'd be here for the show. He had to be.

Eduardo had left a message, saying he'd already given Tanya all the information about the painting, and he said he'd call again when he could, but he was busy. Yesterday, she and Stede had gone to his apartment, anyway, but he wasn't there. Weatherby's swore he was in his office, but they couldn't find him. Tanya believed him, but wanted to double-check anyway, since so much was at stake. Soon, it wouldn't matter. Time was flying by. Running out. And the closer Tanya got to Stede emotionally, the more afraid she became. What if he vanished?

Sighing, she honed in on what Stede was saying. "We'll plan on taking the one o'clock train then."

"My mother," she realized as he hung up. So, it wasn't Ms. Billings, after all.

Smiling, Stede walked toward Tanya, tossing off the sheet and letting it blow behind him like a sail. Although she felt irritated, given how he'd taken another call from her mother, she threw back the duvet covering her, welcoming him into bed. "You and Miss Jean are getting to be best friends."

"No," said Stede. "A woman named Evelyn is yer mudder's best friend. They play bridge on Tuesday, tennis on Thursday. Her son is Timmy, and he's the first boy you ever kissed. You were but a wee little thing then, only seven, and everybody at the country club thought it was cute."

"Hmm. You've become quite the student of Taylor family lore. How long have you been awake?"

"Since the crack of dawn. I went out for a bit."

"Out?" She startled, even though she wasn't sure why she should have. After all, Stede was a grown man. "Without me?"

"Aye. I went to see Julius." He sounded proud of himself. "I took the subway."

She exhaled slowly. "If something happened to you," she warned, keeping the panic from her voice. "I'd never be able to find out anything. You don't have any identification and you're not a citizen."

"True enough. So I hurried back. And then I watched

you sleepin' like a baby. After that, your mother called," he finished on a sigh. "And a sweet woman she is."

"You didn't really tell her we were coming there today," she whispered dolefully as he laid beside her.

"Matthew's pickin' us up at the train station at two-thirty sharp in his automobile," he assured, pulling her into his arms.

Matthew was Brittania's perfect husband, the father of her two perfect children, Matt Junior and Clay. He'd become a legend at the family's club in Short Hills, winning every archery and target shooting contest.

"I meant to call and cancel." Tanya groaned. Swatting Stede, she rose from the bed every bit as naked as he, then headed for the phone. Just as she lifted the receiver from where he'd left it by her easel, his hand appeared from nowhere, staying hers.

She turned in his arms, then backed up, stopping when her behind rested against a drafting table. "Look…we really can't go to my parents' house."

His eyes sparked with anger. "Why not, miss?"

Licking against the sudden dryness of her lips, she tried not to think of the complexity of the situation. "You're going to be a fish out of water."

"Don't you want to know if your family will like me?"

She imagined they'd think he was strange, but she spoke truthfully. "I don't care what they think, Stede. I don't care what anybody thinks. I got past that a long time ago."

Placing a hand on either side of her, he leaned against the table, pinning her. "I don't believe ya, miss."

"Don't get mad." Tossing her head, she shook disheveled hair out of her eyes, and tried not to remember the last time they'd stood in this exact spot. They'd shared a glass of wine, and he'd convinced her that her paintings were wonderful. He'd talked in a language only serious painters knew—about color and form and line—and by the time he was done complimenting her, she'd felt like Picasso. He hadn't been merely boosting her ego, either. He believed in her. And she'd believed him when he'd said she was just nervous about her upcoming show, and that if she didn't quit tinkering with her work, she was going to ruin it.

The conversation had opened a whole new door on their similarities, and she'd realized their passions extended far beyond the bedroom. The same morning, he'd picked up some charcoal and had started to draw her portrait. With the first line, she could see his features relax, how much he loved the craft. "I can't," he'd suddenly said, his hand trembling as he set aside the paper.

"Why?"

"I'm sure my curse is lifted," he'd said, in what might as well have been a declaration of his love for her. "But just in case, I can't start drawin' ya." He'd been creating a self-portrait when he'd wound up inside his painting, after all, and it had touched her that he wouldn't risk sketching her, feeling unwilling to pull her deeper into whatever magic spell Missus Llassa might have wrought.

"You're a little liar, you are," he said decisively now, his eyes closing to slits, the green irises darkening with emotion as he scrutinized her.

She was stunned. "How's that?"

In his eyes, desire and anger seemed to fuse, then so much emotion claimed his face that she could almost forget a naked man was standing in front of her. His lips parted, his eyes narrowed and his free hand circled her upper arm. As he drew her closer, she could feel his breath teasing hers as surely as a kiss.

"You think I'm vanishin' tomorrow night."

She could feel color draining from her cheeks, and tears suddenly stinging her eyes. "I don't want to talk about it." The week had flown by, and she'd shown him around town, kissing him in every most-romantic spot, from the spire of the Empire State building, to the carousel in Central Park, to the herb garden of the Cloisters in Brooklyn.

But time was running out, and maybe not talking was worse. His gaze was dropping down the length of her body possessively, and yet he was staring at her as if he'd never seen her before. "Ya think I don't love ya," he clarified.

"I don't know, Stede."

In a flash, his hands were in her hair. Using his thumbs, he lifted her chin, and those fierce eyes raked down her face. "What do ya mean? Ya don't know?"

The truth was, she'd been living in a state of denial. It was barely conscious, but sometimes she'd pretended none of this was happening, that he hadn't really appeared from a painting like a storybook knight and loved her senseless. "You can't really fall in love in just a week," she insisted. "Not really."

"And where would you be gettin' your information, miss?"

From her heart. From his. "That only happens in fairy tales."

"I see." He nodded. "And what about all these trips ya been takin' me on around town?"

Swallowing hard, she thought of other kisses, near Rockefeller Plaza, and on the second floor of Tiffany's where they'd looked at diamonds, and on the Circle Line as they'd boated around the island.

"Sometimes, when we make love," she found herself confessing, "I try to forget where you came from…where you might go back to, Stede. Sometimes I wish you were just a normal guy. With a normal job. Somebody I met at a party or a coffee shop or online. I…don't want to have to be afraid of…your leaving…"

Hating the judgment in his eyes, she lifted her hands and wreathed his neck, dragging him closer, feeling he could never get close enough. "But then, you wouldn't be you." The man she was coming to love. "So, I accept every-thing." Her eyes locked into his. "Everything."

"But ya don't believe I'm in love with ya?"

"Lust." She tried a smile. "That much I'm sure of."

He stepped back abruptly. Putting his hands on his hips, he simply said, "Just get yourself dressed, Tanya Taylor." As he headed for the bed, he tossed a withering glance over his shoulder. "And as far as yer brother-in-law goes, you'll be pleased to find I can outshoot him at your fancy club, whether his choice of weapon be a bow and arrow, or a musket. I have told your mother to pass along my challenge."

She barely heard. Following him to the bed, she put her hands on his shoulders, forcing him to turn around. "Please, Stede," she said, her eyes imploring. She was surprised such a mild disagreement could fill her with such an overwhelm-ing sense of loss. The man was breaking her heart. "Don't be mad. I can't stand it. We're in uncharted territory."

"All relations are uncharted territory, miss," he returned coldly.

She wasn't backing down. "Not like this."

"You don't think I love ya," he repeated. His eyes had gone liquid now, soft and green. Rimmed with inky lashes, they matched rough whiskers on his jaw that, last night, had left burns on her belly.

"I said I didn't know," she repeated. "We won't know, will we? Not until…"

"Then I'll not be tellin' ya," he muttered. "Sweet Betsy Ross, you're a difficult woman, you are."

"I just want to be sure. For your sake."

Reaching on her toes, she shut her eyes and pressed her lips to his. Tension still hung between them, making the air like something she could cut with a knife. It was the worst thing she'd ever felt, and all she wanted was for it to end. Gliding her hands around his neck, she held him tightly, urgently whispering, "Please be nice. We need to use every single minute, in a way that will help you."

"Back to that again," he muttered. His eyes lasered into hers. "Like I told ya, miss. I'm no woman's charity case."

Maybe not. But she kissed him, anyway. This time, using her tongue to lick the edges of his lips. He must have felt the same distress at their argument, because a moment later he was responding, kissing her back and pulling her with him onto the bed. Right before the heated tip of his tongue parted her lips and plunged as if to savage her, he sighed and whispered, "Maybe this will convince you of my feelin's."

A moment later, he was loving her in earnest.

"THATTA BOY," Clyde Taylor said hours later, clapping Stede on the shoulder as he and Matthew finished shooting bows and arrows on the extensive, well-maintained grounds of the club. "Are there any sports you don't play?"

"A few," returned Stede, looking amazing in one of the lightweight sport coats Tanya had bought for him, which he'd worn over khaki slacks.

Clyde didn't look convinced. "Such as?"

"I'm not keen on in-line skating or skateboarding, sir."

Tanya watched in surprise as her father laughed, thrusting hands deep into the pockets of deck pants. He was tall and lanky, with a loose-limbed gait. "Of course you aren't, old boy," he said agreeably, squeezing Stede's shoulder as if they were old school pals.

"But where'd you learn to shoot like that?" he continued. "Let me guess. Harvard? Yale?" Before Stede could answer, Clyde lifted a sailing cap and dragged a hand through thin wisps of hair. "You know you just beat the club's champion archer, don't you?" he continued excitedly. "Outshot him with a pistol, too. Matthew's held the title to both for three years running."

"Rub it in, Dad," muttered Matthew good-naturedly.

"Congratulations on your awards," Stede said to Matthew, generously. Then to Clyde, "I do believe that's what yer lovely daughter said about yer son-in-law. He must be a champion, indeed."

"Lovely daughter!" tittered Tanya's mother, Jean, as they moved from the grounds toward lace-curtained French doors that opened from a dining room onto a tiled patio where they were to dine. "What a way with words!" Jean glanced at her husband, then spoke as if Stede wasn't within earshot. "I told you this one was a charmer. Isn't he just delightful?" She looked at Stede. "Accents like yours make a woman's knees weak, you know."

"Aye." He chuckled. "So women tell me, Miss Jean."

"Miss Jean," her mother echoed, delighted.

Tanya could only stare. Her mother was a college graduate from the old days when college for women had meant learning how to put a suitcase on the overhead rack of a train without raising your skirt hem. Tall, leggy and blond, she wore her hair in a bob and tended to touch things carefully, so as not to mar her perfect manicures. She was usually extremely talkative, just like her husband, but never flirtatious.

Tanya smiled. She'd never have guessed that her parents' most annoying feature, their endless chatter, would actually come to her rescue this afternoon. Already, she'd caught them up on Izzie and Marlo's news, and told them all about Izzie's show, at least the portion of the evening before she and Stede had met Julius Royle. And since her parents never let others get a word in edgewise, all Stede had to do now was pick up the ball and nod his acquiescence.

One of Tanya's nephews interrupted her thoughts. He'd come from behind, running from his mother's side, and now he tugged Tanya's sleeve. "Auntie Tanya," he said as she swept him into her arms.

"What?"

"You've got to carry me 'cause I'm tired," the three-year-old said with a giggle.

"Looks like I already am carrying you, sweetheart."

Her sister's two boys were a source of pure joy for her. Both had their father's square jaw and strawberry-blond hair, and Brittania's brown eyes. Matt Junior was five, just about to start school, and little Clay was three. He was as endlessly chatty as his grandparents, but far more adorable. As Tanya situated him on her hip and circled a supportive arm around his back, she caught a whiff of pure baby. The scent of powder mixed with something clean and indescribable pulled at her heart, making it swell. Nobody had ever made her feel as needed as these boys had when they were babies, and now both were growing into real people. In only a few years, so much seemed to change. Feeling her heart stretch to breaking, she wondered if she'd ever have her own. Or would Stede vanish?

Catching the train of her thoughts, she realized how much she wanted the opportunity to let their passion develop. Could it lead to having a family? If Clay could change so much in only three years, how could Stede handle traversing centuries? Little Clay waved his arms as Stede sidled closer, and the next thing she knew, the boy's pudgy hands circled Stede's neck. She handed the boy over to her lover, murmuring, "Do you mind?"

"I've held many a babe. My own mama was a wet nurse."

Tanya's mother laughed. "What a piece of nonsense!" she exclaimed, not believing a word Stede said.

"'Tis true, Miss Jean. She suckled many a neighbor's child on her knee, and taught me everything she knew about babes."

"He likes you," Tanya said, interrupting since Stede had already said too much.

"Aye."

Shifting Clay on his hip, as if tending to babies really was as natural as breathing for him, Stede pulled out a chair to seat her mother, further thrilling her. Clearly, Stede meant to keep Clay on his lap throughout the meal, too, but Brittania insisted on shifting him into a high chair. Matt Junior was no less intrigued by the man, probably because Stede had shown him how to tie boating knots, shortly after their arrival. In turn, that had led to a conversation between Clyde and Stede about sailing that hadn't ended until Jean claimed she was, as she put it, perishing from boredom. After that, he'd asked to go on a drive, to try to find the clearing where he'd fought the duel. If he felt any disappointment when he saw a house built on the land, he didn't let it show.

Tanya was happy about how her family was taking to Stede, but she was scared, too. Brad seemed all but forgotten. Her parents hadn't even intimated they missed him, although they'd seemed to like him a great deal. So far today, they hadn't once compared her to Brittania, either, which was unusual. And it was all because of Stede. With every moment, he became more like a dream. A fantasy. He was the perfect man...

Except he could vanish in a heartbeat. Neither of them had any idea how to bring him back, either. In a little over twenty-four hours from now, he could be lost forever.

Under the table, his hand found her thigh. He rubbed a thumb deep into the hollows, and she inhaled, bringing scents of freshly cut grass and nearby flower gardens. Late summer blooms had lasted into the heat of autumn, and now the mingling smells seemed as complex as her and Stede's situation. Those scents were like threads of lilac, rose, and mint woven into the fabric of the landscape. If things came unraveled now, where would she start again? There would be...could be...no other man like Stede. Not in a thousand years. Not ever. When a waiter placed an open menu in front of her, she forced her mind back to the present, then discussed selections with Stede.

"Really," Brittania's husband, Matthew, began after Stede gave their order to the waiter. "Where did you learn to use a bow like that, Stede?"

Stede didn't hesitate. "An Apache taught me."

"On a reservation in North Dakota," Tanya quickly put in.

But her nephews were hardly interested in the lie. "An Apache!" exclaimed Matt Junior. "And you knew him? For real?"

"Aye. I knew him, indeed."

"An Apache!" Jean applauded. "What an imagination! The boys just love it!"

Tanya's father leaned forward, elbows on the table. "Not to interrupt," he said, "but I did want to talk horses with you, again." The conversation had begun earlier, when they'd walked by the stables and it had become clear Stede knew more about horses than many professional breeders. "You say you've been riding since you were how young, son?" Tanya's father asked.

"'Twas two when they put me on my first pony." Stede chuckled. "And quite a ride it was." He plunged into an account of being thrown from the pony, but caught in his father's arms.

"I can't ride until I'm in third grade," Matt Junior announced enviously. "Dad says people have accidents."

"And right he is," agreed Stede. "Just as my story shows ya."

Glancing around the table, Tanya settled her gaze on Brittania. As always, her sister looked impeccable, making

Tanya feel ridiculously trendy for her age, in a short skirt, platform shoes and glittering knee highs. Brittania's long upswept hair and makeup were so well done that she could have just left a salon, and her pantsuit was both practical and elegant. Every time Tanya looked at her, she ceased to wonder how her younger sister could have married and had two children while Tanya, herself, was still struggling with dating. She looked impossibly polished and put together.

Brittania had been staring at Stede, but when she registered Tanya's attention, she looked away quickly. That was just like her sister, Tanya thought. Everyone was falling all over Stede, but Brittania wouldn't give an inch. She had to be the best at everything, the center of the family. It was the exact right time to become conscious of Stede's hand again. It was still on her knee, warm and reassuring, and while her sister's seeming disapproval bothered her, Stede swept that away, too.

The world beyond him was like everything in the periphery of her vision. Like the profusion of blurring colors in the nearby gardens. The world—not the time Stede had spent trapped in the painting—was the nether-world, Tanya thought now. Somehow, in the short span of a week, he'd become the most real thing in her life. Her heart lurched. If he did vanish, she wished she could follow him, but she knew that was crazy.

Then she heard her mother say, "Of course you two will be spending the night. I made up the guest rooms."

Rooms. Plural. "No," Tanya said quickly. "We have to make the seven o'clock train back to the city. We have other plans for later tonight."

When Stede's eye caught hers, it was clear he knew she

was thinking of the bed they shared. "Aye," he murmured huskily. Lifting his gaze, he took in her family. "A gallery engagement," he lied. "We're meeting people who'll be in attendance at Tanya's upcoming show. I can't wait for the pleasure of seeing you again there. Yer daughter's a most wonderful painter. It will be a success, indeed."

Breathlessly Jean said, "My heavens. Don't tell me you know art, too!"

"After the year 1790," Stede gravely admitted, "my knowledge gets a wee bit sketchy. In the colonial period, however, Miss Jean, I assure you I'm well versed. In fact, it's as if I'd known some of the painters, myself."

"O'Flannery," Jean said suddenly. "Of course! Why didn't you just tell us when we were introduced, Tanya! He's got to be related to Stede O'Flannery, the painter. I don't know why I didn't guess. I mean, how many Stede O'Flannerys can there be?"

Tanya gasped. "You know his work, Mom?"

Her mother was taken aback. "How could you even ask, after all the years I've volunteered at the Met?"

Holding her breath, Tanya shakily exhaled, hoping to steer the conversation elsewhere. She hadn't told her parents about buying the painting, since they'd urge her to sell. If she refused, that would only have added fuel to the fire, making her look unstable and impractical, compared to Britannia.

"So, you're related?" her mother pressed. When Stede looked a tad uncomfortable, she gushed, "I'm so sorry. Pardon me for prying. I didn't mean to put you on the hot seat. You don't need to answer—"

"Not a'tall. Stede's an ancestor who did our family

justice, to be sure." Astonished, Tanya listened as he plunged into an account of his own family history, then ended with the duel, which left her nephews spellbound.

"And what do you do for a living?" Brittania asked when he finished.

She would. He paused a second too long, and it was as if some magical spell had just been broken. But then Stede chuckled, and Tanya heard something wicked in the low rumble of laughter that told her he was about to save the day once more. "Every once in a while, I dig up some buried treasure," he assured Brittania.

"Now there's a euphemism for being independently wealthy!" her mother exclaimed. "I don't think I've ever heard that one before. Have you, Clyde?"

Her father shook his head. "Buried treasure you say?"

"Seriously," Matthew said, as the waiter circled around, refilling wineglasses. "What do you do?"

"Buried treasure," Tanya couldn't help but repeat. "I can back him one hundred percent on that one."

"So you've already seen this man's portfolio, daughter of mine?" her father asked approvingly.

In her father's world, that was the only mark of a serious relationship heading toward marriage. She laughed, thinking of the dull silver chest she'd helped Stede unearth in Battery Park. Then she simply said, "Aye. Indeed, Dad."

12

LATE THE NEXT afternoon, Stede frowned. His fork was poised near his mouth, and he stopped eating in midbite, just as Tanya pushed aside her dinner plate. Forcing himself to finish chewing the best steak he'd ever eaten, he dabbed his mouth with a napkin. "What's wrong, lass?"

She looked like she'd rather kill him than look at him. "How can you even ask?"

He shook his head slowly. Sons of liberty, he thought, women would never make sense to him, not even if he lived through another millennium. "How? I don't know. Ya just ask."

"It's after four o'clock."

"Meanin'?"

"We've only got three hours left," she burst out.

He'd been trying not to notice. Now his gaze slid toward the digital clock. Sure enough. It was 4:07. "Now, now," he chided. "Eat up. Finish yer meal."

"Don't patronize me."

"Then stop acting like a child," he suddenly shot back, his own nerves fraying.

Grumpily she pushed her plate further toward the centerpiece they'd made together, after picking wildflowers by the river. He'd arranged the profusion of blue and yellow buds in a coffee tin Tanya had painted. Then they'd closed the blinds against the afternoon sun and combined their artistic efforts in finishing the table, tossing a white, patterned cloth over a work space that had been scattered with tubes of paint and jars of linseed oil. Only the bedside lamp was on, and candles—some tea lights, some tapers—flickered, sending ethereal shadows dancing across the walls.

Sighing, Stede tried not to feel hurt, but why couldn't she understand? He was sure he loved her. From the second he'd seen her, he'd been lost, and for that reason, just as sure he'd never wind up in his painting again. "I'm givin' up on ya, I am," he said.

"You're so cavalier about it," she muttered.

And suddenly he was sorry because he'd never seen a woman look so woeful. Ever since last night, at her parents' club, he'd felt her energy pulling away from him like an ebbing tide. It made him think of the great tidal waves about which seamen and islanders always told legends. Sea monsters, they often claimed, sucked oceans backward, toward the center of the earth, leaving all the world's shell-strewn shores dry, and then the waters would come flooding back all at once, pouring over once habitable land, submerging it.

"Sweet Betsy Ross," he said sourly, studying how her lips had pulled into such a kissable frown. The roundest, china-blue eyes he'd ever seen were now filled with immeasurable sadness. If he wasn't careful, he'd wind up in the same maudlin mood as she, and then where would they be? "Shall I be playin' a violin for ya? Yes indeed, we might as well find pall bearers and hire a grave digger."

She didn't say a word. They'd both dressed up for dinner. He'd worn new pants and she'd put on a pale pink dress that made him think of clouds tinged by morning sunshine. Thin straps hooked over bare shoulders, and she'd draped a loosely woven shawl around her that was sewn with gossamer threads, like a spider web. He felt caught inside it. "You're a breathtaking beauty, ya are," he ventured.

"Sorry," she said, looking no less pitiful. "I know you're trying to cheer me up, but it isn't working, Stede."

"Aye." As if he hadn't noticed. As much as he'd enjoyed the steak, he wasn't hungry anymore, either, and now he pushed aside his plate, too. Leaning, he placed his elbows on the table and studied her. All day, he'd been trying not to let his mind run wild with possibilities about his fate, but she wasn't making it easy.

"If you want to meet the issue head-on," he found himself saying, his eyes capturing hers. "So be it, Tanya." He paused, glancing over his shoulder, feeling dread when he looked at the painting. In a few hours, would he be inside the shadowy, grassy clearing, staring at her from a completely different vantage point? "I don't think I'm goin' back inside that paintin' because I love ya," he explained again.

She merely nodded.

He didn't blame her for feeling glum. They'd found something more bewitching in this room than anything Missus Llassa could have conjured with a spell, passion beyond the reach of a witch's cauldron, and neither wanted to lose the magic. He thought of things he'd seen in the conjurer's shack years ago, toads' eyes and strands of hair, then he forced himself to continue. "But make no mistake, miss. If somethin' happens, and I do vanish, then I'm the one—" lifting a hand, he pointed over his shoulder at the painting "—who's goin' to be livin' inside that picture. And you'll be out here, Tanya Taylor, able to go anywhere you wish." His voice hardened, turning rough and implacable. "So don't ya be ruinin' my last three hours on the planet earth."

Her tears fell then. Maybe he'd known they would. And his heart sank as she jumped up, her shawl falling to the floor. She circled the table, lunged into his arms and flung her arms around his neck, and the next thing he knew, he was cradling her in his lap, pressing his lips into her hair. For a long time, he merely held her while she nuzzled his neck, her tears salting his skin.

"THERE, THERE, miss," he murmured senselessly, but suddenly, he admitted the truth. He didn't know which would be worse, being stuck inside the painting again, or having their positions reversed. What would he do if he were destined to live with her image in a painting in his living room, knowing she was really alive, wondering what she might be able to see or hear? The idea of her standing in front of the painting, trying to reach him, or talk to him was too much to bear.

"I want—" Her voice broke. "To go with you if you go…"

It was a terrible thing to say, but he understood. "I swear nothin's going to happen to me, Tanya."

"I don't believe you."

"Ya must."

Wrenching, she looked at the digital clock by the bedside again. Moments had passed. It was four-fifteen now. Every moment was flying by. Exactly three hours remained, and the stark look in her eyes made clear that every second had become her mortal enemy. "We never even found out how to get you back. We didn't do enough all week. But there were no real clues. Eduardo said we had all the information. Susannah wasn't any help. Julius was trying to leave us alone so we—"

"Could make love day and night, which we did," he murmured, circling her neck with a hand and forcing her to look at him.

"Maybe that wasn't enough."

"I couldn't want anything more than what we've had, lass."

"Miss," she corrected, tearfully.

"Miss," he said. He paused, his throat tightening as his gaze roved over her face. He'd never seen a woman so beautiful, never wanted a woman more. His body ached as much as his heart, his loins swelling while his heart stretched, filling with warmth. His voice was low. "Wait here." Changing his mind, he added in a near whisper. "Go get in yer bed for me, Tanya. When the time comes, we'll be naked in each others' arms, we will. You'll be holdin' me so tight that all the powers in all the witches' spells on the face of the whole earth couldn't break us apart." Lifting his chin and nodding in the direction of the bed, he added, "Now, get on with it."

He watched, feeling strangely overwhelmed as she walked toward the bed they'd been sharing. When she'd almost reached it, she glanced over her shoulder, staring at him as if she was never going to see him again. "You're an artist, ya are, Tanya Taylor," he found himself saying.

And it was true. The more he'd seen of her work, the more he'd realized she had a special talent, a gift like his own. Her show tomorrow night was going to be spectacular.

Tears had dried on her cheeks, but the eyes fixed on his still looked watery.

"And ya know what they say about artists?"

She shook her head.

"We don't look back." People born to create stayed too busy sculpting the future. Stede had learned that a long time ago. "You can't live in the past. Not last week when I came into yer life. Not yesterday when we saw yer parents. Not five minutes ago when you pushed aside yer dinner plate. You can't, no more than I can live in that clearin' where Basil Drake nearly killed me and I last saw Lucinda. When we look back, lass, that's when we die inside. Do you understand me, now?"

But she only started crying again, trying not to, but her chin was quivering, and her lips were trembling. "I'll never know anybody else like you, Stede."

He glanced at the clock. Four twenty-two. In less than three hours, she'd be laughing again—she'd know he was here to stay. "No matter what happens. Promise me one thing."

"Anything."

"Ya won't look back, lass."

In her eyes, he could see that he'd just asked the impossible. If he did vanish, it would break her heart. She'd never forget. She'd pine for him. And suddenly, he wished they'd never met. If he vanished, it could destroy her, and for the first time in his life, he felt he had no answers. None of Poor Richard's aphorisms would fill the void. "Now, turn off the light. I'll be back in a minute, Tanya," he managed to say.

Once they were in candlelight, he went downstairs. When he returned, carrying a bag and an open bottle of wine, it was to find her lying naked on soft sheets. Reaching the bed, he put down the items he'd brought and stepped out of his clothes. They'd never used birth control. Julius had told him of methods in the sixties, of course. And later, he'd talked with her about the issue, but he was glad now...so glad. Leaning, he pressed the flat of his hand to her belly. It was warm to the touch. Gently curved. Beautiful. He said nothing, but he knew she'd read his thoughts. If he vanished, maybe he'd leave her his baby.

"Shut yer eyes, miss," he whispered.

When she did, he studied her for a moment, his gaze slowly dropping over every inch, taking in the arch of her insteps, the flowing lines of legs, the curves of hips and breasts, then her sweet face. He filled his mind with the image of her, for all eternity. His throat constricted, and he felt as if tight bands were wrapping around his chest. Opening the bag he'd brought upstairs, he took out a handful of gems.

"Don't peek," he whispered as he took a necklace, circled it around her neck and clasped it behind. It was dazzling, a ruby surrounded by diamonds, gotten on a raid in the Southeast seas. He looped her delicate wrist with the matching bracelet, then slipped on the brightly shining ring. The center ruby was dark and mysterious. Pure poetry, like a drop of life's blood, and it was surrounded by diamonds that caught the candlelight like prisms, reflecting the colors of a rainbow.

She knew what he was doing, of course. Knew he'd

gone downstairs and opened his treasure chest. Her eyes were squeezed shut, but tears leaked from beneath the lids. Suddenly she fluttered them, the pale, sandy lashes batted, and she inhaled sharply as she looked down, taking in the gifts.

"All my treasure's yours," he said.

When she parted her lips to protest, he silenced her with a kiss. "If I do disappear," he said, emotion thickening his brogue. "Yer to have these things, Tanya Taylor. Who knows when I would return? Or what conditions might be in the future. Truly those are uncharted seas, and not even James's maps might help me then." He paused. "I want to make a baby with ya, tonight."

She looked stunned. "Anything," she whispered again. And then she was in his arms once more, his mouth closing tightly over hers, so nothing could intrude.

HE FELT LIKE HOME. Stede's body was her house and her warm hearth, her picket fence and garden. Tanya had never imagined another body could feel so compatible with hers, that she could move in tandem with a man as if they were truly one. That perfect sexual synchronicity was, she'd always thought, better left for love songs as wild as his appearance in her life, but as soon as they began kissing, she was lost, spiraling deeply into darkness, spinning hopelessly into a netherworld of emotion, tumbling headlong into an eternity of pleasure.

His mouth on hers was intense, like a love long forgotten, then suddenly remembered, and as they wrapped around each other, and he drove his hard, wanting flesh deep inside, decades might have passed. Centuries. Aeons.

She knew then that she wasn't really herself any longer. Because he was pure magic, stepping from a canvas into the real world, he'd changed her, deepened her, making even her notions about time, love ,and reality bend like a pretzel. Surely he was her fate. How many times in history could something so strange happen? And this had happened to her. They were both artists, perfect together sexually. It was a match and he'd expanded the horizons of her mind as surely as those of her body.

After hours of lovemaking, she found herself lying on her side, facing him, still wearing the jewelry he'd given her, their flushed, feverish bodies nearly touching, illuminated by candlelight. Days before, they'd played with some of the toys she'd bought with Izzie and Marlo, but the pleasure was nothing next to this, simply resting skin to skin, heart to heart, with her only clothing the gems he'd buried centuries ago. Their noses nearly touched, their lips, their cheeks. Gliding a palm down his side, she slid it over his open hand and let her fingers fall between his. Curling her fingers, she clasped his hand, and he responded, squeezing hard.

Watching candlelight dance on his face, she felt strangely empty, as if the world was really timeless and devoid of everything except him. Yes…time had stopped. Just once. For him and her. For them. They had just this one moment to smell the roses. His every touch made sexual satisfaction uncoil inside her, uncurling in her veins like an unleashed ball of twine. He'd bound her with it. Blindfolded her. Tied her up. Twisted her in knots.

And now it was as if every moment might end, leaving only the fiery glint of candle flame on diamonds and rubies to tell her he'd been here. It couldn't all be snatched away! This was too beautiful, and she couldn't let any of it go…

She blinked in the darkness. How many times had he made love to her just now? Three? Four? Orgasms melted into orgasms. He hadn't withdrawn from her body before he was hard again. He'd made love to her repeatedly. Now she could feel him, pressuring her thigh, and she felt the bottomless abyss of her corresponding heat, a craving they could try to satisfy until the end of time.

Lifting a finger of her free hand, she slowly traced the lines of his face, touching each asymmetric contour, committing each to memory, knowing she could draw his picture with her eyes shut. As her finger moved over his high cheekbones, she viewed the hollow planes of his cheeks, the aquiline nose, then she brushed her lips over the arches of dark bushy eyebrows and the feathering of inky lashes. Warmth spiked in her veins, flooding into her fingertips. As one hand thrust into the silken mass of his chest hair, something inside her loosened and dislodged. Strands teased the sensitive places between her fingers, and her other hand tightened in his, clasping. No…she'd never let him go.

She looked at the clock.

Seven on the dot now.

Fifteen minutes remained. More or less, she thought. Give or take a minute. After all, who knew the exact time he'd landed in the room? He said he'd looked at the clock, but how cognizant had he really been? Surely he'd been dazed from his journey. Maybe a minute or two had passed before he'd looked, maybe more. Did that mean ten minutes remained now? Or maybe six? Or five?

When would they be sure the ordeal was over? She tried not to cry. She wouldn't let him see her shed tears again. She wasn't some stupid, sappy woman, after all. And she wouldn't think of the future, either. Or the past. He was right in saying artists didn't look back. She'd promised him she wouldn't.

She wanted only to be here. Now. In this moment with him. Heat pulsed inside her once more. Her heartbeat quickened, and she knew he was thinking the same thing…that he wanted her. Against her thigh, his erection was surging now, burning. She could feel his flesh warming, pulsing, and she swallowed hard, as if that might help her steady the roar of emotions.

She'd make him love her, she suddenly thought. She had to. If he didn't already, he would now because she was going to… Hands quivering, she glided them to his shoulders, loving the satiny feeling of his skin. Gently she pressed, guiding him onto his back. Following, she stretched a leg over his, and as she did, he caught her calf, fondling the curve until he was tracing the hollow behind her knee, sending a thrill of longing through her.

"It's time," he whispered simply. "Love me, Tanya."

She straddled him, urgency taking hold when her legs parted. She wanted to make this so good for him that he could never leave. Poised above him, she felt her lower lips open like petals, and she felt cooler air touch where she'd grown warm and moist for him again. Glancing down, she inhaled sharply, unable to believe how he looked, so huge and dusky, his sex engorged and protruding from wild, midnight curls.

At the sight, she climbed, emotions jangling inside her

like discordant bells. Panting, she cried out when his hands molded her hips. He steadied her for a moment. Eyes lit with sexual fire met hers, looking suddenly sharp, needy and determined. A baby, she thought. That's what he wanted most.

Suddenly the corded muscles of his lower arms flexed, and he pulled her down. Her heart came with her body, swirling into an abyss of sensation as she settled over the tip of him. He was almost inside. Right there. So hot and perfect. Her hands tightened on his shoulders as he arched his hips, pushing only the head of his blistering sex inside.

It was excruciating. Her heart beat furiously. He'd said he wanted a baby. With her. Tonight. Yet he might vanish. Waves of emotion assaulted her as she gripped his shoulders and his eyes rolled back. They slammed shut as she sank onto him. She was slick and ready, but each inch of rigid flesh spread her beyond what she could bear. Lowering her upper body, she circled her arms around his neck, hugging him tightly, knowing she'd never let him go, gasping when his chest brushed hers.

Hungry fingers clutched her as he brought her down on him again. Harder. Moving her chest in tandem with her hips, she teased her breasts, touching his tight male nipples, bothering them both until they were breathing raggedly, pattering indecipherable words.

She wanted him crazy with lust. To drive him mad, so she thrust out her chest, nipping his chin with kisses, rubbing her hands between them and pinching the tight buds of male nipples before angling down her head to suckle. Pulling a nipple between her lips, she swirled her tongue, knowing it would drive him to distraction. Using her teeth, she sawed edges of sensitized flesh until he shuddered, his head rearing back on the pillow. His chin tilted and his hands tightened on her waist once more, urging her up…up…up…

Ridges stroked her. Ripples of flesh annoyed and maddened. Each inch burned. Inside he was strumming her. Her heart fluttered crazily at the sound of a harsh breath he sucked through clenched teeth. "Tanya," he whispered hoarsely. "Ya must believe me now."

"I do." Maybe it was true. Maybe they'd be together forever. Maybe he loved her, and this hot, wild passion would never end. Guiding her, he brought her down once more. Even harder this time. Deeper, with a force that almost scared her. And when he touched her womb, another gasp was torn from between her lips. The slick envelope of her body was completely filled with him.

His voice was ragged. "Again Tanya."

Whimpering, she lifted her hips, only to be pulled down again and again, her mind blanking as her mound crushed his pelvis. They were climbing together. She knew his rational thoughts were lost just as hers were, as her need took over, driving her into bliss. Waves of sensation kept coming. They were like white lightning in a summer sky charged with static. The man was electric. Kinetic. As if lashed to the mast of a ship in a storm she couldn't hold on any longer. Suddenly she could see nothing. Everything went dark as the sheer life in him centered into a final wave of raw primal heat. Hips slammed hips again, locked in feverish, desperate craving. She was on the brink, and nothing existed but him, scorching through her center.

Strong arms wrapped her waist, pulling her even more

deeply into him. Legs tangled. Buried inside her, he went taut. Time was suspended, then the release came, exploding. Gushing, he filled her, and her last thought before his bruised mouth slammed onto hers and his tongue plunged was, *a baby.*

"I do love ya, Tanya Taylor," he whispered. Then she skyrocketed over the top, into oblivion.

Then, she gasped.

Had minutes passed? Hours? But she knew better. Only seconds had passed! She blinked, trying to collect her wits. The candles were flickering. Her body still rocked with the afterglow of his lovemaking. But…she'd blanked out when she'd come. Her arms, wrapped around his neck a second ago, were now wrapped around the pillow on which he'd lain his head. She wrenched around in bed. She was still wearing the rubies and diamonds he'd given her, but…

He was gone!

"Oh God," she whispered hoarsely, feeling faint, her eyes darting to the picture on the wall to rove over the grassy clearing and the red leaves bursting over the trees like suns. Basil Drake was running forward, his musket aimed.

"At you, love," she spoke, shoving aside the sheets and running to the picture. Stede stared back. Once more, he was dressed in the clothes he'd worn when he'd arrived, the tight white breeches and tailored coat, his hair drawn back into a ponytail. But he was trapped inside the picture now. Yes, he was staring right at her.

She could swear she saw his eyes move.

13

FLOATING. Drifting. Stede was on the sea at low tide, softly rocking in a boat. But something was wrong, he realized now. Very wrong. He was trapped somewhere. He had to escape, didn't he? Chatter sounded at the edges of consciousness. "Izzie," he heard someone say. "Well…Marlo…not ready for the show…I can't…"

And he saw her weeping. But who was the lovely wench he'd made so sad? Oh, yes… Tanya. That had been her name. Tanya Taylor. She'd lived in New York City. He could almost remember everything now. Had centuries passed? Yes…he'd found himself in another world, another time.

Where he'd fallen in love with her. So, why hadn't the wretched curse been lifted? Pain filled the void. A shadow passed, and he remembered the softness of her skin. "Stede…can you hear me? Can you see me?"

His eyes hurt, and he tried to move them, but he could only remember snatches of rosy flesh, a pale face tilted back, and lips parted in ecstasy. That was over, though. Now she was crying, crouching over Lucinda's diary, seeking answers.

"Julius?" he heard her say angrily. "Why don't you pick up your phone? Call me back!"

He remembered Julius, too. A fine friend who'd moved

the world for him. But the world was beyond his reach now. He could only feel it. It was far off, as distant as the voice he heard, brokenly calling him….

"IT'S A SMASHING success!" Tanya's mother exclaimed, surveying the crowded gallery. By contrast to the owner who'd run Izzie's show, this one had preferred to draw a less trendy group. People milled, and given the way they were dressed, they had money to spend on artwork. A small orchestra provided classical music, and a champagne fountain was in the room's center.

"I had no idea your work would look this good hung," Marlo said breathlessly, squeezing Tanya's arm. "In your studio, everything's so jumbled. Supplies everywhere. But to see the work with white space around it! This is…"

"Amazing," agreed Izzie.

"We're so proud," Tanya's dad put in, his eyes settling on the piece she'd called Shattered World, then her picture of the Empire State Building. "And you look so beautiful," he continued. "I can't believe you're my baby girl."

Vaguely, Tanya was aware that the floor-length dress she'd bought had struck just the right chord. A diamond-patterned, white tank-style bodice was attached to the spangly sequined skirt, and camera flashes followed her around the room, but her mind was elsewhere. She barely heard a word anyone said. Beneath every sentence, her mind played an ongoing mantra. *I've got to get home to Stede.*

He had been gone over twenty-four hours.

"I told everyone at the Met to come tonight," her mother was saying. That had been propitious, too. Drawing buyers from one of the world's most famous museums was no small feat, something Brad would have to note in his article. Not that he'd be any kinder than he had to be. Snidely he'd already pointed out that she'd come alone. Otherwise, everyone was avoiding the topic of Stede, covering for her, since they suspected a nasty breakup she didn't want to discuss.

As Marlo, Izzie and her mother and father dissolved into the crowd, Tanya absently lifted a hand to her neck where she'd used makeup to cover the marks left by Stede's kisses and whiskers. It was all she had left. That, and a treasure chest. She'd opened it, stunned to see gems that had to be worth a fortune. Where could she keep such things? She couldn't make use of James's safe once he returned, could she? And what would Stede do now, if he came back in another time? How could she help him?

She clutched her wineglass, curling fingers around it so tightly she expected it to break. She had to get home. She couldn't stand having the painting out of her sight, not even for a moment, not when Stede was trapped inside.

She'd called Julius, but he hadn't returned her call until this morning. He was the only person who'd believe her story. Izzie and Marlo had visited her apartment today, and she'd almost told them. They were her girlfriends, after all. But they'd thought she was crying because she was undergoing stress, due to her show, maybe even the breakup with Brad. How could she tell the truth? What could she say? That she'd been sitting in her room alone, talking to a painting because her lover was trapped inside?

No wonder Julius had been committed. And if anyone decided she'd gone crazy, then Stede would be lost, maybe forever. No…she had to keep her mouth shut. She couldn't easily forget what had happened to Julius Royle.

Panicked, she racked her brain, mouthing the words to the curse. "In your own painting you will be, perchance for all eternity. Awakened through the century's, until love's currency does free." She pondered the missing words, too. What came between, "you and thee?" And how did the phrase end that began, "You must say you…"

A trumpet sounded and she quickly dug into her purse for her phone. Just as she flipped it open, she simultaneously recognized the caller's number as Julius's and realized Brad was beside her again. "Decent show," he remarked. "I'm still looking, of course, but—"

Tears were pushing hard at her eyes now. "Sorry," she interrupted. "I've got to take this call."

"Only boyfriend trouble could put you in such a snit on your big night," he said.

"I don't see Sylvia Gray here," she couldn't help but say, turning away, determined to find somewhere quiet. She wound up edging behind the champagne fountain. "Julius," she said in a hushed tone. "Where have you been?"

"I went to my sister's," he explained. "I thought it might do us some good to have the receipt for the painting, if she still had it. And if she'd give it to me. Moon Beam… Susannah Billings, gave me one years ago, and I had a canceled check, of course. After my siblings moved my things, and the painting disappeared, I was more worried about Stede than the receipts, and now I just thought…"

So he'd been busy trying to help, after all. "Look," she said, still feeling frustrated. "I need you. I left a message

last night. Like I said, Stede's in the—" She lowered her
voice, feeling desperate. "In the painting," she finished.

Julius sounded crushed. "So, you weren't able to make
him love you. Sorry," he quickly added.

But it was too late. Pain sliced through her. She managed
to find her voice, anyway, and kept talking, blinking back
tears. "I've been thinking about the curse, trying to make
out what it means. And I have to ask you…" She paused.
"You bought the painting on the West Coast, right?"

"Yes."

"But Stede appeared in your living room in New York.
On the East Coast. When did you get the receipt? And how
did you pay for the painting?"

"Moon Beam, I mean Susannah, sent me a receipt after
my check cleared."

"You paid by check then?"

"Probably, she cashed it after I was back east. What are
you thinking, Tanya?"

"Love's true currency," she began, hoping she wouldn't
start crying again. "Maybe the important word is currency,
not love. And maybe the currency doesn't refer to love, but
money. I bought the painting a week before Stede showed
up, but now I remember. My credit card didn't go through
immediately, and the night he came, May called from her
shop, Finders Keepers, saying she'd put it through. I was
asleep at the time and didn't remember. Maybe Stede pops
out when currency for the painting changes hands."

"But Missus Llassa told Lucinda that Stede had to fall
in love during the week he was set free."

Her heart felt shattered. She tried not to think about it,
but she knew the truth. He hadn't loved her, not really. Not

in his heart of hearts. Tears gathered in her eyelashes, but she refused to let them fall. She loved Stede. That was what mattered most. She would get him back, give him another chance to love someone else.

"I believe that's true, also," she explained. "Anyway, Susannah said the painting was in storage for years. Her parents were interested in collecting, not displaying, so even though they bought the painting from the Wilsons, they didn't remove it from storage immediately. They only took possession and hung it in their living room after the break-in at the storage unit. And that's when their daughter took it and sold it to you, over ten years later. Then there was a time lag between your taking the picture and the check clearing, just as when May charged my credit card after I'd taken possession."

"And your point is?"

"I'm going to risk it. I'm going to sell the painting."

"Oh, no," said Julius. "I don't know if that's the best idea. I think—"

"I have another call," she said. "I've got to take it. It could be Eduardo. I've tried to call him ten times today, and James is due back in another couple days, so he'll probably call soon. I'll call you right back." She clicked to the other line. "Hello?"

"It's Eduardo. I'm really sorry, Tanya. It's been the week from hell. Nonstop auctions, and I just wanted you to know I'm sorry about not being more available. Right now, I'm on my way to your show. It was nice of you to invite me—"

"I've got business for you."

"You're selling?"

Inside, she was crumbling. She could only hope this was the right thing to do. "Yes."

"I knew you'd find your internal shark, Tanya."

Nothing could have been further from the truth. Greed was her last motive. "How soon can you sell the painting?"

"I've got a list of interested parties. Enough for a private auction. As I told you, O'Flannery's work has a fan-club following, and you only want to sell one piece, so people won't have to scramble to find the cash to buy from a larger collection. We can discuss strategy when I get to your show. I'm about to get into a cab."

"I need to sell it now," she forced herself to say. "Forget coming to my show."

There was a pause. "When the shark comes out," he said, "it has teeth. Tell you what. Give me an hour. I think I can piggyback the painting into another small, private auction we've arranged. It just depends on whether enough bidders want to fly in or arrange for someone to place bids. The auction's the day after tomorrow."

She felt faint. "So soon?" James wouldn't even be back by then. Somehow, she'd imagined weeks in which she could live with the painting…and Stede. How could she let it go, knowing what she did? And what if she was wrong, and this didn't buy Stede a week, after all? Then somebody else, somebody who wouldn't understand the significance of the work, would own it. Stede would be trapped in the painting, hanging in the home of some wealthy family, such as the Wilsons or the Billings.

"Tanya? Are you still there?"

"I'm here. Don't worry about making my show," she repeated, knowing she was gambling with somebody else's life. She just hoped she'd had a flash of brilliance, not lunacy. Keep moving, she thought. She couldn't afford to stop and let her feelings in. Stede hadn't loved her. The words of the hex and what Missus Llassa told Lucinda jibed, along with the general legend. And that meant he'd have stayed if he loved her. But he'd been wrenched from her arms. "Try to set up the sale for the day after tomorrow."

"You're really getting buyers for your work," Brittania said as she hung up.

How could she concentrate on such inane conversation when her soul was shattered? When she was so confused? When her lover had vanished? She realized Brittania had overheard the end of her call and thought it concerned one of the pieces in the gallery. According to the owner, she'd sold others tonight, so she simply said, "Yes."

"It's a great show," Brittania offered.

Her smile wasn't exactly insincere. And she looked as she usually did, her hair neatly pulled away from her face, the makeup around her liquid-brown eyes impeccable. She'd chosen the perfect simple black dress, which she wore with a single strand of pearls. It was hard to remember all those years ago, when their four-year age difference had meant so little. They were only sisters then, playing dolls and dreaming of their futures. Stede's words played in her ears. She could almost hear him whispering in her ear, saying, "Don't look back."

How could she do anything else, though? The last week of her life was one she didn't want to ever forget.

"Thanks," Tanya managed to say, coming back to the present. Even now, the mantra was playing. *I've got to go home. I've got to be with Stede.* In a few minutes she could play sick and leave. She'd talked to everyone, met the gallery owner's friends. Yes…she'd pretend to get ill. *I've got to get out of here. Get home…*

"I'm happy for you," Brittania added.

Loss was mingling with loss. Stede was gone. So was the Brittania she'd once known. She felt like nothing was left between her and her sister but lies. They'd lost what was truest between them, the love they'd shared as kids. Maybe they could start a new relationship now and begin with something fresh, without all the jealousy. In the end, she was sure the more negative emotions would prove to be the ones that were skin deep. Love would win out. Not just for her and Brittania, but for her and Stede, too, whatever their future might bring. Now she could hear Stede's voice in her ear, whispering, "Don't look back." She had to heed the words, even if he wasn't here now. Maybe he'd thought he'd loved her….

But she couldn't recapture their hours of passion any more than the years of playing dolls with Brittania. "Thank you for coming," she said, the words sounding hollow, her mind on Stede. "I appreciate the support."

Brittania said the last thing she expected. "Matthew and I are getting a divorce."

Her lips parted in astonishment. "What?"

Suddenly Brittania was talking faster than Tanya's mind could follow. "I always looked up to you," her sister said. "I wanted to grow up too fast, maybe. To be like you. You were so free. Mom and Dad always let you do anything you wanted. And when they didn't, you never cared. You followed your heart, anyway. They wanted me to be perfect. Another version of you. Didn't you ever wonder why they called me Brittania and you Tanya? It's almost the same name."

"Brittania was Dad's sister's name," Tanya said, feeling stunned. "And Mom's favorite aunt was Tanya. They felt the names were different enough. They loved both people, and wanted to name us after people they cared for."

There was a long silence.

Tanya's mind was reeling with what Brittania had said, but she wanted to get home, too, to Stede. "We're all different," she began. "And I thought you were happy. You've got Matt, the kids."

"We used to be. But we were only twenty when we got married, and now…I just don't know, anymore. I feel like I'm missing out on what everyone else does in their twenties." Pausing, Brittania shook her head. "I just want you to know I'm sorry. I've been jealous of you."

Tanya didn't have any idea what to say. "Don't be."

"And that guy you were with," Brittania added. "You could feel the passion between you. It was like something that was meant to be, while Matt and I seem so apart from each other right now…"

Blowing out a stunned sigh, Tanya reached and simply pulled her sister into an embrace. Over Brittania's shoulder, she saw her own paintings, and how the shattered landscapes seemed like something from the distant past. With Stede, she'd found her map, her compass. Whatever she painted tomorrow would be truly different. Yes…Stede had come into her life, and even without him in her arms—holding her sister instead— she felt transformed.

But he hadn't loved her.

She broke inside, then tried to push away the thought and couldn't. She squeezed her sister more tightly, knowing if she didn't, she'd begin to cry again.

"Where is he?" Brittania asked. "I want to say hi."

"Who?"

"Stede."

"Gone," Tanya said simply.

"NINE-HUNDRED and fifty thousand," the auctioneer called into a microphone two days later, his English accent and tweed suit lending an air of dignity to the proceeding.

This was hardly how Tanya had imagined a small, private auction. At least a hundred people were seated below. Since she was the owner, she was alone in a glass booth on the balcony above the auction floor, so she could watch the bidding. It had started at a half million dollars, and now everything she'd eaten all month was spinning around in her tummy. When her eyes fixed on Stede, she wanted to scream that she'd changed her mind. No one could buy this particular work by Stede O'Flannery. It was hers. He was in it.

But if she didn't sell, and if she was right, he'd be trapped inside forever. Not that they'd be together. She had to get it through her thick skull, no matter how much it hurt. Eduardo was downstairs, pacing near the door through which they brought out the works for sale. Now he vanished through another doorway. Six paintings had already been sold, and now Stede's was displayed on an easel beside the auctioneer's podium. Even from here she could see his eyes. They followed her everywhere…eyes she now knew were wickedly green and charged with devilish humor.

"We have one million dollars," the auctioneer said now.

A hush fell over the crowd. Tension was thick. Her eyes swept the crowd. Who was spending so much money? Along the walls were phone banks manned by people sent to bid for anonymous buyers. She watched one speak into the phone. He was a cultured man, slender and balding, wearing wire frame glasses and a tan tailored suit. He lifted his hand.

"A million-one," said the auctioneer. "That's one million, one hundred thousand. Will anyone counter the offer?"

Slowly but surely, people had dropped out. Now another man from the phone bank raised his hand. He was short and pudgy, but well-dressed and tenacious-looking.

"A million-two," said the auctioneer.

Immediately the slender man countered. "A million-three." Then the short, pudgy man. They were bidding against each other now. No one else was left. When the auctioneer called, "A million-six," Tanya felt the air whoosh from her lungs. Eduardo was right. The painting was bringing in a fortune.

Who were the mystery people on the other end of the phones? she wondered. She hadn't counted on them. She'd imagined easily discerning the identity of the buyer. And she had to know who it was. She intended to camp outside their home, just as Julius had camped outside hers. It could take days for checks to clear. With sums as high as this, maybe even longer. Tanya had no idea what to expect. Would Stede pop out in another state? Another country? And what if she was wrong? And he only wound up living in some strange rich person's home? This was such a long-shot…. The slender man was winning. "A million-nine," the auctioneer said.

The short pudgy man countered.

"Two million." Then the auctioneer said, "Our other party is not going over two million. Two million it is. Going once. Twice." Lifting a gavel, he brought it down on the podium. "Sold. To the party at the phone bank."

Just as people began to rise from their seats, the auctioneer smiled. "Weatherby's extends special congratulations to both buyer and seller of this unique work. As you know, sales of this magnitude require parting remarks. O'Flannery's paintings have always been shrouded in mystery. An enigmatic figure, the artist, himself, was said to have countless lovers. A privateer and child of the American Revolution, Stede O'Flannery was rumored to be the victim of a witch's hex, as well. Some say that a figure in one of his paintings—no one knows which one— is Stede, himself. That he is destined to live inside a work of his own art."

The auctioneer paused. "Perhaps one of the men represented in this painting is Stede himself," he finished. "It is said, too, that many of those associated with his paintings have gone mad. After a break-in at a storage facility which housed it in the 1950s, a crate in which the painting rested was mysteriously destroyed, although the painting was not moved. A guard swore he'd been attacked by a man who looked like the dark figure in this very painting. Days later, he vanished before the man's very eyes."

That was new information. Tanya could merely stare as the auctioneer continued. "I'll end by reading the hex put on the painter's head by that most mysterious of colonial witch's, Missus Llassa, about whom you may have read in the flyer we prepared. 'In your painting you will be, perchance for all eternity,'" he intoned. "'Awakened through the centuries until love's currency does set free both you and thee. And then you must say you will marry me.'"

So Eduardo had lied! How had the hex really read? She was so angry that she barely registered the words. All along, Eduardo had known a rumor existed that Stede was trapped in one of his own paintings. It was the wrong time for the door to swing open, and for Eduardo to come inside. "Liar," she spat. Jumping to her feet, she tried not to panic. "You didn't tell me everything."

"Calm down, Tanya. We dug up some more history and used it to sell the work for you. It's our job."

"For a hefty percentage of the sale price."

"What's your problem? They're only crazy stories."

"The shark gene," she said simply, realizing Eduardo and his buyers thought the stories were exactly that—stories. But they weren't. "I need to know the name of that buyer."

"No can do. It was a private sale, Tanya. That protects you, too. You asked that we not release information about you, remember?"

She was furious. It was in his best interest to hype the mysterious history of the work and he had. He'd release any information, as long as it was to his own benefit. Nothing was going the way she planned. She was shaking with worry. Quickly she brushed past him, thankful no one was in the upstairs hallway. Because she'd been here before, she was aware of employee entrances. Pushing one open, she ran downstairs, wishing she hadn't worn high heels with her suit. She had to get to the painting. But what then? Would she say goodbye? All she knew was that she wanted her painting back. More than that, she wanted Stede's love.

She was breathless when she reached the room where she'd last seen it. Fortunately, the man guarding the door recognized her. "Tanya."

"Eduardo said I could see the painting one more time," she lied, hoping she could do so before Eduardo caught up with her.

"You'll have to hurry," he said uncertainly. "It was a cash sale."

"Cash?" she echoed.

"Some really rich guy. He brought the dough in suitcases, then directed the sale from his cell phone in the lobby. He was talking to a guy on the phone bank, but he didn't want to come inside. Stede O'Flannery's work always draws a weird crowd."

"I'll just be a minute."

He used a key to open the door. "Enjoy your last private viewing."

She stepped inside the climate controlled room and closed the door, her heart hammering. There was nothing inside, except the painting. No other doors or windows. The work was propped on an easel, draped in black velvet. An edge of the gilded frame showed; she'd recognize it anywhere. Swiftly crossing to it, she lifted a corner of the velvet. Just as she whisked it away, wind seemed to lift her from her feet, throwing her backward. She felt as if she'd been punched.

What had hit her? Staggering, she lost her footing. Wrenching to catch herself, she slammed her hand on the floor, crying out. She pushed herself up again, unable to believe her eyes. She was staring at a cartoon ghost. But instead of a man wearing a white sheet over his head, this one wore black velvet. He was punching his way out, and she thought she'd start weeping when she heard him mutter, "Sweet Betsy Ross."

The money must have just changed hands.

STEDE WAS SURE he'd been hit by a hammer. That, or the scoundrel Basil Drake really had killed him this time. Blinking, trying to get his bearings, he tossed off the black shroud obscuring his vision, then he pressed a hand to his forehead. That's when he saw her. "Damn you, miss!" he exploded. "Sellin' me, are ya? I thought you said I was the man for ya!"

"You don't love me," she countered, looking stunned. "You vanished. But I kept reading Lucinda's diary, and thinking. I realized that if the painting was sold, you'd pop back out. That's the key. You come out when money changes hands."

His green eyes softened. Yes, he was getting his bearings now, and he was remembering everything about their last night together. "That's why you sold me, miss?"

She nodded. "I wanted to give you another chance. Another week..." Her voice trailed off. "With another woman, if that's the way it's got to be."

"Another woman?" he said hoarsely, just as someone knocked on the door outside. Ignoring it, he said, "I don't want another woman, Tanya Taylor."

"You don't?" Her eyes were tearing, and she looked almost as forlorn as she had the last time he'd seen her.

He shook his head, then suppressed a smile. "You must love me something fierce if you popped me out just to give me a chance with someone else," he said, looking touched.

Another knock sounded. "Tanya," the guard called in a stage whisper. "The buyer's coming down the hallway now. You'd better come out. I don't think he'll want to find anyone with his painting."

She gasped, her eyes darting to the black velvet in the floor. "You've got to hide, Stede."

But there was nowhere to go. Sans the easel, the room was empty. No other doors. No windows. It was climate controlled, and hermetically sealed. How could they explain his presence? Or tell the buyer why the painting was missing one of the figures? Was someone else about to realize that the myths surrounding Stede's work were all true?

The door swung open. And when it shut a second later, Stede could barely believe his eyes. His heart swelled and he knew he'd never really understand his good fortune. "Sons of liberty," he murmured. Just moments before, he'd been so afraid, floating in the netherworld, knowing he'd be trapped forever. But now Julius was here. And lovely Tanya Taylor hadn't sold him, after all. Or she had, but for all the right reasons. "Julius?"

He was wearing a dapper gray suit, probably bought during his younger, more affluent years. "You're the one who bought the painting?" Tanya asked. "How?"

"The other morning, Stede brought me some jewels," Julius explained. "So, when you called, saying you thought Stede would be freed if you sold the painting, I started hawking some of them. I figured using cash was the best bet. Sorry," he added, glancing at Stede. "But there was no other option, and what way to better spend your money than getting you back. Right my friend?"

Before Stede could answer, he went on. "I didn't want to tell you—" Now he glanced at Tanya. "Just in case I couldn't come through, since you sounded so depressed. But I got the money a few hours ago. When I arrived here, I realized I couldn't be seen, though. Everyone in the art world knows I was committed, and most have heard about my financial circumstances, so they'd never take my bids, so I had to work with a bidder at the phone banks." Pausing, Julius blew out a frustrated breath. "Art dealers," he muttered. "A nasty lot. Anyway, did you two hear the rest of the hex?"

"Aye," Stede said. It was coming to him as if from a dream now. Just as he'd heard the auctioneer recite the hex, Stede had felt himself being carried, and now he realized he'd been stuck in the painting and Weatherby's employees must have been bringing him into this room. He shook his head to clear it of confusion. Being inside the painting was truly disorienting. The only other thing in life that had twisted him into such knots was having relations with Tanya. "…Awakened through the centuries until love's currency does set free both you and thee," he murmured, his eyes settling on Tanya.

His breath caught. She was as beautiful as ever, and his fingers itched to touch her, just as they had while he'd been trapped earlier. How could he explain the feelings? He'd known he'd miss her for all eternity, and now he felt he'd die if she wasn't in his arms soon. When he spoke, his voice was husky. "And then you must say you will marry me."

"It's okay," she whispered, glancing away. "I mean, if you'd loved me in your heart of hearts…"

Closing the space between them, he cupped her chin in his hands and lifted her face to his. Quickly he seared her lips with a kiss. "No, I think I won't go back if I ask ya. And I was gonna ask ya, Tanya Taylor," he assured throatily. "But my circumstances aren't exactly stable. And as Poor Richard said, 'Never take a wife till thou has a house to put her in.' Besides, I only met your papa once, and it didn't seem polite on the first meetin' to ask for your hand."

She looked stunned, then touched. "You were going to ask my father if you could marry me?"

"Of course I was," he returned, feeling mildly offended. "What kind of a man do ya take me for?"

She came into his arms then, wrapping hers tightly around his neck. "The best kind in the world," she said between the kisses she peppered on his lips. "Mine."

Disengaging himself, he dropped to his knees. Lifting her hand, he brought it to his lips, kissed the back of it, then looked into her eyes. "Will you be my wife, Tanya Taylor?"

She offered a shuddering breath. "Yes," she whispered.

FLOATING. Drifting. Tanya was coasting in a netherworld, rocking on a sea, but this wasn't a wave, only the rise and fall of Stede's chest. Her eyelashes fluttered against his skin and she opened her eyes. Her first thought was that she was hungry for him, her body already burning.

"Top of the mornin', Mrs. O'Flannery."

Chuckling, she stretched her arms around his waist, then shifted her weight, feeling heat flush through her system when she registered his sexual excitement. "We're not married yet."

Only a week had passed since he'd asked her. And he still

insisted nothing would be final until he'd spoken with her father, officially asking for her hand. Now his arms circled her waist, and he lifted his hips. His smile broadened as a hand found her breast and stroked. "I *feel* married," he assured. "Besides, I've a right to be tryin' out yer new name."

And more. Always a breast man, he was rolling a nipple between a thumb and finger now, and as desire took hold, she exhaled a shaky breath. "A lot of women keep their old names nowadays, you know."

"But you want mine, don't ya, Tanya?"

Actually she did. Shifting her weight, she snaked both hands around his neck, teasing the nape before thrusting them into the most silken hair she'd ever felt. Then she felt his hand between their bodies, slowly guiding himself to where she was so open. At least that's what she hoped.

But he only stroked her there, and she sighed in pure bliss as he rolled on his side for better access, using his fingers to part the delicate folds and find her clitoris, driving her wild. Leaning back her head, she lost herself to the sensation as the recent past receded into the far distance.

Much had happened in the past week, since she and Julius had recovered the painting. Draping it in velvet, they'd marched through the front doors of Weatherby's with it, waving the receipt and using the canvas to shield Stede's face. Julius, who had more contacts than money, had found documents for Stede, including a birth certificate and social security card, which meant Stede would be able to get other papers, such as a driver's license. In turn, Stede gifted him with a bit more of his treasure. Accustomed to horses, Stede said he felt ready to leap into the age of automobiles, too, and he'd started studying for his learner's permit.

When her parents had called, Stede apologized profusely for missing them at the gallery opening, which had been a success beyond Tanya's wildest dreams. Brad's review had been bad, but other reviewers had disagreed, and one noted his romantic history with Tanya, so she'd come up smelling like roses. Brittania had called, too, apologizing for baring so much emotion at Tanya's opening, but Tanya was glad about that, as well. If her sister could learn to be more honest, maybe they could start becoming friends again. As it turned out, Brittania wasn't divorcing Matthew, after all, but they were going to counseling, trying to find ways to make their relationship more satisfying.

Even James had things to look forward to, since he could begin his renovation. He'd been shocked when he arrived home to find Tanya packing. With a man in the picture, she'd explained, her love nest above Treasured Maps was getting a little crowded. Regarding their new place, she and Stede had hired a Realtor and were looking at condos. Between his buried treasure and the proceeds from the art show, as well as the canvases and vintage wine he hoped to retrieve from Killman's cave, they figured they'd have no trouble making a down payment.

Otherwise, Izzie and Marlo kept attempting to make plans, but both understood what female friends always did, that sometimes a new man in a girl's life took precedence, no matter how much they were dying to hear, as Izzie always put it, "Every dirty little detail."

And there were many. Stede had started painting again, and his first project had used her body for a canvas and paints from the pleasure chest at the foot of her bed.

Catching his gaze now, Tanya stared deeply into eyes the color of a green sea glittering in sunlight. He was so talented, so interesting, and now that Julius had helped set things up so that he could pretend to be his own ancestor, the sky was the limit for Stede O'Flannery. There was no reason he couldn't sell any new paintings he produced, not to mention his collector's items in Killman's cave, and he wanted to go to galleries, to get a sense of today's art world. Already, he'd sniffed around the nearby piers, too, deciding he might want to work on one of the private yachts or tourists boats, or as he called them all, local pleasure crafts. Already, her father had signed him on for competitions at the Short Hills Country Club, convinced that Stede would win trophies in everything from horseback riding to target shooting.

And he was probably right.

But now, the man looked sleepy, his eyes half shut. "What time's it gettin' ta be, lass?" he whispered lazily, arching his hips suggestively and watching her face register pleasure as his fingers continued working their magic. In a moment, both knew, speech would be impossible. Already, her heart was starting to beat a tattoo, stealing her breath.

"Seven-fifteen." She paused significantly. "In the morning."

Lowering his head, he settled his mouth on hers, his tongue exploring. "So, we made it through the night?"

Every muscle ached, and she strained now, stretching… reaching…climbing for the ecstasy. Once more, they'd made love last night. On Friday night. Seven-fifteen had come and gone. "Looks like you're here to stay," she murmured, sucking in a sharp breath when his maddening fingers quickened, taking her to the edge.

She whispered, "Maybe we should quit talking."

His chuckle warmed her. "You have a better idea about how to occupy our time, miss?"

"Why don't you and I have…" Her voice trailed off as he thrust a finger inside her. "Proper relations?"

"One thing I learned a long time ago," he murmured, testing her readiness a final time, then preparing to guide himself inside. "Smart fellows never argue with a lady. So, when one insists on proper relations, a man better deliver the goods."

"Poor Richard?" she guessed.

"No, miss," he said, his lips against her ear. "That would be an O'Flannery original."

Before she could answer, he entered her, thrusting inside with a long, unbroken stroke, shattering her last impulse to keep talking. But she did manage to whisper one last thing. "Sweet sons of liberty, I'm really glad you're back, Stede O'Flannery."

* * * * *

RUN, ALLY! Don't be fooled by him. He's evil. Don't let him touch you!

But as the forbidding figure came through the mists toward her, Ally knew she couldn't run. His features burned with dark malevolence, and his physical domination of everything around him seemed to hold her like a net.

She'd heard the tales. She knew all about the Wolverton legend and the ghost that haunted The Willows, an elegant old mansion lost by Micha Wolverton nearly a hundred years ago. According to folklore, the estate was stolen from the Wolvertons, and Micha was killed, trying to reclaim it. His dying vow was to be reunited with the spirit of his beloved wife, who'd taken her life for reasons no one would speak of, except in whispers. But Ally had never put much stock in the fantasy. She didn't believe in ghosts.

Until now—

She still didn't understand what was happening. The figure had materialized out of the mist that lay thick on the damp cemetery soil. A cool breeze and silvery moonlight had played against the ancient stone of the crypts surrounding her, until they joined the mist, causing his body to thicken and solidify right before her eyes. That was when she realized she'd seen this man before. Or thought she had, at least.

His face was familiar. . . so familiar, yet she couldn't put it together. Not with him looming so near. She stepped back as he approached.

"Don't be afraid," he said. His voice wasn't what she expected. It didn't sound as if it were coming from beyond the grave. It was deep and sensual. Commanding.

"Who are you?" she managed.

"You should know. You summoned me."

"No, I didn't." She had no idea what he was talking about. Two minutes ago, she'd been crouching behind a moss-covered crypt, spying on the mansion that had once been The Willows, but was now Club Casablanca. And then this—

If he was Micah, he might be angry that she was trespassing on his property. "I'll go," she said. "I won't come back. I promise."

"You're not going anywhere."

Words snagged in her throat. "Wh-why not? What do you want?"

"If I wanted something, Ally, I'd take it. This is about need."

His words resonated as he moved within inches of her. She tried to back away, but her feet were useless. "And you need something from me?"

"Good guess." His tone burned with irony. "I need lips, soft and surrendered, a body limp with desire."

"My lips, my bod—?"

"Only yours."

"Why? Why me?" This couldn't be Micha. He didn't want any woman but Rose. He'd died trying to get back to her.

"Because you want that, too," he said.

Wanted what? A ghost of her own? She'd always found

the legend impossibly romantic, but how could he have known that? How could he know anything about her? Besides, she'd sworn off inappropriate men, and what could be more inappropriate than a ghost? She shook her head again, still not willing to admit the truth. But her heart wouldn't play along. It clattered inside her chest. The mere thought of his kiss, his touch, terrified her. This wildness, it was fear, wasn't it?

When his fingertips touched her cheek, she flinched, expecting his flesh to be cold, lifeless. It was anything but that. His skin was smooth and hot, gentle, yet demanding. And while his dark brown eyes were filled with mystery and wonder, there was a sensitivity about them that threatened to disarm her if she looked too deeply.

"These lips are mine," he said, as if stating a universal fact that she was helpless to avoid. In truth, it was just that. She couldn't stop him.

And she didn't want to.

* * * * *

Find out how the story unfolds in…
DECADENT
by
New York Times *bestselling author*
Suzanne Forster.
On sale November 2006.

Harlequin Blaze—Your ultimate destination
for red-hot reads.
With six titles every month, you'll never guess
what you'll discover under the covers…

nocturne™

Save $1.⁰⁰ off

your purchase of any
Silhouette® Nocturne™ novel.

Receive $1.00 off
any Silhouette® Nocturne™ novel.

Available wherever books are sold, including most bookstores, supermarkets, drugstores and discount stores.

Coupon expires December 1, 2006. Redeemable at participating retail outlets in the U.S. only. Limit one coupon per customer.

5 65373 00076 2   (8100)0 11265

SNCOUPUS

Save $1·⁰⁰ off

your purchase of any
Silhouette® Nocturne™ novel.

Receive $1.00 off

any Silhouette® Nocturne™ novel.

**Available wherever books are sold, including most
bookstores, supermarkets, drugstores and discount stores.**

Coupon expires December 1, 2006. Redeemable at participating
retail outlets in Canada only. Limit one coupon per customer.

52607136

SNCOUPCDN